W9-DCH-910

"Hugh, what *are* you doing?"
She thumped her fist on his chest, scandalized. Hugh liked baiting her, but this was ridiculous.

A large hand reached for her, whispering across her cheek. Her hood was pushed back. They were kneeling facing each other. On her bed. Because of her lack of height Hugh had to stoop his head and the motion brought his lips very close to hers.

Despite the poor light, everything snapped into sharp focus. Hugh's eyes were very dark, his expression arrested.

"Hugh?"

She could hear their breathing; she could hear the mutter of voices in the hall and the soft hiss of rain in the mud outside. Time seemed to slow.

He slid his hand round the back of her neck and carefully, eyes never leaving hers, he brought her closer.

"Hugh, you really should not have climbed in here." Aude's thoughts raced. She was an unmarried lady and her reputation here in England was unsullied. It simply was not done for a lady to have a man in her bed—even though he was her brother's friend and it was perfectly innocent.

Hugh smiled.

* * *

Her Banished Lord
Harlequin® Historical #296—November 2010

Author's Note

Crèvecoeur Château in Normandy still exists, although in the eleventh century it would have looked very different. There would have been wooden buildings and a motte and bailey—a defensive mound and a yard within a palisade.

A little before the year this novel begins, the real Lord of Crèvecoeur was banished; he spent many years in exile. This is *not* his story. The characters in these pages are entirely fictitious, although the themes of disgrace and injustice proved rich sources of inspiration.

On marriage rites: in the early middle ages, many marriages were solemnised by a church blessing—but a church blessing, although desirable, was not yet mandatory. In the eleventh century, a marriage simply had to be declared before witnesses to be considered binding.

During the course of the eleventh and twelfth centuries the Church began to regularise the varying traditions. The need for clear inheritance laws helped speed this process along, and over time more and more weddings took place under the auspices of the Church.

HER BANISHED LORD

Carol Townend

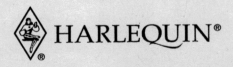

HARLEQUIN®

TORONTO • NEW YORK • LONDON
AMSTERDAM • PARIS • SYDNEY • HAMBURG
STOCKHOLM • ATHENS • TOKYO • MILAN • MADRID
PRAGUE • WARSAW • BUDAPEST • AUCKLAND

If you purchased this book without a cover you should be aware that this book is stolen property. It was reported as "unsold and destroyed" to the publisher, and neither the author nor the publisher has received any payment for this "stripped book."

Recycling programs
for this product may
not exist in your area.

ISBN-13: 978-0-373-30605-3

HER BANISHED LORD

Copyright © 2010 by Carol Townend

All rights reserved. Except for use in any review, the reproduction or utilization of this work in whole or in part in any form by any electronic, mechanical or other means, now known or hereafter invented, including xerography, photocopying and recording, or in any information storage or retrieval system, is forbidden without the written permission of the publisher, Harlequin Enterprises Limited, 225 Duncan Mill Road, Don Mills, Ontario, M3B 3K9, Canada.

This is a work of fiction. Names, characters, places and incidents are either the product of the author's imagination or are used fictitiously, and any resemblance to actual persons, living or dead, business establishments, events or locales is entirely coincidental.

This edition published by arrangement with Harlequin Books S.A.

For questions and comments about the quality of this book please contact us at Customer_eCare@Harlequin.ca.

® and TM are trademarks of the publisher. Trademarks indicated with ® are registered in the United States Patent and Trademark Office, the Canadian Trade Marks Office and in other countries.

www.eHarlequin.com

Printed in U.S.A.

Praise for
Carol Townend

THE NOVICE BRIDE

"*The Novice Bride* is sweet, tantalizing, frustrating, seductively all-consuming, deliciously provocative… I can't go on enough about this story's virtues. Read this book. You'll fall in love a hundred times over."
—*Romance Junkies*

"From the very first words, this story snatches the reader from present day, willingly pulling hearts and minds back to the time of the Norman conquest. Culture clash, merciless invaders, innocence lost and freedom captured—all wonderfully highlighted in this mesmerizing novel."
—*Romance Reader at Heart*

AN HONORABLE ROGUE

"Ms. Townend's impeccable attention to detail and lush, vivid images bring this time period to life."
—*Romance Reader at Heart*

"Anyone who wants to read a very satisfying and heartwarming historical romance will not go wrong with *An Honorable Rogue* by Carol Townend."
—*Cataromance*

To my brother David, with particular thanks for all the photos,

And to Dad for so many happy memories of the Yorkshire Dales.

CAROL TOWNEND

has been making up stories since she was a child. Whenever she comes across a tumbledown building, be it castle or cottage, she can't help conjuring up the lives of the people who once lived there. Her Yorkshire forebears were friendly with the Brontë sisters. Perhaps their influence lingers....

Carol's love of ancient and medieval history took her to London University where she read history, and her first novel, published by Harlequin, won the Romantic Novelists' Association's New Writers' Award. Currently, she lives near Kew Gardens with her husband and daughter. Visit her website at http://caroltownend.co.uk.

Chapter One

The river port of Jumièges, Normandy

Lady Aude de Crèvecoeur eyed her brother in some dismay. It was early morning and she and Edouard, Count of Corbeil, had left their lodgings at the Abbey and were walking along the quays. Judging by the set of her brother's face, Aude feared that he had already discovered what she had done. Why else would he be steering her to that particular jetty?

Edouard's squire, Raoul, was following a discreet distance behind them. Aude had the lowering feeling that Raoul might be under orders to catch her should she make a run for it.

Oh, Lord. She had been planning to confess the whole today in any case, but perhaps she should have been honest with Edouard from the first. A light breeze was playing with her veil, teasing a strand of copper-coloured hair from its plait. Behind them the Matins bells rang out from the Abbey towers.

Her mind raced. *What best to do?*

Edouard loathed it when people kept things from him. And that of course, was exactly what Aude had done. She had been too cowardly to tell him that she was not ready to fall in with his plans for her.

Under an immaculate summer sky, the port was coming to life. Bales of English fleeces were being offloaded from one of the barges. They skirted round them. She had long been dreading this moment, but Edouard must be made to realise that she was serious about leaving Normandy. She had booked passage to Honfleur, and from there—England!

Did he know? She would not rush to confession until she was more certain of his mood. They walked on, towards the very barge on which she had booked her passage. Lord. Edouard must know. It was obvious something was bothering him.

The port was relatively peaceful. The water was at a very low ebb—at the mouth of the Seine, near Honfleur, the tide must be out. On the opposite bank a small ferry was making ready to cast off and cross the shrunken river. Behind the ferry, white cliffs reared heavenwards, blinding in the morning sun. It had always struck Aude as odd that here in the port the bank was so low, while on the other side, there were those tall white cliffs.

Face set, looking neither to right nor left, Edouard came to a halt next to the river barge that was bound for Honfleur, the very one on which Aude had reserved her place. She braced herself. 'Edouard, I have a confession to make…'

But Edouard's attention had been caught by a sudden

burst of activity on the barge so he hadn't heard her. Guilt tightened Aude's stomach. Edouard would be furious, he had plans for her, plans which did not include her touring her recently acquired estate in England.

Lifting her green skirts clear of a coil of ropes, Aude kept her eyes fixed on her brother's face. They had passed the night in comfortable beds in the Abbey lodge; she had seen to it that they had eaten a filling breakfast at one of the inns. She had hoped to put him in a good mood. Edouard *must* be made to understand. To Aude that English estate represented a hard-won freedom: freedom from duty, freedom from convention, freedom to be herself. Acquisition of that English estate had given her the independence she had dreamed of, and she was not going to give that up, for anyone.

'Edouard?'

'Mmm?'

Her brother was fascinated with the barge. A bare-chested sailor was tossing orders in all directions, brusquely indicating that some of the cargo should be shifted from one side of the deck to the other. Shocked, Aude gave the sailor a sidelong glance, wondering why the ship's master permitted this man to work half-naked; it simply was not done.

By his looks, the man had Viking ancestry. He had thick brown hair which had been burnished blond by the summer sun and he was most beautifully formed. Those shoulders, those back muscles—the Duke's champion would kill for a body like that...

A sharp quiver that Aude was unable to identify ran through her. The half-naked sailor seemed vaguely familiar, but how could that be? She knew no common sailors. Aude frowned, but with his back to her, the man's face was hidden.

With a wrench she tore her gaze from the beautifully formed sailor and tucked her arm more firmly into her brother's.

'Edouard?'

'Hmm?'

'I am trying to tell you something important. It would help if I had your full attention.'

Edouard reached across to tuck a coppery tendril of hair back beneath her veil.

'A confession, you say?' His eyes gleamed, and though that tightness had not left his face, Aude could see no anger in his expression, not for her. Some of the tension left her. 'Hadn't you better wait until our appointment with the Abbot this afternoon? He will be only too pleased to hear your confession, I am sure.'

Aude swallowed. Her throat remained dry, as though she were nervous, which was ridiculous. Edouard might be Count of Corbeil, but he was also her brother. Would he insist on imposing his will over hers? This was Normandy in the eleventh century, and noblewomen were expected to obey the male head of the family.

'Edouard, this appointment with the Abbot—you would not force me into a convent?'

'Force you? Lord, no. But, Aude, we have discussed this many times. You have had over a year to mourn your Martin. It is time you got on with life.'

She removed her hand from his arm. In that perfect blue sky the swifts were screaming and Aude felt like screaming too. 'I am getting on with life! I have been helping *you*! Heaven knows, you needed someone to run the household. Crèvecoeur was little better than a midden when I returned.' Realising that an all-out argument would do her no favours, she moderated her tone and replaced her fingers on Edouard's arm. 'You said you appreciated my assistance.'

'I did. I do.' Edouard's gaze rested for a moment on the dazzling white cliffs on the other side of the Seine. He sighed. 'Naturally, I appreciate your hard work, but as I said, it is over a year since Martin's death—'

'Sometimes I think the shock of it will be always with me,' she said, slowly. 'One moment Martin was leaving the Great Hall all laughter and smiles, and the next he was brought back on a hurdle. *A hurdle.*' Aude fixed her brother with her eyes; Edouard had heard this many times before, but she could not stop herself. 'His horse threw him, how could that have killed him? Men are thrown by horses every day and they survive.'

'Martin had internal injuries, Aude. There was nothing you could do to save him.'

'I did my best, but I shall always wonder. Did I miss something?'

'You missed nothing. Aude, it is not healthy to keep looking backwards. Martin would want you to have a future.'

'Would he?'

Edouard smiled. 'Indeed he would. And it is time you gave it some thought. I cannot keep you hidden away at Crèvecoeur for ever; you are no longer young.'

'I am eighteen,' Aude murmured. 'That does not feel so old to me.'

'You know what I mean, you are not a child. You are old to be…unsettled.'

'You want to lock me away in a convent…'

'At the least you should be wed.' Edouard's expression

was hard. 'Aude, we need to make an alliance, a good one. I beg you to remember that our family's position is not secure.'

'You are referring to Grandfather's disgrace? But I thought…after Beaumont…' Aude's brows snapped together. 'Surely Duke William cannot still be holding what happened in Grandfather's time against us? You fought for him in England five years ago, and last year you…*we* both gave his favourite Richard of Beaumont our full support. Why, I even agreed to marry the man!' Aude's voice was in danger of breaking and for a moment her brother's face was lost in a mist of tears. Blinking rapidly, she fought for control. This was not a good start and she had not even begun her confession.

Absently, Edouard patted her hand. 'I know and I appreciate the sacrifices you were prepared to make.'

Aude cleared her throat. 'I should hope so. Poor Martin had barely been laid to rest, but I knew my duty. I agreed to marry Richard de Beaumont, and so I would have done, if he had held me to it.'

'For that I am grateful.'

'Nevertheless, despite my reluctance, you will use me to forge *another* alliance.'

'It would certainly help.' For an instant Edouard's eyes strayed to the barge behind her. The barge on which Aude had booked passage to Honfleur. Passage for herself, her maid and a small personal escort. Edouard's lips tightened. That Viking sailor was probably still flexing those impossibly fine muscles. Aude could certainly hear him, throwing commands at the other sailors. She was *not* going to look at him.

A fleeting expression of anxiety crossed Edouard's face. It was quickly masked to be sure for Edouard had never been one for worrying her, but she knew him. Something was bothering him. She did not think it concerned her. Edouard had been scowling at that sailor… the one she was *not* going to look at.

'Something has happened, I can see something is wrong.' Aude squeezed her brother's arm. 'Don't tell me our family's loyalty has been called into question?'

Edouard shifted his attention back to her and shook his head. 'Not precisely.' His voice was clear in the warming summer air. 'Aude, I won't beat about the bush. One of my friends has been denounced as a traitor.'

Her breath caught. 'A friend? Who?'

'Aude, hush, for pity's sake!'

'What did he do, this friend?'

'So far as I can judge the accusations against him are completely false, but I can say no more. I am telling you this, Aude, because it is important for you to realise that over the coming months we shall have to be particularly careful with whom we are seen to associate.'

It felt for an instant as though the sun had gone in. But there it was, still gleaming on the trickle of water in the riverbed. It was low tide, but the Seine was especially low this morning—it had been a dry spring and an even drier summer.

'Mind your back, fool!' The voice of the distracting sailor—she was certain it was he—cut into her thoughts. Aude turned in time to watch that bare-chested form take up a small packing case and heft it on to a wide shoulder. He ran lightly down the gangplank and on to the jetty.

Aude's jaw dropped. Her heart missed its beat. She could see his face properly and she knew him!

This was no sailor as she had assumed, but she had

been right about his ancestry; Viking blood did indeed flow in this man's veins. She was looking at Hugh Duclair, Count de Freyncourt. No wonder that naked torso had caught her attention. Hugh had always been so…so vibrant. Whenever Aude was with him she could see no one but him. It was a little unsettling to learn that Hugh had the power to fascinate even when being mistaken for a deck-hand.

She clutched Edouard's arm. *'It's Hugh!'*

Aude had not seen Hugh for over a year. A friend of her brother's, she had met him several times when she had been a child. Notwithstanding the cloud that had hung over her family, Hugh had always been kind to her. True, he had enjoyed teasing her more than she found comfortable, but when he hadn't been baiting her, she had liked him. Too much. Indeed, as a child, she had woven many a childish dream about him. But goodness, he had changed since those days. He was so tall, so large, and with that gilded brown hair shining in the sun…

Edouard's lips tightened. 'Aude, you are *not* to acknowledge him.'

'I beg your pardon?' Aude stared. 'You cannot mean it, Hugh is a particular friend.'

'Not any more,' Edouard said, in a clear, cold tone that Aude was afraid must carry to where Hugh was directing operations a few yards away. No wonder the ship's master had not commented on Hugh's lack of attire, he would not dare. A ship's master—criticise the Count de Freyncourt!

'What do you mean?'

'Haven't you heard? Hugh has been banished from the Duchy.'

'Hugh is the one who was banished? *No*!'

'He has been accused of conspiring against Duke William.'

Aude drew her head back. Her skin was icy, as though someone had doused her with cold water. 'That cannot be true, Hugh would never do such a thing, never.'

'It was Bishop Osmund of St Aubin himself who gave testimony against him. He swore a sacred oath, over relics.'

'I do not care who testified against him, I am going to speak to him.' Aude picked up her skirts.

Edouard caught her wrist. 'Don't you *dare*!'

'Edouard, release me!'

'*No!*' Her brother lowered his voice. '*Mon Dieu*, we are still shadowed by the accusations made against our family in Grandfather's time.'

Aude clenched her teeth. 'But Grandfather always maintained his innocence! The charges against him—'

'Serious charges,' Edouard murmured, leaning closer, 'of plotting to overthrow the Duke.'

'They were never proven! Grandfather was falsely charged, and you know it.' Aude lifted her chin. 'Just as Hugh is being falsely charged.'

'In a sense it does not matter whether we believe Hugh to be guilty or not, we cannot afford to recognise or be associated with him. You are not to speak to him. Ever.'

'Hugh is our friend!'

'Not any more,' Edouard muttered under his breath, before raising his voice loudly enough to be heard on the ship. 'But should Hugh Duclair be reinstated that would, of course, be a different matter. Then we might acknowledge him.'

'Why you…you…' Words failed her. Her eyes were drawn back to that strong, lithe torso. Why had it only just dawned on her that watching the play of a man's muscles could be so stimulating? She was flushing all over, hot where moments ago she had been cold. This was not right, she could not bear it. *Not Hugh, merciful Lord, not Hugh.*

It was only when Aude felt her brother's hand catch hers that she realised she had stepped towards Hugh. Blindly, instinctively, wanting…what? To give comfort? To take it? Her brother's revelations had thoroughly upset her.

'Aude, let the man continue with his preparations,' Edouard's voice came at her, seemingly from afar. 'He is cutting it fine as it is. He only has a day to get out of the Duchy.'

'What will happen if he is delayed?'

'His life will be forfeit.'

Aude's heart beat hard as Hugh came down the gang-plank with another packing case. How galling to have to leave Normandy under such a cloud, how ghastly to have lifelong friends ignore you…

Her frown deepened. That packing case on Hugh's shoulder, surely it was one of hers? Biting her lip, hobbled by Edouard's command not to acknowledge him, Aude watched as Hugh set the box down—yes, it was definitely hers—next to a couple of travelling chests. Travelling chests which Aude also recognised, since they too belonged to her. But they should all be on that barge…

Eyes narrowing, Edouard's strictures forgotten, Aude stepped forward to block Hugh's path. His sun-kissed hair was ruffled and, thanks to his exertions, a fine

sheen of sweat gleamed on his splendid chest. Heavens.
Those childish fantasies she had once built up around
him; those dreams she had had only last year of kissing him, of cuddling him—well, she couldn't possibly
apply them to the man standing before her today, she
wouldn't dare. Spring fever, it had been spring fever.
Breath constricted, Aude found herself staring into
stormy eyes that were mid-way between blue and grey.
Dark lashes, such long, dark lashes… Hugh's eyes had
always been breathtaking. To look at them was to ache
with longing.

'Excuse me, *ma dame*.'

His voice was curt. Rude. It hit her like a slap in the
face. His voice was a stranger's voice, and it reminded
her that in the past Hugh had irritated her as often as
not. She stiffened. Hugh *must* recognise her; she had
known him, despite only seeing him a couple of times
in recent years.

A chilly ball formed in her stomach. Hugh and
Edouard might once have been close as peas in a pod,
but times had changed. Today Edouard was refusing to
acknowledge Hugh—or was he…?

There! Hugh and her brother exchanged the briefest of
glances; indeed, Aude was almost certain she saw Hugh
gave Edouard the slightest of nods. She frowned. Maybe
it was only in public that Edouard was not acknowledging Hugh. What happened in private?

She sighed. Whatever was going on, it seemed she
must follow her brother's lead. Count Hugh de Freyncourt, or rather, the *former* Count Hugh de Freyncourt
was in enough trouble, there was no point drawing attention to him. She would act as though she took him for a
common sailor.

'That packing case,' Aude pointed, her tone was haughty. 'And those travelling chests—why have you removed them from the ship?'

'They were in the way.'

'You can't do that!'

The wide shoulders lifted. 'I just have. Excuse me, *ma dame*.'

Aude inserted herself between Hugh and the plank. This was not quite the way she had envisioned informing her brother she had brought her plans forward, but that could no longer be helped.

'Those are *my* belongings you are throwing about,' she said, grandly. 'And since I have paid for my party's passage to Honfleur, I demand to know why you have seen fit to unload them.'

At her side, Edouard caught his breath, but Aude ignored him as she was focused on Hugh.

Hugh's jaw clenched. A large hand was shoved through the sun-bleached hair; stormy eyes pierced her to the quick. A strange awareness made itself felt in the region of Aude's belly, like a slow tightening. It was not unpleasant. *Sweet Mother*, one thing was inescapable. Hugh was disconcertingly well favoured, even when he was scowling.

'As I told you, *ma dame*, they were in the way.' He strode past her and on to the gangplank, only to return to the jetty with yet another of her travelling chests.

Aude turned to her brother, somewhat surprised she could actually think with Hugh parading that fine body before the entire port. 'Edouard, your support here would be most welcome.'

Edouard simply folded his arms and looked blandly at her. Truth to tell, he looked more amused than angry to have had her secret out of her. And, yes, he was clearly relieved she had not acknowledged Hugh by name.

'My support? I think not. When did you plan to leave?'

'This afternoon.' She gestured at Hugh. 'Please, Edouard.'

He shook his head. 'You intended to sneak off to Honfleur without so much as a word to me, and you expect me to back you up? No, Aude, I would have your full confidence before I give you support of any kind.'

'I was going to tell you!'

'Before or after your interview with the Abbot?'

'Before! I was about to tell you when Hu…that clod starting tossing my belongings all over the quayside.'

While Aude and her brother had been talking, Hugh Duclair reappeared. With studied care he put the last of Aude's travelling chests down next to the others. He was about to step back on to the gangplank, but this time she stopped him by placing her hand in the centre of his chest. He felt hot and he was muttering under his breath, something which sounded like, 'If you want something done, sometimes you must do it yourself.'

She caught a faint whiff of male sweat, fresh male sweat. Oddly, it was not displeasing. Hugh might have adopted the manners of an angry barbarian but he was heart-stoppingly attractive. Even at Beaumont, tales of his wild ways with women had reached her. Aude had heard that even the most chaste of women found him irresistible—today she could believe them all.

He was affecting not to have the slightest idea of her identity or status. It hurt to see those breathtaking eyes look down at her with undisguised irritation. In the past, behind the teasing, she had sensed warmth and affection, but she could sense none now. Had the events of the last year changed him so much?

'I must speak to the ship's captain,' she said, clearly and slowly.

Strong fingers peeled her hand from his chest. The curl of his lips was so arrogant it was nothing less than an insult. Regret pierced her. Had Hugh taken against them because they were not openly acknowledging him?

'The ship's captain,' Hugh said, and there—again—she thought he exchanged the briefest of glances with Edouard, 'is at the Abbey negotiating a price for shipping out a consignment of wine. When he returns, I will give him a message, if it pleases you.'

Behind her, Edouard let out a snort.

Aude whirled on him, anger rising. 'Really, Edouard, you might help, rather than standing there sniggering.'

'No, no.' Edouard's eyes were laughing. 'This is far too entertaining. To see my sister, Aude de Crèvecoeur, brawling with Co...a common sailor...you do not need my help.'

Aude fixed Hugh with her eyes, wishing with all her might that he could see into her heart, that he could understand she had no wish to ignore him. 'I have booked passage to Honfleur. You will be so kind as to return my things to the ship.'

'Not a chance. This vessel is fully laden.'

'It wasn't earlier.'

'It is now.' Hugh made no attempt to hide his annoyance. 'You will have to find another, *ma dame*; this is not the only river barge going as far as Honfleur.' He pointed upriver. 'Try that one.'

He was indicating the furthest jetty, but from her

standpoint Aude could only see a rowboat stranded on the mud by the falling tide.

'That is far too small, I need a proper river barge.'

'There's a barge there, take my word for it. It is tucked out of sight behind the jetty, and it sails tomorrow at high water.'

Take his word for it? Aude set her jaw. 'But I paid passage on this one. Leaving *today*.'

Heaving a sigh that unfortunately drew Aude's eyes to his magnificent chest, Hugh dug into the purse at his belt. 'How much?'

His arrogance took her breath away. It was not that she was standing in such close proximity to his half-naked body. No, no, what was she thinking? Marshalling her wits with some difficulty, Aude scowled at Edouard. 'Surely he cannot get away with it?'

'Clearly he is a man of some influence with the captain,' Edouard muttered dryly.

Hugh made an impatient movement. His eyes were bleak. 'How much did you pay? Come on, woman, I am not at leisure here.' He thrust some silver at her, and before Aude had time to think up a suitable reply, was back on the barge ordering the crew about as though he were the Duke himself.

Aude blinked at the silver in her hand. 'Why, the insolent b—'

'Careful, *chérie*,' Edouard murmured in her ear. 'That is not a word one would expect Lady Aude de Crève-coeur to be casting about the docks.'

'As if I cared for that.' Foot tapping, Aude frowned at the trunks and travelling chests Hugh had stacked on the jetty. Inside, her heart was breaking—for Hugh, for the loss of her friendship with him—but that did not prevent her from feeling angry at what he had done. 'He had no right to remove my things.'

'Well, I for one am grateful, as it gives me a chance to make you change your mind.'

'That will not happen. Count Richard gave me the Alfold estate and I need to see it for myself. Apparently it is much run down. I would like to set it to rights.'

'That might not be as easy as you imagine. Think, Aude. England remains unsettled. Since Duke William took the crown, it has been a country in ferment. Remember what Count Richard told us, what happened up in the north—'

'Alfold is in the south.'

'The entire realm is unsettled,' Edouard pressed on, wrapping an arm about her and giving her a conciliatory hug. 'And irritating though you are at times, I do not want to lose you.'

'Edouard, you are wasting words, I will not change my mind.' She threw a dark glance towards her brother's erstwhile friend, powerless to prevent herself from running her gaze one last time over that magnificent physique. Holy Mother help her. 'He had no right.'

'There is no arguing with a desperate man.' Edouard took her by the elbow and guided her from the dockside towards the market square. 'Besides, you really do not want to become entangled with Hugh Duclair. Remember, I do not want you speaking to him.' His expression lightened. 'Looks the part though, doesn't he? Exactly like a river pirate.'

'A river pirate? You think so?' Aude hung back. What with that stunning masculinity, those angry, flashing eyes—the word Lucifer sprang to mind. 'Edouard, my things! We can't abandon them on the dock…'

Edouard gestured for his squire. 'Raoul, be so good as to have my lady's travelling chests returned to the Abbey lodge.'

'Yes, my lord.'

As Raoul called over some porters, Aude allowed her brother to place her fingers back on his arm.

'Now, Aude, I would like you to complete that confession of yours. You were about to tell me, I think, that you had booked passage to Honfleur.'

Edouard's voice was stern, but amusement lit his eyes, it was lingering in the corners of his mouth. Aude hung her head. She did not feel particularly contrite, not when her brother seemed intent on making decisions on her behalf, decisions that were blatantly wrong, but perhaps a small show of meekness might help.

'I am sorry to spoil your plans, Edouard, but I really have no wish to become a nun. I did try to tell you back at Crèvecoeur.' They began walking towards the Abbey gates. 'Believe me, the life of a nun does not appeal.'

Edouard gave her a searching look and grunted. 'I do realise that, even though after Martin's death I clearly recall you saying something about retiring from the world.'

Crossing the thoroughfare, they nodded a greeting to the abbot's sentries at the gatehouse and passed under the arch and into the Abbey courtyard. The church of Our Lady stood before them with its two massive towers. The façade was bright with fresh paint—the reds and blues glowed like jewels.

Aude grimaced. 'Yes, I remember. A person says many things in the first throes of grief that later they come to see are untrue.'

'I can understand that, you loved Martin a great deal.

Relax, Aude, I can't see you in a convent myself, that was not my main reason for arranging the interview. I was hoping that you might be ready to consider marriage.'

'Marriage? *No!*' Suppressing a shudder, she moderated her tone. 'One day perhaps.' Immediately her unruly mind presented her with a disturbing image of a half-naked deck-hand. Swallowing hard, Aude thrust it to the back of her mind.

'Aude, it was not easy arranging this appointment with the Abbot, I had to call in a few favours to get it. I insist you speak to him.'

She stiffened her spine. 'Very well. Since you wish it, I shall meet with the Abbot. But I want to make it quite clear, I will not be forced into making vows of any kind.'

Chapter Two

Downstream at Château de Tancarville, a lookout high in the clifftop tower was idly staring at an eagle as it glided over the river below.

He yawned. Despite the wind that whistled round the heights summer and winter alike, the man's helmet was hot and tight, and he couldn't wait to remove it. But he was proud of his position as castle guard, so he stood firm. Duke William's own tutor had made this castle what it was today, a defensive watchtower with clear views of Normandy for miles around.

On one side you could see the Seine gleaming like a silver snake as it wound out to the sea, and in the other direction the port of Quillebeuf. Generations ago, Viking dragonships had hidden out between raids there, as they sacked and pillaged their way inland. Jumièges, Rouen, Paris….

Nothing half so exciting had happened that morning and the sentry was bored, glad his stint was almost over.

A bell sounded the noon hour.

A rowboat was drifting at the midpoint. The rower had shipped oars and his head was turned in the direction of a mysterious wave which had formed right across the water. The lookout could not see the rower's expression, but his stomach gave a sick lurch. He had never seen a wave like that, not on a river. It stretched from one bank to the other and it was powering upstream towards Quillebeuf and the rowboat like a serpent from hell.

A wave? Coming upstream?

'Here, Gérard, is that a tidal bore?'

'Can't be, Pascal. Wrong time of year.'

'Well, I might have had too much Rhenish last night, but that looks like a tidal bore to me. Come on, man, quick!' he said, pointing.

Gérard looked and went grey. He swore and hastily crossing himself, leaned out over the parapet. *'Tidal bore!'* He grabbed the rope of the alarm bell. 'Tidal bore! *La barre!'*

'That rowboat,' Pascal added, shaking his head in horrified fascination. 'Will it make it?'

It looked unlikely. Forced upstream by the incoming tide, the wave was gathering height as well as pace. It whipped along, bearing down on the boat faster than a man could run. Foam sprayed out along the riverbanks.

The noon bell had stopped ringing. Gérard's alarm bell died away. Down by the river, the screaming began.

It seemed there was no escaping the interview with Abbot Bertram. Aude was determined it would not take long.

Shortly after noon, she and Edouard went to meet the Abbot in the old church, St Peter's. They stood in the shady cool of a side passage as the chanting faded, and watched the monks file out. The rich scent of incense lingered in the air. Shafts of sunlight were falling in perfect lines through the narrow windows, illuminating here a carved bird, there an angel in full flight.

Abbot Bertram was sitting on a stone wall-bench, a compact, stern-faced man with little hair; whether this was because of his tonsure or because he was bald it was impossible to say. His face was elongated; he had strong features and startling black eyebrows that gave him a somewhat surprised air. Gems glittered in the polished gold cross that hung at his breast.

'Lord Edouard, it is good to see you.'

'Thank you, Lord Abbot. I trust you are in good health?'

'Never better. Please sit.' The Abbot waved Aude and Edouard to cushions on the bench. The windows above their heads were unglazed, but since it was the height of summer, the breeze playing over their heads was a blessing rather than a curse.

'So, Lord Edouard, this is the sister I have heard so much about.'

'Yes, my lord, this is Lady Aude de Crèvecoeur.'

'My lady.'

'Abbot Bertram.'

'Lord Edouard, when your letter first arrived, I assumed you to mean that your sister had a vocation and that you wished me to find a suitable house in which she might live out her life.'

'Lord Abbot,' Edouard said, 'I apologise if you were put to any trouble.'

'My son, it is never a trouble to find places for any of our sisters who have a true vocation. And it is never wrong to test that vocation before binding vows are made. Such vows are sacred; once made they are irrevocable. It would be a grievous sin for someone to make them only to discover later that they have changed their mind and that they no longer wish to offer their life to God.'

Aude met the Abbot's gaze. 'Abbot Bertram, if I may say something?'

'Speak freely, my lady. You have considered how you wish to spend your days?'

'I have. You must know that my fiancé, Martin de Beaumont, died just over a year ago?'

'Indeed, your brother informed me of his untimely death. Please accept my sympathies.'

'Thank you. Abbot Bertram, it is true that after Martin's death I considered taking the veil. But deeper thought has made me realise that the contemplative life is not for me.' *It was Hugh*, Aude realised with a start. *Hugh with his teasing smile, the smile that could lift me out of my grief, the smile that could startle because last spring it made me wonder what it might be like to kiss him…*

'Are you certain, my lady? The Church would welcome you. Perhaps one of the less…austere orders might suit you?'

Aude's every muscle tensed and she had opened her mouth to speak when Edouard cleared his throat. 'My lord, I am sorry if there has been any misunderstanding, but I must make it clear, my sister is not to be coerced. I have given my word that her will should be respected.'

Aude sent him a grateful smile.

'Of course, of course.' The abbot was beginning to sound irritable. 'Compulsion would negate the offering to God. Anyone giving their life to the Church must do so freely. But I would hate to see your sister idle away her days. She has many strengths and talents, and to waste them would be a sin against the very God who gave them to her. Perhaps Lady Aude needs further, more focused guidance—a retreat, perhaps?'

'*No!*' Aude knew her voice was sharp, but she could not help it. 'My apologies, Lord Abbot, but there would be no sense in that. I have no vocation and that will not change, however many retreats you may offer me.'

'Your mind is fixed.'

'On this matter it is.'

'Perhaps you think to marry?'

'One day, perhaps.'

The Abbot pushed himself to his feet and held up his hand in brief blessing. 'I shall leave you to your meditations. Ponder well on the benefits that would accrue to your family should Lady Aude make a good marriage to a reliable man, a man whose loyalty to Duke William is unquestionable. With that in mind, there is someone I should like Lady Aude to meet. In view of the clouds that still hang over your brother, my lady, I would beg you to ponder hard on the merits of what I have suggested. May God guide your decision, Lady Aude, and may He bless you both.'

'Farewell, my lord,' Edouard said.

'He's after my dowry,' Aude muttered, frowning at Abbot Bertram's back as he left the church.

'He will be sending in one of his knights next,' Edouard said.

'You are not serious!'

'Never more so. Listen, Aude…' Edouard lowered his voice '…I can understand you not wanting to enter a convent, but I do think you should consider marriage, and soon. Some time this year.'

'This year? Edouard, there's something you are not telling me. What have you done?'

Her brother looked steadily at her, saying nothing. Her fingers had clenched into fists; deliberately, she uncurled them. *Today was not turning out as she had hoped it would. Hugh—banished! And now this…*

'Edouard? It would help the family if I made a good marriage?'

He sighed. 'An alliance with one of the Abbot's more trusted knights would cement our position in Normandy. No one would ever question our loyalty to the Duke.'

'I really do not—'

'Aude, shut that mouth for once and meet the Abbot's man. You never know, you might find that he suits.'

'The Abbot's man? Edouard, have you arranged something behind my back?'

Edouard cleared his throat. 'Just meet the man. We shall proceed from there.'

'*No*! Edouard, you…you… I *hate* you!'

'No, you don't. Aude, you have to marry some time. It is, as Abbot Bertram says, the moment to make your choice.'

'Some choice! You present me with a man I have never laid eyes on! Edouard, you *worm*! You planned this all along. I feel betrayed, betrayed!'

In the distance, a door slammed.

'Hush, Aude, for the love of God, here he comes.'

Brisk footsteps drew closer, Aude couldn't bear to look. *If only it could be Hugh.* But that, a wish so secret she had barely acknowledged it even to herself, had always been a vain hope.

'Good day, Lord Edouard.'

He had a pleasant voice. Unfamiliar. Aude lifted her eyes. A blue tunic. The Abbot's knight was tall with dark eyes and curly brown hair. His smile was friendly. Slightly reassured, she rose to greet him.

Everyone stood to benefit if she married this stranger. This knight would get his reward—Aude and her dowry. Yes, it would be a fine arrangement. If Aude de Crèvecoeur married one of the Abbot's knights, everyone would be happy. Everyone except her…

'Sir Olivier!' Edouard smiled. 'Good to see you again, man, good to see you. Aude, may I present Sir Olivier de Fougères? Sir Olivier, my sister Aude.'

'*Enchanté, ma dame.*'

'Sir Olivier.' Aude made her voice cool.

As the Abbot's knight bowed over her hand, a peculiar fancy took her. Hugh Duclair was standing in Sir Olivier's place, and he was no longer a banished man. Hugh was wearing a silk tunic banded with intricate embroidery, gold gleamed on the pommel of his sword, and his eyes were glittering with laughter as they had done that spring at Crèvecoeur…

'Abbot Bertram suggested I spoke to you.' Sir Olivier's voice brought her crashing back to reality. 'And that your brother approved our meeting.'

'Indeed?' Carefully she withdrew her hand. *Not Hugh. Heavens, what was happening to her?* She bit her lip.

'My lady, both the Abbot and your brother speak highly of your qualities.'

'It is good to hear my brother values me.'

'And why should he not? But not only your brother, my lord Abbot speaks highly of you too. Word has spread of your competence at Beaumont, not to mention the changes you have wrought at Crèvecoeur.'

'Oh.'

'Lady Aude, I would be honoured if you would care to walk with me in the orchard. We might get to know each other a little better. You don't object, I take it, Lord Edouard?'

'Be my guest.' Edouard had a definite smile in his voice.

'My lady?'

Aude put her hand on the knight's arm and he led her out of the church.

The tidal surge roared along. It was only a few miles short of Jumièges and it was larger than ever. The wave spanned the Seine; it burst over the banks. White crests foamed and frothed at the margins, churning the mud, snatching at dead branches.

The surge pushed on, unstoppable. Boats rocked at moorings, the wave broke over them, filling them to sinking point in a moment. River barges were ripped away, stolen by the great press of water. This was *la barre*, also called the *mascaret*.

At the Ételan riverbank, a woman's eyes widened and she ran to snatch her daughter clear of the foreshore.

Near the harbour at Villequier, a little boy murmured, 'Viking wave,' and stuck his thumb in his mouth, eyes round as pennies.

At Caudebec-en-Caux, a monk made the sign of the cross when he noticed the white horses racing upriver. He shouted a warning at a woman hauling eel-traps in from one of the jetties. She never heard him. Foam sprayed in her face; the wave swirled round her ankles, tugged at her skirts and bore her away. There was more screaming. Choking. A mouth full of river water mixed with brine. The river swallowed her.

Jumièges lay around the next curl of the river. Only minutes away, *la barre* drove relentlessly towards it.

Bees were humming in the lavender hedge that bordered the Abbey orchard. Butterflies wavered past, drunk with nectar and sunshine. Walking sedately through the orchard with the long grasses brushing her skirts, Aude shot the Abbot's knight a sidelong glance.

Sir Olivier was, as Edouard no doubt knew, well favoured and attractive. He had good teeth, he was powerfully built and he had a smile that might charm the larks from the sky. He had tucked her arm into his and she could feel strength under the broadcloth of his tunic. So far, she had seen nothing to dislike, and it was a pity she could not warm to him. *Hugh. What would it be like to be walking in this orchard with Hugh Duclair?*

Sir Olivier reached to pluck an apple from a tree and passed it to her.

'My thanks.' The fruit was red and unblemished. It held the heat of the sun, but Aude did not want it any more than she wanted the man. The memory of a teasing smile held more allure.

Firmly, she put the memory behind her. *Hugh had no smile for her today.*

Brown eyes gleamed as they looked at her, and with

practised ease Sir Olivier manoeuvred her against one of the lichen-covered tree trunks. When his eyes darkened, she realised he was going to kiss her.

Aude lifted her lips. She had to admit, she was curious. Despite two betrothals and a hopeless yearning for a certain banished lord, she was sadly lacking in experience with regard to kissing. The only man to have kissed her had been her Martin. She had adored Martin, but she had only been thirteen when they had become betrothed and they had pledged to remain chaste until their wedding day.

That was no doubt why Martin's kisses had been so brief; he had not wanted to tempt either of them into breaking their vows. Affectionate but chaste, Martin's kisses had left her entirely unmoved. And as for her second fiancé, Count Richard had known she was grieving—he had not touched her. Besides, Count Richard had had a Saxon mistress to entertain him…

Sir Olivier bent his head.

Aude did not know this man; never mind that his handsome features left her unmoved, she would try for her brother's sake. Edouard thought she had been grieving too long, that grief was her habit and it needed to be broken. Perhaps he was right. This knight might teach her to enjoy his touch. *Well, let us see. If I find you pleasing, an alliance might be possible…*

A tall, broad body blotted out the sun. Aude felt herself go stiff. It was not Hugh's body, she felt no desire to touch it.

Her nose wrinkled. Sir Olivier's blue tunic smelt faintly of sweat, stale sweat that made her want to turn her head aside. Not all men had this smell, she recalled, as the naked shoulders and finely sculpted musculature of Hugh Duclair came into focus in her mind.

'My lady, I swear if you were to honour me with your hand, I would cherish you all my life.'

The eyes of the Abbot's knight were almost black and as she tipped her head back Aude could see her own small self reflected back at her. *What was he seeing? Herself? Or the lands and the dowry she would bring him?*

The body of the Abbot's knight pressed against her, flustering her, hemming her in. Her apple fell to the ground and she forced herself to stand still while his lips touched hers.

Nothing.

Aude felt nothing but a sense of unease. No, it was stronger than that, it was irritation and it was growing stronger with every second that his mouth was on hers. Smothered—he was smothering her. Her hand came up to push him away. He caught it in one of his. She swallowed down a protest.

Sir Olivier pressed closer, pushing her back against the tree. *Think of our family*, she told herself, *we need to make a good alliance.*

Aude held firm as he pressed closer. Her veil snagged on a twig and her sense of irritation increased.

'*Ouch*! Sir Olivier!'

He could not have heard for he went on kissing her. He was trying to insert his tongue between her teeth. A shudder, and it was entirely of revulsion, went through her. Martin had *never* done anything half so repulsive. Aude twisted her head. There was a ripping sound as the twig tore the delicate fabric of her veil. Her hair felt as though someone was pulling it out at the roots.

'*Ow*! Please, sir!'

His body smelled sour. Sir Olivier might be wearing a pretty tunic but it was better suited to winter than summer and it needed rather more than an airing.

He lifted his head and Aude no longer felt suffocated. The sense of irritation faded. He smiled; it was a very charming smile, his best feature. Boyish and vulnerable, his smile told her, for all that he was a knight, this man was malleable. He would never bend her to his will.

In that instant Aude recognised that if she and Sir Olivier were to make a match of it, he would defer to her. Thoughtfully, she looked at him. She might not warm to him, she might never yearn for him, but it seemed he was a rarity among the knightly class. He would not forget that the lands that came with the marriage belonged to her.

'Oh, your veil! I am sorry, my lady, I wouldn't have had that happen for the world, except...'

'Yes?' Aude felt as though she were not really here in the orchard, she was watching Sir Olivier from many miles away. *This Abbot's knight, this landless knight wanted her dowry.* Her hair had come loose, a strand was gleaming in a patch of dappled sunlight; when he reached to caress it and sighed, laughter formed inside her.

'Your hair, it is so beautiful, I had no idea,' he murmured. 'You are a goddess, a golden goddess of beauty.'

Yes, a giggle was definitely rising, Aude sank her teeth into her lips to keep it in. Sir Olivier had a fine opinion of himself, but she could not take him seriously. And as for his touch, his kiss...

What would Hugh's kiss be like?

Unhooking her hair from his fingers, Aude turned

away and set about straightening her veil. *Stop thinking about Hugh! Give this knight your full attention. If he is indeed malleable, he might be useful.*

When Aude had set her appearance to rights, Sir Olivier was leaning against the tree, biting into an apple.

'My lady, it is your brother's wish that we marry.'

'Yes, I know, but—'

Sir Olivier tossed the apple aside and reached her in two strides. 'It is my wish also.'

'Sir, my dowry is not large, but nevertheless I think you are more interested in my lands than my person.'

'Not so!' He took her hands, kissing each in turn. 'I admit that was the case before I met you, but now that I have met you...'

Aude pulled free. 'You are very glib, sir. You know I have a manor near Crèvecoeur?'

'Yes.'

'And my grandfather left a chest of money with the Abbot here. That is my dowry.'

'I know about that, but—'

'I also,' Aude swept on, 'have been gifted a small estate in Wessex. Did you know of that?'

Sir Olivier's handsome face crinkled into a frown. 'Where the devil is Wessex?'

'It is in England, sir.'

'Your brother gave you this estate?'

'No, my fiancé gave it to me.'

'Count Martin? I was not aware he had lands in England.'

'No, Sir Olivier, it is Count Richard I am referring to.'

The Abbot's knight tipped his head to one side. 'The

man who stepped into Martin's shoes? I never realised you were promised to him too.'

'Only briefly. We soon agreed that we should not suit, and as a parting gift Count Richard granted me this estate in England.'

Sir Olivier looked puzzled. 'Well, that is all to the good, my lady, but I meant it when I said I wished to marry you and not your lands.'

'I am telling you this,' Aude softened her voice, 'because I want you to understand my intentions. I am currently on my way to Wessex.'

His eyes widened. 'I see.'

'I hope that you do. I wish to tour my estate there and ensure that it is in good order. And whatever my brother may say, I am not going to make any decisions regarding my future until my return.'

'And when might that be?'

Aude shrugged. 'That will largely depend on what I find in England.' She gave him a straight look. 'My brother thinks to sway me, Sir Olivier, but—'

'You cannot be swayed.' He grinned.

Not by you, Aude thought, which, oddly, was the very reason she might consider marrying him in the future. If she had to… 'No, sir. I shall tour my estate; there are matters there that need my attention. With luck I will be back at Crèvecoeur by Advent.'

'You will risk a winter crossing? Is that wise?'

Aude made an impatient movement. 'I will not travel if the weather is inclement. What I am saying, Sir Olivier, is—'

'No. You are saying no. You will not have me.'

Aude was startled to see disappointment written so clearly on the handsome face. And she would swear it was more than the loss of her dowry; this man appeared to genuinely want her for his wife. *Malleable indeed.*

'Yes, Sir Olivier,' she spoke gently but firmly. 'I am afraid that I am.'

His nostrils flared and she found herself at the receiving end of another of those charming smiles. 'When do you leave?' he asked, politely offering her his arm.

As they started walking back to the church, tension seeped out of her, and Aude realised she had been braced for a churlish reaction. Her heart warmed to him. There were not many knights who would accept her decision so well. Charmer he might be, but Sir Olivier was genuinely likeable, which was all to the good. Particularly since Edouard would be more agreeable about her visiting England if she went in the company of the knight he had chosen for her husband…

'I had planned to take a barge to Honfleur this afternoon, but another passenger took my place and had my baggage thrown off the ship.'

He missed a step. 'Surely not?'

'Really.' They resumed their slow progress towards St Peter's church where Edouard was waiting for them.

'What will you do, my lady?'

'Find another ship.'

'Does Lord Edouard know what you have in mind?'

'Yes, but I fear he may try to delay my departure.' Aude gave him a straight look. 'I should like to trust you, sir. May I?'

Brown eyes looked earnestly into hers. 'It would be my honour to assist you, my lady.'

'There is no need to feel compelled.'

'Lady Aude, it will be no trouble.' His smile broadened. 'I want to help. You see, I hope to prove myself worthy of you.'

Firmly, Aude shook her head. 'My mind is made up, Sir Olivier. I will not marry you.' *Unless I have to...*

'You will forgive a man for hoping.'

The brown eyes held hers steadily, and after a moment Aude nodded. 'I will not change my mind, but I will accept your help. I am told that another river barge is due to set out tomorrow. In order to avoid an argument with Edouard—he wishes me to delay, and I am for leaving as soon as possible—I shall be needing new travelling chests.'

She was sent another of those charming smiles. 'My lady, I know the very place where they might be found.'

Chapter Three

Owing to the need for discretion, Hugh Duclair had three horses stabled at one of the quieter inns a little downstream from Jumièges. The inn was small and in need of repair, daylight was visible through the stable roof. It was not a place in which he would choose to stable horses in winter, but since it was summer and a hot one at that, he had known the animals would be snug enough.

Having paid their accounting with the innkeeper, Hugh and his squire, Gil, were riding back along the riverbank towards the port. The river was almost at the full, and swifts screeched across the sky, fast as arrows.

Hugh was thinking about Aude de Crèvecoeur. Great God, it had knocked him back seeing her this morning. Edouard, Hugh had been half-expecting to see, but his sister… No, seeing Aude had been a surprise.

Each time Hugh saw Aude it seemed that she was

becoming more and more beautiful. Little Brat, he had
called her, years ago, and the name had stuck, much
to her irritation. There had been no trace of the Brat
today. At first Hugh had thought Aude was ignoring him,
as well she ought given his present circumstances—it
would not serve her well to recognise him. But what had
startled him most wasn't the way his heart had lifted at
sight of her—he had always been fond of little Aude—
it was the way his gut had twisted when she had not
immediately acknowledged him.

The matter of his banishment had hardened him;
Hugh had learned to inure himself to his friends reject-
ing him. Politics—he knew it was just a question of
politics. But it would seem that Aude was an exception;
he had thoroughly disliked it when she had not recognised him.

Might Aude come to believe that the accusations
against him were true? That there was no smoke without fire? Hugh's jaw clenched. He could only pray, could
only trust that she would remember their past friendship.

He grimaced and glanced down ruefully at his horse,
an unremarkable bay gelding. Aude might not recognise
him if she saw him now. The previous time they had
met, he had been riding into Crèvecoeur on Shadow,
his warhorse. With a full escort.

Hugh forced his thoughts back to the present. His
warhorse had been left at Freyncourt—Shadow was far
too showy for a man not wishing to attract attention to
himself. After midnight tonight, he should be out of the
Duchy. Which was why he was wearing a worn grey
tunic and was astride a gelding he hadn't bothered to
name, an animal that had more temper than manners.

Gil was mounted on a small black, a brown mare on a leading rein trotted beside him. The mare belonged to Hugh's thirteen-year-old sister Louise.

Louise was, if she had done as Hugh had ordered, waiting for them back at the barge. Hugh loved his little sister and enjoyed her company, but in the dark days ahead, he was going to have to part with her. He had no right to drag his sister all over Christendom while he fought to clear his name.

'I hope Louise hasn't taken it into her head to explore the market,' he said. 'We shall be casting off at high tide; the ship won't wait for her. Besides, she really must learn that we have no coin to spare until we regain what the Bishop has stolen from us.'

'No, my lord,' Gil murmured. 'I am sure Lady Louise understands.'

Hugh looked bleakly at his squire. 'Are you?'

Anger burned deep within him. Anger at the calumnies spread against him, anger that the Bishop's lies had been so readily believed. He and his sister were reduced to penury, because the Bishop of St Aubin wanted to keep the silver his father had deposited with him for safe-keeping. Family silver. Freyncourt silver.

Hugh might be a Count, but he was discovering it was not easy proving his innocence. He had, so the word went, supported Duke William's enemies in the recent power struggle in Flanders. And the documents that would support the deposits his father had left with the Bishop had gone missing. At first Hugh had thought, naïvely, as it turned out, that it would be a simple matter of proving his innocence, of finding those documents. How wrong he had been.

His Holiness, the Bishop of St Aubin, vehemently denied the existence of the Freyncourt silver.

And the document that proved it?

Missing from his father's strongbox.

'I wish I had your confidence, Gil; we only have a few hours to quit the Duchy.'

'I am sure she will be waiting at the barge, my lord.'

Hugh frowned. 'Gil?'

'My lord?'

'You really must dispense with my title from now on. It will be important you use my Christian name in the days to come.'

'Yes…Hugh.'

Against all the odds, Hugh felt a smile forming. 'And for God's sake, try to use it more naturally, you sound as though it might choke you.'

'I am sorry…Hugh…but I think that it might. I will endeavour to try harder.'

'See that you do. Today we hired ourselves out as ship's porters to save a coin or two. But tomorrow? Who knows what part we will have to play tomorrow? If you cannot address me as an equal—and my sister, too, for that matter—I shall have to dismiss you until I am reinstated.'

Gil's expression of horror was eloquent enough to make further words unnecessary. His squire would, Hugh was sure, get it right from now on.

They lapsed into silence. Hugh was lost in his plans when an alarm bell jerked him out of them.

Gil yelped and pointed downriver. 'Holy Mother, what is *that*?'

A wave was rolling along the river. Couldn't be, but it was.

A wave?

Hugh's heart began to thud. He dug his heels into the gelding's ribs. *'La barre,'* he muttered.

The wave was rushing upstream towards the port. White crests foamed at both banks. In the centre, a wall of water reared up.

Behind him, Gil began to babble as he spurred his horse. 'My l—Hugh! The boats! The jetties!'

'More to the point—*Louise*!'

Hugh gave the gelding his head. They pounded up the track towards the quays.

In the port ahead, others had noticed the wave. People were crying out, pointing, dragging pack animals away from the water side, darting forwards to drag bales of wool clear of the water-line. The tocsin rang on, louder than before.

Louise! She should be on the barge. The blood thumped in Hugh's ears as beneath him the gelding's hoofs drummed the ground. The wall of water was closer, almost level with the port itself. Hugh had heard tales about tidal surges, had heard of the damage they caused, but until this moment he had thought them exaggeration. Now as he stared dry-mouthed at the approaching surge, he wasn't so sure.

Louise! As the gelding thundered towards the port, part of him was praying that his sister had disobeyed him. She often did. But the cold lump in his belly was telling him that this time, Louise had done as she was told. 'Stay in the boat,' he had said. 'Be good.' *Mon Dieu.*

'We're too far away!' The despair in Gil's voice

sounded like Louise's death knell. 'Impossible to get there!'

Hell! The surge was a mere five yards from their barge which, since it was moored at the end of the jetty, would be one of the first to be struck. Hugh focused on a slight figure in a brown gown and his blood turned to ice—*Louise*! There she was, she had heard the commotion, had run to the ship's rail to stare.

'Get out, Louise!' Hugh yelled. 'Get out!' But it was hopeless, Louise could not hear him. It was too late, he could never reach her in time.

Hugh Duclair had told Aude the truth; another river barge was indeed moored downstream, in a shady inlet behind the far jetty. Sir Olivier—he was being most useful—had helped her find it.

Aude had booked passage on it for the following morning, and with the knight's assistance had covertly acquired new travelling chests. Aude's maid, Edwige, had quickly transferred most of Aude's belongings to the new chests.

The old trunks had been plain wood, studded and banded with iron. The new ones were painted, the surfaces covered with daisy-like flowers. Once Edwige had finished packing, Aude and Sir Olivier had between them supervised their safe stowing on the barge in the backwater.

That being done, Aude and Sir Olivier were walking arm in arm along the riverbank back to the main port.

'I do not think Lord Edouard suspects you are intending to leave tomorrow, my lady,' Sir Olivier said.

'No, I hate to deceive him, but I must confess I am glad you have agreed to accompany me.'

Sir Olivier smiled. 'You know the reason for that, my lady. My time with the Abbot has come to an end and—'

'Sir, you know I will not marry you; you will not persuade me.'

'Perhaps, perhaps not…'

'Sir, you *must* believe me. But I do hope to use some of my English revenues to pay your knight's fee. I will need support in Alfold.'

His face brightened. 'You would like to hire me?'

'Yes, I—'

A piercing scream cut through the air. A tocsin was sounding.

'What on earth…?' Aude lifted her hand from Sir Olivier's arm.

More screaming. Hairs prickled on the back of Aude's neck. Snatching up her skirts, she started running towards the quays.

She took in the approaching wave—*coming upstream*?—and the panicky scurrying on the jetties. People were shoving past her, faces blank with fear. Spray arched skywards, droplets glowing like a rainbow. Someone else started screaming; everyone was screaming.

And there, alone in the barge nearest the oncoming water, stood a little girl—a child—in brown homespun. She was looking at the wave, frozen with shock, forgotten.

The wave reached up like a living thing. The barge lurched sideways, the mooring rope snapped. The girl's shriek rose like a gull's above the clamour and the wave thundered down, dragging the girl into a swirl of frothing, seething foam.

Hissing snakes, Aude thought, as something clicked

inside her. There was no time for thought, she tore the veil from her head and hurled herself forwards.

'My lady, *no*!'

The river swooshed past, flooding the jetty. There was noise, Aude's ears were full of it: rushing, screaming, bells. So much noise, it deafened. Water hit, came up to her calves. The river roared, drowning out the snakes. Cold.

Water slapped her legs, almost toppling her. The ancient river gods had come alive and they were out to get her. Aude held her ground. One hand found a mooring post and she clung. The other reached for the girl as her barge was swept away, bucking and rocking out among the white horses.

'Take my hand!' Aude cried.

The girl in brown was being tossed about like a bundle of rags among the packing cases, but the water was bringing her closer. She was barely managing to keep her head above water; if she let the incoming tide take her, she wouldn't last more than a minute.

Someone else was in the water. A woman wailed. 'Didier! *Didier!*'

Aude fixed her whole attention on the child. A barrel thumped into her and her knees buckled. She held her ground. The girl vanished beneath the surface before reappearing a few yards nearer, water steaming down, hair stuck to her skull. A small hand reached for hers.

'That's it!'

Bracing herself, Aude stretched forwards.

Their hands met and clutched. Held. The girl's body swung round; the river was determined to carry her upstream. Aude gripped that small hand as though her life depended on it. Her arm felt as though it was being ripped from its socket.

And then she was no longer alone. Sir Olivier was at her shoulder, catching the child's other hand, the brown skirts. Together, they wrestled her out of the water.

The wave had passed Jumièges; it was ploughing on upriver, but the danger was not over.

'Be careful, my lady,' Sir Olivier gasped, as they got the girl clear of the water and he lifted her into his arms. 'There's a fierce wake. Mind the wake.'

Even as he started back to shore, a packing case thudded against Aude's shin.

Aude's legs buckled. She fought to find her footing and slipped head first into the boiling river.

Galloping flat out along the high water-line, Hugh had arrived in time to see that Louise was safe. The havoc the surge had caused at the port had almost stopped his heart. A couple of rowboats, their moorings severed, were being tossed about on the river; barges were drifting midstream without oarsmen or steersmen; upturned boats were being carried towards Rouen, but *Louise was safe*.

Aude had saved her! It had to have been Edouard's sister; Hugh recognised that green gown. The pristine whiteness of her veil stood out in a crowd, *she* stood out in a crowd, risking herself to save Louise. She had handed Louise to Sir Olivier. And now she herself was gone.

He had to find her. Little Brat. She must be saved, she *must*.

Breathing hard, Hugh fixed his eyes on the spot where he had last seen Aude. Nothing. He shifted his gaze a little upstream. Still nothing. The branch of a tree.

Something that looked like sacking. A white…her veil, surely?

No, no, she had torn that off, had flung it aside.

Yes! There she was, several yards behind the crest of the wave, in the churned up, muddy waters of its wake.

As Hugh narrowed his eyes, the main front of the bore reached him. He held the gelding steady as the wave crashed on to the bank. Spray fanned out in all directions, droplets gleaming pretty as dew in the morning sun. His horse shifted, shaking his head, legs trembling. Hugh held him steady. So deadly, that river. The front raced by, soaking him, his horse, and doubtless Gil, who was swearing colourfully somewhere behind him.

Hell, where was Aude? He had lost sight of her again. Desperation gripped him, he couldn't breathe. *Where? Where was she?*

The river was seething and choppy, broken up into thousands of wavelets as the wave forged its way inland. The gelding shifted; he was afraid of the river today, and Hugh could not blame him.

Where was she?

There! A few yards out, Aude's head had reappeared next to a bundle of straw. Both were sinking.

Hugh kicked his heels, guiding the gelding into the water. *The river shall not have her!* The force of his feeling rocked him, but then he had long had a soft spot for Aude de Crèvecoeur. Despite appearances, her life had not been easy. This morning by the barge, Hugh had been occupied, but he had noticed her the moment she had stepped on to the quayside. And he was almost certain that, despite Edouard's orders to the contrary, Aude had wanted to speak to him. She hadn't wanted to speak to the surly deckhand who had removed her belongings from the barge—she had wanted to speak to him, to Hugh Duclair. Foolish, *foolish* girl.

Edouard's sister, like Edouard, had a loyal heart, and he would be damned before he saw her bravery rewarded by drowning. There was enough injustice in Normandy without adding Aude's death to the scales. Edouard's strictures, his own resolution not to drag Aude into his affairs must, for the moment, be set aside.

'Careful, Hugh, that river has power.'

Thanks to Hugh's urging, his horse entered the water faster than was safe. Its flanks shuddered, its eyes rolled, it fought Hugh's commands, but it obeyed.

Aude was clinging to an oar, a wavelet breaking over her. Her plaits had unravelled. Her hair streamed out, dark red against the cloudy water.

'Let go!' Hugh took the gelding in as far as he dared. It would help no one if he were swept away too. 'Strike out for me!'

Hugh doubted that Aude could swim—no lady of his acquaintance could—but she seemed to understand that the oar would carry her away. She let go and surrendered herself to the water.

Determined to intercept her, Hugh angled his horse sideways. It wasn't particularly deep here. The gelding was still on its feet, but the force of the water would have been too strong for a person to withstand. The rush of the river filled his ears.

Aude was blinded by water. Her mouth was full of brine and it was choking her. Cold. It was so cold. How could river water be so cold when the day was so warm? The horseman who had waded in after her—she could not see him clearly for the stinging in her eyes—must be quite mad. Her hair, too, was blinding her. She spluttered and choked.

The horseman was shouting, but Aude couldn't hear him for the roaring—whether it was the roaring of the river or her own blood, she could not tell. Her lungs ached. Water slapped her in the face.

He was getting close, thank God. Her legs tangled in waterlogged skirts, her arms refused to obey her. Heavy, everything was heavy, pulling her down. But even as Aude felt herself sinking, she was carried towards him, the madman on the bay horse.

Yes! Only a little further.

'Come on, Aude!'

He knew her name?

Feebly Aude kicked her feet—her shoes had gone almost as soon as she hit the water. Her toes scraped the bottom, but it was impossible to stand. Too fast, the river was running too fast.

She hit the horse's flank, the horseman's leg. Glimpsed red cross-gartering. Another wave tried to drown her. Blindly, she groped for a well-muscled calf and hooked her fingers into his cross-gartering.

'Hold hard!'

A madman, clearly. Why else would he be commanding her to do the obvious? More water found its way into Aude's lungs and a fit of coughing took her as he turned the horse and she was dragged ignominiously towards the river bank like so much wet washing.

On dry land, she let go and fell on her knees. Someone was talking. Aude couldn't make out the words; it sounded as though bees were buzzing. Blackness was swirling at the edges of her vision, exactly as, moments ago, the water had swirled about her. She retched and retched again. Warm hands were on her shoulders, supporting her. He was sweeping her hair back to keep it clear of her face. Her chest ached.

'That's right, Aude,' her rescuer said. 'Get it out. All of it.'

Aude? More retching. Her stomach burned. And still he was holding her.

'Better?'

Nodding, Aude sat back down, panting. She looked into his face.

'*Hugh*!'

Hugh Duclair's stormy blue eyes were anxious and his thumbs were making tiny caressing movements on her shoulders, but even as she watched the anxiety faded. He released her and shifted away. '*Ma dame*, I do not think you know me.'

'Oh, yes, I do, I—'

'*Ma dame*, your brother has forbidden you to acknowledge me.'

She gripped the frayed edge of his sleeve. It was that or reach for Hugh's hand and the look in his eyes warned her that such a gesture would not be welcome. 'Don't be ridiculous, Hugh, you saved me! Besides, you proved you know me when you called me by name.'

Sighing, Hugh sat down on the bank beside her. He was almost as out of breath as she was. Someone else was riding up, a young man with another horse on a leading rein. His squire, Gil—Aude recognised him from last year. She flung a weak smile at him. Thank God, not all Hugh Duclair's friends had deserted him.

'In any case, I thank you,' she said, as another fit of coughing overcame her. She put a hand to her throat, she felt hoarse. 'I was never…never so glad to see anyone in my life.'

Hugh grinned and for a moment his face transformed and he was his old self. A handsome Viking of a man who was her brother's closest friend; a man who was—thank goodness—utterly oblivious of the fact that while Aude had been a girl, she had put him at the centre of many a romantic dream.

'No, my lady, I should be thanking you.'

Still panting, Aude shoved her hair back. 'Me?'

Hugh's sun-gilded head nodded in the direction of the port. 'That was my sister in the barge back there.'

'Your sister?' Aude had heard of Louise, naturally, though she had never met her.

'Yes, indeed. My one and only little sister.' Hugh put his hand on his heart and his eyes held hers. He was regarding her so warmly that the heat rushed back into her cheeks and for a moment she could not look away. 'Aude, I owe you more than I can say. My sister is—'

'Hugh! *Hugh*!'

'Gil?'

'Some monks and a couple of the Abbot's knights are heading this way.'

'*Merde*, they cannot be allowed to delay us.'

Aude could practically see Hugh's cares fall back on his shoulders: banished with time running out on him; concern for his sister; the loss of his baggage on that barge…

He pushed to his feet, and Aude found herself staring at a pair of strong male legs. His boots squelched.

'I got you wet, Hugh, I am sorry.' There was a cold lump under Aude's breastbone. There was so much she longed to discuss with him, she wanted to wish him well...

But already Hugh was moving away. 'It is of no matter,' he said. 'You have my eternal thanks. The good brothers will see to your welfare while I go and find Louise. And, Aude, if they should ask, remember that it is best that you do not know me.' He gave her a brief bow, and in a couple of heartbeats he and Gil had gone.

Aude was sitting alone on the ravaged foreshore when the monks arrived to exclaim over her and offer her their assistance.

'Haven't you had enough of the river today, my lady?' Edwige asked, curling her lip as she edged round a stinking tangle of fish nets. The wave had strung much debris along the river path and the two women were carefully making their way upstream, towards the concealed inlet.

'Believe me, I have, but we won't be long.'

Aude had bathed and washed the salt and mud from her hair and put on a dry gown and veil. 'As soon as we have reassured ourselves that our property is still on that barge, we shall return to the Abbey.'

On the foreshore, some boys were hauling a half-sunk rowboat out of the river, scraping and bumping it across the stones as they dragged it in. With a grunt and a heave they tipped it on its side and the water poured out. *Where was Hugh now? Had he found his sister? How was he going to prove his loyalty to the Duke?*

Edwige touched her arm. 'Where did you say this barge is?'

'A little further on the left, there's a backwater and...

there!' Aude pointed at a mooring in the shade of an overhanging alder. The barge looked intact. 'See, it is exactly as I left it! I hoped it would be, tied up out of the way as it is. Come along, Edwige, stop dawdling. Don't you want to see for yourself that your trunk is safe?'

It wouldn't have been the end of the world for Aude and Edwige to have lost their belongings; everything they were taking to England could easily have been replaced. Which likely could not be said for Hugh Duclair. Hugh had lost so much when he had lost Duke William's trust. His lands and his revenues had been confiscated, and today the river had snatched what little remained. When the money in his purse ran out, he would have nothing. What must that feel like?

'What's *he* doing here?' Edwige's sharp whisper cut into Aude's thoughts. 'Is he following us?'

Aude glanced back. A masculine figure in a threadbare grey tunic was striding purposefully after them. She went very still. *Hugh.*

The soon-to-be exiled Count de Freyncourt was rolling down his sleeves as he came and when he reached within a couple of feet of her, he bowed his head in that slightly ironic way he had. 'My lady.' Aude had the fleeting impression that he was pleased to see her again; she was certainly glad to see him.

'Hugh, was Louise all right?'

'Perfectly, thank you. Gil is looking after her.'

So tall. And when the sunlight gilds the tips of his hair, he really does look like Lucifer. Her eyes fell on the fraying sleeves of his grey tunic. *A beautiful, albeit rather shabby Lucifer...*

'I should not really be speaking to you, my brother will disapprove.' Aude softened her words with a smile.

She really did not understand it, but truly it was impossible not to smile when Hugh looked down at her like that. His eyes were soft and unguarded, as they had been before his banishment. His mouth had gone up at the corner, exactly as it used to when laughter between them was but a breath away. Aude was beginning to think that one could not help but smile whenever Hugh did. His coldness when she had first seen him on that barge that morning had been particularly distressing.

Hugh Duclair seemed to have a strange effect on her these days. She felt fluttery when he was close by, most unlike her usual calm self. It had not always been so; when they were younger there was only ease between them. Aude had liked him then and she liked him still. Except….well, there was that inauspicious encounter early this morning. She had heartily disliked him when he had taken it upon himself to remove her baggage from the other barge!

Hugh lifted a brow. 'Wise man, your brother.'

His voice was dry. Deep. Surely it had not always been as deep? And his mouth—when had that begun to fascinate her? Hugh had a full lower lip which hinted at a sensual nature; his upper lip had a slight dip in the centre. On his cheeks there was the slight shadow of an incipient beard. Heavens! Why ever was she examining Hugh like this? *A kiss. What would his kiss be like*? It was an extraordinarily compelling thought, it would not be pushed to one side. *She would enjoy Hugh's kiss…*

Jerking her gaze away, Aude stared at a tree past Hugh's shoulder, painfully conscious that her eyes wanted to linger on his face, to study that nose, so strong and straight, to memorise the exact curve of those high cheekbones. Her eyes wanted to learn his features in a way that was new to her. It was extremely unsettling, not unpleasant exactly, but deeply unsettling.

Fond though Aude had been of Martin, she had never felt the slightest inclination to learn his features; her eyes had not wanted to linger on him. This reaction to Hugh Duclair was baffling. It must be because she was so worried about him. The future of a man with a day to get out of the Duchy and only a small purse between him and penury could only be bleak. Fortunately, Hugh did not appear to have noticed either her interest or her confusion.

Some swallows were diving low over the river. As they swooped up past the white cliffs on the opposite bank, Aude forced herself to concentrate on the patterns they were tracing in the air.

'I would not want you to court your brother's displeasure on my account, particularly when he is in the right,' Hugh said softly.

Slowly, as though he were fighting himself, he touched her hand. Tingles raced up her arm.

'Take care, Aude. The river has taken a bite out of the path here, you and Edwige must watch your step.'

Sure enough, a section of the bank had broken away.

Hugh flashed a grin at her, revealing strong white teeth. 'Wouldn't want you falling in twice in a day. Aude, my banishment is not effective till midnight, so I think you may safely allow me to escort you one last time. In any case, there is no one else about.' He offered her his arm. 'Edouard need never know. If you manage to remain silent, you may truthfully tell him that you only spoke to me when absolutely necessary.'

Chapter Four

Hugh lifted an eyebrow, daring her to follow his lead.

If you manage to remain silent.

The wretch, he was needling her!

'There must be more of the devil in me than I had thought,' Aude murmured, laying her fingers on the worn grey sleeve without the slightest hesitation. 'For this afternoon the thought of disobeying Edouard is most attractive.'

Hugh's eyes lit up. 'I am relieved to hear it.'

The path narrowed as they entered the shadowy inlet. Branches brushed Aude's clothes, clear sunlight became dappled. Aude was conscious of Edwige following a couple of paces behind, listening with avid curiosity to their every word.

'I am also glad to see you are fully recovered from your…swim earlier,' he added softly.

'Yes.' Like Hugh, Aude responded quietly. It had the

effect of making this, a walk by the river in full day, feel oddly clandestine. 'And your sister—I take it you found her without any difficulty and that she really is fully recovered?'

'Yes, thank you, Louise is well.' He glanced pointedly at the river. 'Aude, why have you chosen to walk this way? Wouldn't a ride along the inland pathways be more congenial after this morning?'

'Indeed, but after you tossed my baggage off that ship…' She scowled at him, caught the tail end of an unrepentant grin, and continued. 'I took your advice, Hugh, and found another.' She gestured at the barge moored to its post in the riverbank. Leaves rustled overhead.

They stared at the barge.

Something flickered in Hugh's eyes and he looked sharply away. 'I am sorry about that, Aude.' His voice had an odd inflection to it.

'Don't give it a thought. In truth you did me a favour, for the wave did not penetrate the inlet. This ship and my baggage are quite safe.'

Blue-grey eyes travelled the length of the ship, from the snarling wolf carved on the swooping prow, to the finial on its rounded stern. They were more than a little troubled. 'It is small for a river barge,' he commented.

'It is one of the smallest, but my travelling chests are safe.'

A sun-burned hand came to rest on hers. 'I am glad my advice meant you didn't lose anything.' He gave her an intent look. 'Did you intend to go to Honfleur?'

'I still do intend it, Hugh.'

'I see.' He cleared his throat.

Whatever was the matter with him? Aude might not

have seen much of Hugh lately, but she knew him well enough to be certain that something she had said had given him pause. What on earth could it be? His lips were curved, yet she would swear he was concealing something.

Their eyes met. Aude's thoughts became tangled; Hugh had a way of looking at her that disordered her mind. His gaze skimmed over her—brow, eyes, cheeks, lips, nose…she could feel it as one might feel a caress. Yet his expression remained shadowed as he turned his attention back to the barge. It was impossible to shake off the impression that something she had said worried him.

She must be mistaken. Naturally Hugh was troubled, he was weighed down with so many problems it was a miracle he remained standing. That pensive look had to be connected to his banishment. Yet the thought remained, Hugh was unhappy about her desire to go to Honfleur. Why on earth should that be?

'Aude, didn't Edouard send your baggage back to the lodge?'

'Yes, but afterwards I recalled you mentioning this boat, so I had everything carted here.'

'Does Edouard know that you have no intention of abandoning your plans?'

Aude's chin inched up. It was no business of Hugh's what she had told her brother, but perhaps that explained his change of mood. Her disobedience disturbed him. This was the eleventh century and women were meant to be obedient. Women were little more than chattels and men did not allow their chattels to display wills of their own.

Which was the very reason she was so eager to reach Alfold.

At Alfold, which Count Richard had gifted *wholly* to her, she would be her own mistress. For the first time in her life, she would only have herself to answer to.

'I am not one of my brother's men that I must rush to obey his every whim.'

Hugh removed his hand from hers. Aude felt a distinct pang; she liked it when he touched her. It had felt as though he was her particular friend, that he was concerned for her and would stand by her if he could. Which, given his disgrace, was utterly absurd.

'You had best go aboard,' he was saying. 'To make quite certain nothing is lost.'

Ever the courtier, even when being hounded from the Duchy, Hugh handed her politely up the gangplank and on to the deck. High in an overhanging willow, a blackbird was singing.

The ship's master had left a boy on board to act as a guard, he was dozing in the shifting shadows on a couple of empty grain sacks. Hearing their footfall, the boy leaped to his feet and rushed into speech.

'Lady Aude! I...I didn't hear you. There is no need for concern; as you see, the wave didn't get us.'

Hugh nodded pleasantly at him. Several packing cases were roped into place, but Hugh didn't recognise any of them as being the ones he had unloaded from the other barge back in port. 'All accounted for, Aude?'

'Yes.'

Really, Hugh thought, running his gaze over the crowded deck, *there will scarcely be space to breathe when this ship is full.* 'Are you taking horses, Aude? It will be very cramped. And what about an escort—you are taking an escort, I assume?' *Lord, it looked as though he was going to have to repeat his actions of this morning, and unload her baggage from this barge too. There will be hell to pay when she finds out.* It struck him that he had yet to see Aude truly angry. The thought of Aude in a fury was unexpectedly tantalising. And extremely distracting. It stirred his blood—in truth, the thought of Aude in a fury stirred him in places that had no place stirring when he was planning to steal her place on this barge.

For a moment Hugh could barely think. He found himself fighting the urge to pull Aude into his arms, to tug that veil from her head and press his lips into the curve of her neck. Suddenly Aude was temptation incarnate. Bemused, he gazed at her mouth. He wanted to taste it while she was smiling; he wanted to taste it while she was angry. *When she learns what I have done, will her eyes spark with a fire to match that glorious hair? Now that*—he bit back a smile—*would surely be worth seeing...*

'An escort?' Aude put her nose in the air. Hugh's questions struck her as impertinent. 'I have thought of that, thank you.' She went over to the larger of her new, painted trunks and nudged it with her foot. It seemed secure.

Conflicting thoughts tugged at her. She was conscious of an impulse to trust him, to open her heart to him, but that would be folly indeed. Men usually stuck together, so the less she told Hugh, the better. He and Edouard might not be acknowledging each other in public, but she had seen the looks they had exchanged this morning. Hugh's banishment had not extinguished their friendship.

Yet the impulse to confide in Hugh remained powerful. Aude had long nursed a fondness for Hugh Duclair, and had thought that if ever there was a man she might trust, it would be him. Yes, men generally stuck together and while she had a fondness for this one, he was—unfortunately—not in the least bit malleable.

These days Hugh's looks…really, he had become terrifyingly attractive. Those wide shoulders, that thick sun-kissed hair that betrayed his Viking blood-lines, that careless manner, that easy confidence. He seemed to draw her to him; the same thing had happened last spring. She wanted to reach out, to touch, to stroke…

Sinful, sensual thoughts.

But being with Hugh did not simply put sinful thoughts into Aude's head, other thoughts were also taking shape. Strange half-formed longings for a world in which there were men who formed genuine friendships with women. What an extraordinary idea—of course it was possible for men to form friendships with women! Ladies might be considered chattels by their menfolk, but that did not prevent friendships from developing between men and women, as she herself knew. Her betrothal to Martin might have been made for political reasons; none the less Martin had adored her. Even though at times—here, a shockingly disloyal thought startled a frown out of her—Martin *had* seemed somewhat distant…

Was Hugh fond of her? In the past Aude had had her hopes. And then, without warning, the past rushed back at her and the tumultuous events of 1066 were sharp in her mind. Painfully sharp. Aude nibbled her finger. She did not understand it, but in some way Hugh Duclair's impending banishment made the events of 1066 seem even more poignant…

It had been a fateful year. It was not only the year that Duke William took the English crown, it was also the year that Aude's father, Sir Hamon, had died.

With her grandfather in exile and the family lands confiscated, her father had been a landless knight like Sir Olivier. Sir Hamon had longed to inherit Crèvecoeur and Corbeil, but with his father's lands held under stewardship for the King, he had never lived to see that hope fulfilled.

Poor Father. Tears pricked at the back of Aude's eyes.

In 1066, the Duchy had been buzzing like a hornet's nest; talk of war had been on everyone's lips. Her father had resolved to go to the seaport of Dives where he would enlist with the invasion force. He had been full of optimism concerning his future.

'*Mark my words, Aude,*' Sir Hamon had said as she had ridden up with him to a bustling inn near the Dives shipyard where Duke William's fleet was being built. '*This venture of the Duke's will be the making of our family.*'

Blinking firmly, Aude dismissed the memory. It only made her sad. That night near the Dives shipyard had been the night her father had died, killed not while fighting gloriously for his Duke, but in a squalid tavern brawl.

She had been thirteen years old.

Aude shot Hugh a sidelong glance. *Sweet Mother, let Hugh forget me as I was at the time. The shame of it*! For in 1066, Aude had been serving her impoverished father as his squire, and when Hugh and Edouard had arrived to join the mustering troops they had found her clad in boy's clothing—a short tunic and cross-gartered hose. Her cheeks warmed as she remembered. She had only been thirteen, of course, but...

'Aude?' Gently Hugh removed her finger from her mouth.

'Mmm?'

'Is something wrong?'

'No. No, not at all.'

In truth, far from appearing shocked at the sight of her, Hugh had been kindness itself in Dives. He had taken the trouble to endorse her childish wish to become Countess of Beaumont, even going so far as to encourage Edouard to arrange for her betrothal to Count Martin. Hugh had not mentioned her clothing, but she had sensed his disapproval.

Had what happened that year affected the way Hugh thought of her?

Aude's pulse jumped. It could be her imagination, but it seemed to her that the liking she and Hugh had always felt for each other might be changing. Another surreptitious glance revealed him to be studying her, running his gaze up and down her body.

Her pulse began to do more than jump, it began to race.

Did Hugh like her looks now she had grown into a woman? Another brief glance confirmed that he did. Hugh Duclair was drawn to her. Some of the worry had left his expression, his eyes were watching her warmly. The careful way that he had handed her into this barge told her that he respected her, while his gaze told her that he liked her looks. For her part, Aude liked him, far better than Sir Olivier, for example. And as for Hugh's form... She sighed. The image of that lithe, half-naked body tossing her belongings about the docks was only too easy to recall.

It was a pity Hugh was leaving under such a cloud, she could do with a friend who liked her for herself, and even though her brother had forbidden her to speak to him, she yearned for his friendship. This man attracted her in many ways. She stole another look at him. Wide shoulders, strong limbs, upright posture...

Hugh was noble by birth and noble in his bearing and nothing, not even banishment, would take that away from him. Perhaps it would not take him long to prove he was innocent of the charges against him.

She felt adrift. She must be realistic. There were many reasons why Hugh was out of bounds to her and, given his banishment, it was impossible that their childish friendship would survive, never mind grow. From midnight tonight he should not even be in the Duchy. Anyone caught helping him after then would be in serious trouble.

After midnight, anyone associating with Hugh Duclair could be brought to court to answer charges of aiding and abetting a traitor. At best they risked disgrace, at worst, execution. Aude's relationship with Hugh might have been a bright thread running through her life, but she must resign herself to the loss of it. Much as she might wish otherwise, their childish friendship was over.

She would never kiss him.

Holding down a sigh, she moved to the ship's handrail. 'You will stay out of Normandy?' Knowing Hugh, he would fight like a demon for his reinstatement. 'I don't want you to get yourself killed; if you come back to the Duchy, your fate will be uncertain.'

'I will do what I must. As well as clearing my name, there is a matter of some family silver which has gone missing. And in order to regain my lands I will have to take the kiss of peace from King William in person.' His mouth twisted. 'Given that our Duke has been neglecting his Norman territories in favour of his English kingdom, I may have to travel to England for that.'

'Yes, I hear the Duke has been fully occupied with enforcing his authority as King.' With a heavy heart, Aude stepped on to the ramp. 'Hugh, wherever you go, I wish you well. It is not likely that we shall meet again and I am sorry for it.'

'No, we shall not meet, and I too have my regrets. I beg that you remember that.'

What an odd thing for him to say. She stared blankly into his eyes, but they were unreadable.

'Aude, there is something else.' A simple touch on her arm had her stopping in her tracks. 'Do not let a rift form between you and your brother—he means well. He wants the best for you and one day you will realise that.'

'Hugh, Edouard barely knows me. After he went to be fostered with you at Freyncourt, we rarely saw each other. Why, I saw him no more that I saw you.'

Blue-grey eyes watched her. Mysterious, breathtaking eyes, eyes that dropped briefly to her lips and lit up every time he smiled. 'He wants the best for you.' Taking her hand, he lifted it to his lips. Another tingle flew up her arm. Aude's throat worked; it was dry as dust.

Darting a glance at Edwige, Hugh lowered his voice, rubbing his thumb over her knuckles. 'What are you going to do in Honfleur?'

'What, apart from escape Edouard's plans for me?'

'Aude—' strong fingers tightened on hers '—Edouard would never force you.'

How could Hugh know that? No matter. 'I sail to England,' she said.

'England?'

Those tiny caresses had started again. Hugh's thumb was moving gently over her knuckles; she wondered if he realised what he was doing. It was very distracting, it made her heart pound. And the air in this inlet…it must be the heat of the day, because there didn't seem to be enough of it.

'Mmm, I have an estate in Wessex.' She watched his thumb, back and forth it went, back and forth. She let her hand relax in his. Hugh's touch was most pleasant, once one got used to the unsettling effect it had on her senses. And why on earth was it so hard to concentrate on their conversation? She looked up in time to see that Hugh's eyes had narrowed in that intent way he some-times had when something caught his attention.

'You have an estate in England? That's the first I have heard of it—I didn't know your family has interests in England.'

'We didn't until recently. Count Richard gave me the estate when he broke our betrothal agreement.' The way Hugh was watching her mouth was making Aude absurdly self-conscious. Cheeks burning, she tugged at her hand, but he would not give it up.

'Aude, what's the matter?'

'N…nothing.'

'Count Richard married a Saxon, I hear.'

'Yes, he married Lady Emma of Fulford. Count Rich-ard insisted on giving me the estate by way of compen-sation, though I assured him there was no need. It is called Alfold and I hear it is much run down. I should like to set it in order.'

'Alfold, you say?'

'Yes.'

'And it is in Wessex? Is it anywhere near the city of Winchester?'

'I believe it is. Why?'

The broad shoulders lifted. 'I heard the King has a residence there. Aude, were you very upset?'

'Upset?'

'When Count Richard set you aside. I assumed you were not because I know how you cared for Martin.'

'No, I was not upset. I like Count Richard very much, but it is as you say, Martin was the man for me.' Even as Aude spoke, the words seemed to freeze on her tongue. *Was that the truth? Was Martin truly the man for me? Did I ever feel half the sense of...connection that I feel with Hugh Duclair?*

Hugh's gaze was steady, but a line had formed between his eyebrows. Aude became conscious that the soft caresses had stopped as suddenly as they had started. 'He still is, I think.'

Aude gave a little nod, but it felt like a lie. *Is Martin still the man for me? Had he ever been? True, I enjoyed talking with him, but there had always been that sense of distance. Have I been living a dream?*

Carefully, Hugh released her. 'Does Edouard realise you are determined to set out to this Alfold of yours tomorrow? Surely he has noticed your belongings are missing from the lodge?'

Grimacing, Aude waved to where her travelling chests were roped together on the deck. 'As you see, I have acquired new baggage.'

'Ah.' Hugh's forehead cleared as he took in the boxes. 'So your old ones have been emptied and left behind as decoys?'

'Yes.'

'And these painted coffers here, they are yours?'

'Yes, they are mine.'

'When do you leave?'

'Tomorrow morning.'

Hugh's mouth curved. 'Poor Edouard, he doesn't stand a chance, does he?'

At twilight the Abbey wall cast a thick shadow. Striding to the place he had appointed for the rendezvous, Hugh Duclair settled himself on the grass and leaned against it. He had his cloak on and his hood up, because both he and Aude's brother—the person he was meeting—did not want it generally known that they were on speaking terms.

A moth fluttered past.

While he waited, Hugh looked towards the port. Aude would doubtless be in the Abbey Lodge behind him. Perhaps she would be settling down for the night. Did she sleep with her hair loose? Was it soft to the touch? Little Brat, who would have thought it? Such a slender waist, and those breasts…

Heat rushed to his loins. Hard in an instant, Hugh was rampantly—and extremely inappropriately—aroused. Those breasts, they were even more fascinating than when he first noticed them…

Aude's breasts had long been something of a distraction—Hugh had first noticed them when he had been seventeen. He and Edouard had arrived at Dives to enlist with the Duke's war party. Since Edouard had been fostering at Freyncourt, Hugh had come to see him as a brother.

But before they embarked for England, the two young men found themselves arranging Sir Hamon's funeral.

At the dockside inn, Aude—dressed in a scandalous short tunic that did little to shield her rapidly developing body—had flung herself into Hugh's arms and wept her grief out on his tunic.

'What happened, Aude?' Hugh had asked, gently stroking her shoulders while the questions lined up in his mind. What had Sir Hamon been thinking about to allow her to continue acting as his squire? Yes, Sir Hamon loved his daughter and wanted her with him, but surely the man must have seen that the time for their masquerade was long past?

Aude had wriggled closer, and the soft young breasts pressing into Hugh's chest had pushed his indignant questions to the back of his mind.

'I didn't see. I had gone to bed, was deep asleep.' Aude had lifted her face to him, amber eyes glassy with tears. 'Knives were used. I am told that Father didn't suffer, that it was quick...'

Hugh had murmured sympathetically, even as he felt his body betray him. A heaviness was gathering in his loins. Afraid of frightening his friend's innocent little sister, he had edged carefully back. Aude's breasts, Lord, that tunic scarcely contained them...

Gently, shocked at himself, he had transferred Aude to her brother's arms.

Grimacing, Hugh shifted against the cool stone of the Abbey wall and forced his attention back on to his surroundings. A row of houses adjacent to one of the quays, glared violet in the last of the light. Above a stand of trees a cloud of starlings formed and reformed, making swirling black shapes in the dusky air.

A couple of minutes passed and the flare of lust subsided, but Hugh's thoughts were lingering in that inn at Dives. After Sir Hamon's funeral, Hugh had been concerned for Aude's future, which was why he had encouraged Edouard to arrange for her betrothal to Count Martin de Beaumont.

He winced at how blunt he had been, but he had been young and hot to go to war. And time had been short.

'Have you given any thoughts to marriage, Aude?' he had asked. *'Is there anyone you particularly like?'*

Aude's face had frozen; she had given him the strangest of looks. Then she had laughed, before finally saying, 'I like Count Martin de Beaumont.'

Edouard's eyes had widened. 'Count Martin? But he's—'

Hugh had kicked his friend into silence. 'I wasn't aware you had met Count Martin?'

'Yes. Father and I attended the Easter Mass in Beaumont, and afterwards Count Martin found us a place in his household. He was kind to us and I like him.'

Given that Aude had to be sent somewhere safe while he and Edouard went to England, the betrothal to Count Martin had seemed ideal. Martin of Beaumont had been one of Duke William's most trusted nobles, one of those chosen to remain in Normandy to guard the Duke's interests while the Duke was abroad.

At that moment, at one of those houses by the quays, the dusk seemed to solidify as a man in a cloak separated himself from the shadows. Edouard.

Smiling, Hugh rose to his feet.

'Hugh.' Edouard nodded a greeting at him. 'Aude told me about Louise. I am glad she is safe.'

'Yes, I am very grateful Aude got her out of the river.'

'And I have to thank you for saving Aude.'

'It was my pleasure. Edouard?'

'Hmm?'

'I daresay I shouldn't tell you this, but you do realise that Aude is still set on leaving?'

Edouard's face went still. 'I thought we agreed that you would not speak to her!'

Hugh grinned. 'That became somewhat impossible after what happened at the river today. Anyway, I thought you might care to know, she is determined to get to England, to see that estate she has been given.'

'Yes, I knew that, she and I have discussed it.'

'Did you realise she is planning to leave tomorrow?'

'So soon? No, I wasn't sure, she was rather evasive... but I thank you for telling me.'

'At least she has sense to have arranged for an escort.'

'That is a relief,' Edouard said. 'And what about you? Are you set to go?'

'I plan to leave at dawn tomorrow.'

'You have found another barge? Good.'

'Yes, and that brings me to a slight problem I thought I ought to mention.'

'Yes?'

'It is Aude's barge,' Hugh said. 'She has booked it to take her to Honfleur; already her baggage is stowed on board. And like the last one, there is not enough room for both our parties...'

'You are not thinking of offloading her baggage again?'

Hugh spread his hands. 'What would you suggest?'

Edouard flung his head back and gave a crack of laughter. 'Hugh, she will want to kill you!'

'Quite probably.' Hugh sighed. 'Edouard, I want you to know, I am grateful for your support.' In his present circumstances, it ought not to matter that he was running the gauntlet of Aude's anger again, but...damn it, it did.

'Lord, man, I have done nothing.'

Hugh shook his head. 'You are making enquiries on my behalf, and at the moment, believe me, that is not nothing.'

'It seems little enough.' Edouard frowned. 'I would like to do more.'

'Keep your ear to the ground. The man I am searching for is Brother Baldwin. He was last seen at St Aubin, but one rumour puts him in Rouen, another in England. In short, he seems to have vanished without trace.'

Edouard rubbed his chin. 'He may be dead.'

'That is possible, but make enquiries for me, will you?'

'Assuredly. Where will you go?'

Hugh grimaced. 'I don't like it, but if nothing solid turns up, I shall have to go to England.'

Edouard lifted a brow. 'To plead your innocence before the King? That's a dangerous strategy.'

'If all else fails I will have no choice. The King scarcely sets foot on Norman soil these days, I will have to face him in England.'

Edouard grunted. 'I wish you well. In the event of my discovering anything to your advantage, we need to arrange how to keep in touch.' His expression became thoughtful. 'All roads seem to be leading to England. I can see that shortly I will be visiting my sister at Alfold.'

Hugh's face darkened. '*No*! I don't want Aude dragged into my affairs.'

'I agree——believe me, that's the last thing I want. Surely we can meet without Aude knowing it? At summer's end I will visit her in Wessex. Send word to me at Alfold and I will quietly arrange to see you and give you any news.'

Hugh looked doubtfully at Edouard. 'Aude need not be involved? It will be bad enough implicating you if things turn sour, but I will not risk Aude too.'

'I swear it, man, Aude need *not* be involved.'

Chapter Five

The sun was not yet strong enough to cast more than a greenish pall over the river barge under the overhanging willows. It was so early that the bell for prime was in competition with the dawn chorus. In the trees, blackbirds, doves and robins were stirring, and on a ledge on the cliff opposite, a cormorant had spread its wings out to dry.

Hugh's boots sounded hollow on the deck as he strode to the ship's master. 'Here.' He tipped coins into the waiting hand. 'I will double it if you can cast off *within the hour.*'

Gil and Louise were waiting on the bank with the horses, wrapped in their cloaks against the early chill.

'Oh, no, my lord, I am sorry, but I cannot do that. Our other passengers are not expecting us to leave until after noon.'

Hugh sent him a straight look. 'I'll double whatever they paid you.' *And may Aude forgive me.* But these were desperate times. He had hoped to be out of Jumièges already, but the *mascaret* had put paid to his delicately laid plans, forcing delay on him when delay could be disastrous.

And at the rate money was draining from his purse, they would be short of silver within the week. If they survived that long. Time had finally run out, and he was no closer to proving his innocence. Louise must be got safely away before the fight to clear his name could continue.

He must be realistic. If he were caught breaking the terms of his banishment, he would *never* prove his innocence, he would be executed. And then what would happen to Louise?

On the bank, Gil swore softly. 'Hang it, Hugh, Lady Aude will go up in flames if the ship casts off without her.'

The ship's master jerked his head at Gil and Louise, a crease forming in his brow. 'I take it you want those two to accompany you?'

'Certainly.'

'I doubt there's space.'

'We shall make space. Come, give me a hand with these travelling chests.' Clapping the captain on the shoulder, Hugh grinned. He would die before he let this man know that desperation was clawing his insides to bits. 'What harm? The river is calm this morning; other ships are certain to be leaving for Honfleur later in the day, your passenger will find a place on one of those.'

'But the lady paid the fee in full,' the captain muttered. He was weakening, Hugh could sense it. His eyes were lingering covetously on Hugh's purse, weighing the likely profit.

Hugh jingled more coins. 'Give me the lady's fee and I shall send Gil here back to the Abbey to return it to her.'

The captain's eyes narrowed. 'Oh, no, you don't! How do I know I can trust you or your man? He could pocket the money and say the job was done.'

Hugh drew himself up. He must be more on edge than he had realised; his hold on his temper was slipping. 'Do you know who I am?'

'A nobleman who by rights should be close to the borders by now. It strikes me, my lord, you have little to bargain with.'

Hugh inhaled slowly, reaching for calm. 'On my honour, Gil would obey me.' He gave an easy shrug. 'But if you are in doubt, send one of your oarsmen along with him as witness.'

The ship's master stroked his chin. 'Double the usual fee, you say?'

'Yes.'

'And you will lend a hand unloading her baggage?'

'Assuredly.'

'Done.'

With a wry grimace, Hugh unbuckled his sword and set about removing Aude's belongings from the barge. It was the second time in as many days.

Mon Dieu, *Gil is right*, he thought, as his squire and an oarsman took the path back to the abbey. *When she finds out, she will go up in flames.*

Her recently bought travelling chests were lighter and less weighty than the old ones. Daisies, he thought, noting the flowers painted on the wood, *Aude likes daisies.*

An image of her took form in Hugh's mind. Aude

was awaiting her husband in her marriage bed. A long auburn plait was trailing over one shoulder, her eyes glowed like amber in the flare of a rushlight. She wore the most delicate of nightgowns, the silk was so fine it was almost invisible and….

Diable! His loins were throbbing. Hastily hefting Aude's packing case on to his shoulder, Hugh thrust the image firmly behind him.

In the Lady Chapel, it was cool and quiet and dimly lit. The windows were tall and slender, and beeswax candles gave the softest of lights. It was the perfect place for reflection and Aude had much to reflect upon. Kneeling in front of the altar, she stared up at a candle she had lit for the repose of Martin of Beaumont's soul.

More than a year had passed since Martin's death, and every day Aude prayed for him. A hard chill was coming up from the stone-flagged floor; she folded her skirts under her knees.

How long will it be before I stop missing him?

It was true that Aude's relationship with Martin had been unusually chaste, but that, she was beginning to realise, had been no bad thing. Martin's tall, rangy form had not drawn her in the same way that Hugh's had done yesterday. Aude had never found herself gazing fascinated at Martin's mouth, she had never found herself wondering what it might be like to kiss him.

If only she had a female relation with whom she could discuss the welter of feelings Hugh Duclair stirred inside her. The man had her completely bemused, but she could hardly discuss Hugh with her brother, one of Hugh's oldest friends.

While Aude genuinely missed Martin, she was begin-

ning to see that the affection she felt for him was perhaps
not the sort of affection a woman ought to feel for her
husband. Martin's touch had never evoked the confused
yearning she had felt yesterday when Hugh had taken her
hand. Thank goodness! If Martin's touch had affected
her in the same way, it might have been a trial to keep
to the vow of chastity he had imposed on them.

'*Until our wedding day,*' Martin had said. '*We shall
be chaste in thought and word and deed, until our wedding day.*'

And so they had. She had only been thirteen when
she had been betrothed and the vow had been an easy
one to make. Martin had been, first and foremost, her
friend.

And Hugh?

Despite her anxiety for him, Aude's lips curved—
Hugh was her friend too.

In the past he had been something of a reprobate;
Hugh enjoyed shocking people, Hugh was a tease. Hugh
enjoyed women too. Martin had not kept her entirely
cloistered; rumours of Hugh's roistering had reached
her at Beaumont.

With a shiver, Aude adjusted her skirts under her
knees, Hugh was more than a mere reprobate nowadays.
Banished. Stripped of his lands and title. Poor Hugh.
He would shrug aside her pity—Hugh had the pride of
a king—but it was impossible not to feel sympathy for
him.

Hugh, a traitor? It did not bear thinking about. What
would he do? Where would he go? How would he set
about proving his innocence?

The candle sizzled, an impurity in the wax reminding Aude of her purpose—she had come to the Lady

Chapel to pray for Martin. Hugh's affairs were not her concern. Setting her hands together, she closed her eyes and bowed her head.

She had not been long in prayer when a draught teased the hem of her veil. Her eyes opened as the flame of Martin's candle wavered and winked out.

'My lady?'

Edwige was standing under one of the arches.

'Is something wrong?'

Her maid drew nearer. 'I am sorry to disturb you, my lady, but I thought you would want to know at once.' She opened her palm to reveal a handful of silver.

'Goodness, I didn't know you had so much money, Edwige.'

'I don't. My lady, it is *your* money.'

'Mine?'

'The river barge—the one in the inlet—it is leaving early. Your payment has been returned.'

Frowning, Aude held out her hand and Edwige tipped the coins into it. 'This is my money? Are you saying that someone has taken my place?' *Heavens, was she never to get away? Freedom, it seemed, was always around the next corner...*

'So I was given to understand.'

Aude rose. Taking up Martin's candle, she rekindled it from one nearby. 'That cannot be; the ship's master seemed reliable to me.'

'He has changed his mind. Hugh's man said—'

Aude stiffened. '*Hugh*'s man?'

'Yes. Gil said that Hugh conveys his apologies and said to tell you that he had no choice—'

Aude stalked to the splash of light by the doorway. 'Hugh Duclair has taken our place on the barge?'

'I believe so.'

'Holy Mother, that man!' Aude picked up her skirts and crossed the yard with unladylike speed. She hurried past the bemused guards at the gatehouse with an even more unladylike word falling from her lips. 'The *devil*! Hurry up, Edwige!'

Two minutes later, Aude and Edwige were standing, chests heaving, on the edge of one of the quays.

Edwige pointed downriver. 'See? There it is, my lady.'

There it was indeed. *Her barge.* Out in the middle of the Seine, its oars lifting and falling. The fierce carving on the prow made a Norse dragon ship of it as it cut through the sparkling water, heading towards the sea.

'We are too late.'

'Thank you, Edwige, I have eyes.'

Aude glared at the ship. The demon! She had booked with time to spare, she had paid in full, she had even given that boy extra to guard her baggage. She gritted her teeth. 'How *dare* he?'

Hugh Duclair was standing in the stern looking directly at her, the image of his Viking ancestors, may God blast him. So handsome, with that bright hair ruffled by the breeze. He grinned across the water. So confident, even in the midst of his current humiliations, with those strong shoulders, that assured stance.

'The wretch.' Aude scowled and raised her voice. 'You wretch!'

He lifted his hand, he bowed.

'He's a wretch, Edwige.'

'Yes, my lady.'

'Yesterday…' Aude's words were tripping over themselves. She felt sick, betrayed. 'Yesterday…all that so-called concern, all those warnings about the river bank being too dangerous to walk on as he escorted us to the barge…I thought him charming, but all the while he was waiting to clear the deck of my things…ooh, that man!'

Edwige's eyes were pensive as she worked it out. 'Yes, I see. He was looking for a ship. My lady, when he met us after the wave struck, he must have been planning to take our place.'

'Indeed.' Aude clenched her jaw. The ship was drawing swiftly away and the girl she had pulled from the water, his sister Louise, had moved to Hugh's side to take his hand. Aude judged her to be about the same age that Aude had been when she had been betrothed to Martin of Beaumont.

Hugh's squire was also visible on the deck and three horses were tethered amidships. *Where her baggage had been.*

Her hands had become fists, her nails were gouging into her palms. Once again a man had put his needs before hers; once again, her wishes were unimportant. This was *exactly* why she would never marry. Not even a malleable man. When she reached Alfold, which, thanks to Richard of Beaumont's generosity, was hers and hers alone, she would *never* marry.

Hugh's bright hair gleamed in the sun as he sent her another ironic bow. She could just imagine the grin on his face, the lights in his eyes would be dancing and…

'Wretch!' she murmured, but already she was calming down.

In truth her heart was twisting, and there was the most terrible pain in her chest. Hugh was at the end of his tether, she understood that. And for friendship's sake she must not begrudge him safe passage. *Lord knows, he needs it.* 'I only wish you might have asked, Hugh.' Had he thought she might refuse him? Did he think so little of her? It hurt to think so.

'What's that, my lady?'

'Nothing.' The barge grew steadily smaller as it approached the bend in the river; when his head was no longer visible Aude turned away, shoulders drooping. She would not see him again, and much as she misliked that thought, it was probably just as well.

Edouard had been right to forbid her to associate with him. Even setting his banishment to one side, Hugh Duclair was far too unpredictable. Not to mention disturbing. Her anger was fading, but uncomfortable emotions remained. Hurt. Sadness. Regret. And—she would not be honest if she did not admit this to herself—a pang of longing for something that would never be hers.

'My lady, what shall we do?'

Aude looked across the square towards the Abbey. 'First, you will show me where they put my baggage, then we will find Sir Olivier; he can help us find another ship to take us to Honfleur.'

'So you are not abandoning your plans to go to this Alfold Hall?'

She glared fiercely at Edwige. 'Most certainly not!'

Wessex, England—several weeks later

Hugh kicked his gelding into a trot, sending up puffs of dust in his wake. He was riding along a chalky track with Gil and Louise. They had been told it led to Alfold. They had also been told that Lady Aude de Crèvecoeur had taken up residence there about a month earlier.

Hugh was not here to see Aude, far from it. Seeing Aude was the last thing he wanted. He was here to learn the lie of the land—and to discover if her brother had arrived as he had promised. He and Edouard had not communicated since that evening by the Abbey wall in Jumièges. With luck, Edouard might have news for him.

The track ran long and straight at the foot of a ridge. Thick beech woods had sprung up on one side, while the downs lay on the other, dotted with sheep.

Sweat prickled between Hugh's shoulder blades; it was too warm a day to be swathed in his cloak and hood, but he could not run the risk of being recognised. The Count of Freyncourt had been banished from *all* of Duke William's lands; he was no more welcome here in England than he had been in Normandy.

Was it possible that Edouard was already in Alfold? It would be good to see a friendly face again.

'Hugh?' At his side Louise tossed back her hood and huffed out a sigh. 'Is that Alfold? It doesn't look much.'

She was pointing down the slope to where a cluster of cottages sat near the edge of some field strips. The field strips were edged with clumps of hazel, and beyond the hazels yet more beech trees had grown up. They must be looking at the other side of Crabbe Wood. They had made their camp deep in Crabbe Wood, but Hugh had never approached it from this side.

'Louise,' Hugh said. 'Please keep your hood up as we agreed. I can't run the risk of Aude seeing me. We simply need to know if her brother has got here.'

'And if he has?'

'I return to Crabbe Wood. And then, when I am safely

out of the way, you and Gil can take Edouard a message.
There is no reason why you two shouldn't be seen, but
me...that is another matter entirely. And remember, it is
dangerous for anyone to be seen in my company. Until I
have exchanged the kiss of peace with the King, anyone
who helps me is putting themselves at risk.'

Louise's eyes were dark with suspicion. 'I know your
mind, Hugh. You are trying to get rid of me. You will
give me the message and desert me here.'

Hugh said nothing, Louise was right, Hugh had hoped
Aude might take her in. 'Louise, I do not wish to desert
you, I want to see you safe.'

'I would rather be with you.'

What could he say? 'Best guard your tongue while
we are in the village.'

They continued along the track with the sun beating
down on them. Hugh shrugged deeper into his hood. If
Aude should chance to see him... Lord, he might have
thought of her every now and then in the past few weeks,
but he had no desire to compromise her position here in
England. He must *not* be recognised.

Several times when Hugh had been lying on the edges
of sleep and his guard on his imagination had been at
its weakest, his mind had presented him with images of
Aude. Why, he could not fathom. These images—and
they were usually of Aude in her bed—had been so allur-
ing that he had been reluctant to dismiss them. Also, they
had a tantalising way of shifting, of becoming inexorably
more intimate.

One night, when they had been waiting for the ship
that would carry them to England, Hugh had envisioned
Aude lying in her bed as though awaiting a lover. Her
beautiful hair had been unbound, it had trailed like

tongues of fire over her breasts. Those amber eyes had glowed with welcome. And as for her nightgown, someone had unfastened the ties at the neck and...

The last time the image had presented itself had been last night in Crabbe Wood. Aude had been wearing little save a secret smile; Hugh's imagination had gifted him with clear sight of her naked shoulders peeping up over the bedcovers.

And now, despite the sweat trickling down his back, merely to recall those images had the edges of his mouth curving up...

These imaginings meant nothing. And if he had not dismissed them as quickly as he ought to have done, it was only because they helped him find sleep when lying on a lumpy pallet.

'Hugh?'

'Mmm?'

Louise was giving him her mutinous look. 'I can see why you must hide yourself, but I have not been banished. Nor has Gil. Why must poor Gil and I hide our faces like outlaws? We are boiling to death in our cloaks. I really don't understand why Gil and I can't simply go and ask Lady Aude if her brother has arrived.'

A hot summer was turning into an even hotter hot summer's end. Louise was tired and irritable and not thinking straight. She was very young. Guilt knotted Hugh's insides. Louise's face was streaky with dust; they had been riding too hard, for too long. Hugh did not need Louise to tell him that she had had enough; he could see that for himself. There were shadows under her eyes where there had never been shadows. Also, since leaving Normandy his sister had lost weight, her cheekbones were far too prominent. This life was not for her.

'I told you, I need to see the lie of the land for myself. And while you are with me…hang it, Louise, I will not have you questioning my every decision. I really think we have come to a parting of the ways.'

'No! I want to stay with you!'

Firmly, Hugh shook his head. Louise must be made to understand. 'This is not what I want for you. It was a mistake to permit you to accompany me for so long. I have been watching out for somewhere safe for you to stay, and Alfold might be the very place. It is small and out of the way, yet it is close to Winchester. When I have made my peace with the King, it will be an easy matter to come and find you. And you will be among friends here.'

'Your friends, not mine. Anyway, that place in the trees seems safe enough to me.' Louise loosened the tie of her cloak and pulled the wool of her gown away from her neck with a grimace. 'Holy Mother, Hugh, it is far too hot to be wearing a cloak. I'm sticky and dust seems to have got everywhere.' She stuck her chin out. 'I repeat, Gil and I are not outlaws.'

Sometimes his sister was like a dog with bone. Hugh sighed. 'This argument is tired, Louise. But I did warn you that you could not stay with me for ever. King William is away from Winchester at the moment. As soon as he returns I plan to beg for an audience, the outcome of which is far from certain. If matters go badly, it will be better for you not to be associated with me.'

'You are my brother, I am not about to desert you!'

His heart softened. 'Your loyalty does you credit, Louise, but I repeat, I do not wish to be worried about you.' He made a point of looking towards the village. 'I wonder where the hall is…'

* * *

'That is Alfold Hall?' They were in the heart of the village, and Hugh was staring in disbelief in the direction the villager's soil-blackened finger was pointing.

If this villager, an elderly peasant farmer, was correct, Alfold Hall was a ramshackle wooden longhouse set in the middle of a village, which was itself run down to the point of collapse. It was fortunate that Hugh had been in England a number of times before. His command of English, though not fluent, was passable. Certainly the Saxon hoeing between cabbages in one of the field-strips had understood him.

'Yes, sir, that is Alfold Hall.'

Hugh leaned on the saddle pommel. With the exception of the church, Alfold Hall was larger than the other village buildings. In all other respects, however, it was depressingly similar. Its thatch was green with age, moss and rot, just like the nearby cottages. The door of the hall had been removed—there it was, propped up against one of the walls. On the ground nearby was a ladder, several bundles of reeds, and various vicious-looking agricultural implements the exact use of which Hugh was hazy about.

'They wouldn't look amiss on a butcher's bench,' he murmured, even as the sun bounced off the tine of a pitchfork. 'Or on a battlefield.' And Saxon peasants, as Hugh could most vividly recall from 1066, could wield agricultural implements most fearsomely when called upon to do so.

'Hmm?' Louise had thrown off her ill temper and was gazing about with wide-eyed interest. 'This is it?'

'Alfold Hall,' the villager repeated, in his slow English.

'My thanks.' Kicking his horse back into a walk, Hugh exchanged glances with his squire. '*Mon Dieu*, I didn't think it possible to find anywhere in a worse state than Crèvecoeur was when Edouard took possession. It looks as though Aude has exchanged one midden for another.'

'Lady Aude will knock it into shape soon enough,' Gil said. 'If she managed at Crèvecoeur, she can do the same here.'

Hugh ran disparaging eyes over the settlement. Set halfway down the hill in a sunlit clearing in a beech wood, Alfold did have a certain simple charm. The wheat in the strips was heavy and golden, the apple and pear trees were weighed down with fruit. Dust was floating out from one of the less derelict barns and Hugh could hear the distinctive *thwack, thwack, thwack* of a flail. However... 'The defences are appalling.'

Gill grinned. 'What defences?'

'Exactly. It would have been much better to have built the hall on the top of that rise. You would have visibility for miles up there—why, on a clear day you might even be able to see Winchester. But here...' Hugh grimaced '...it is scarcely worth bothering with. Poor Aude, I wonder if she realised what she was taking on.'

'I expect the hall was built in more peaceful times,' Louise said, thoughtfully.

Sometimes Louise startled Hugh with her perceptiveness. She was right, of course. Alfold Hall had not been built by England's conquerors. A Saxon thane would have built it, a noble who had probably expected to live out his life cheek by jowl with his neighbours.

What had happened to that thane? Had he been killed in 1066? Since his lands had been handed over to one of the conqueror's most honoured knights, Sir Richard of Asculf, this seemed likely. Did these people bear resentment against Normans?

A woman had heard the horses and had come to watch them from her cottage doorway. She had a baby in her arms and her eyes were like narrow slits as she stared into the afternoon sun. Hostile? Or was the sun dazzling her? Her expression was blank, Hugh could not read her.

It had been five years since William of Normandy had seized Harold's crown. Did the people of Alfold yearn for a Saxon king? Did they mourn their dead Saxon thane?

An ear-splitting shriek brought his head round. It had come from inside the hall.

Hell, the villagers wouldn't be avenging themselves on their new Norman lady, would they? In this out-of-the-way place, who would find out if they did?

Gil shot him a look. 'What the devil is that? They wouldn't hurt Lady Aude, would they?'

Another cry flew through the doorway, more agonised than the first.

Hell, hell, hell. I must not get involved, I must not! But if Aude is being hurt, I would never forgive myself…

Louise blanched. 'Hugh, whatever's happening?'

'God knows, but I have to find out.' Shoving his hood back, he dismounted and thrust his reins at Gil.

'Hugh, do be careful,' Louise said.

Hugh nodded. He ought not to engage with anyone in the village, but he could not ride by when Aude might be at risk. *Merde.* 'Gil, take the horses over to that smithy, and keep an eye on Louise. Neither of you are to come near the hall unless I signal that it is safe to approach.'

Chapter Six

Hand on his sword-hilt, Hugh paused on the threshold as another shriek rose to the rafters. A boy of about seven years of age was lying on a cloak that had been spread out before a hearth ringed with stones. It was the boy who was screaming. *Not Aude.* He felt the tension lift away. *Aude was not being hurt.*

She was kneeling on one side of the boy, worry lines marring her clear brow. Sir Olivier knelt across from her. *Sir Olivier de Fougères, here?*

The boy moaned. And *no wonder, poor lad, with his arm at that angle.* Hugh's stomach gave a sick lurch as he strode towards the fire. Several people were watching from the shadows. There were a couple of women, one wringing her hands—the boy's mother? A handful of men.

And Edouard, Count of Corbeil? There was no sign of him. Damn.

Several faces turned towards Hugh, but he ignored them, he found himself watching for Aude's reaction.

'*Hugh*!' Aude's face cleared and something within him eased. She might still be angry about him stealing her place on that boat in Jumièges, but she seemed happy, even relieved, to see him.

'Be careful, my lady,' Sir Olivier muttered in a low voice, as he jerked his head towards two men—knights?—sitting on a wall-bench. Hugh strained to catch the rest of his sentence. 'It will be dangerous for your friend to be recognised.'

Aude's eyes widened and the subtlest of nods told Hugh that she had grasped what Sir Olivier was saying, namely that Hugh was banished from England as well as from his native Normandy. The Duke's writ ran on this side of the Narrow Sea too, for here in England, William was King.

Aude was gripping the hand of the boy's good arm, fingers white as she tried, not altogether successfully, to stop him thrashing about.

'Thank God you are here, Hugh, your English is better than mine.'

Aude's hair was uncovered and wound in a loose plait, but her struggles with the boy had taken their toll and several shining strands had worked loose. They hung about her face with the warm glow of copper.

'That may be so.'

'Oswy here has dislocated his arm. Olivier was trying to put it back, but Oswy doesn't understand and he will keep screaming. Hugh, will you explain?'

'Assuredly.' Smiling at the boy, Hugh nodded easily at Olivier as he took his place opposite Aude. Time enough to learn why the man had followed Aude to Alfold and, perhaps more to the point, why she had apparently abandoned all formality and was on first-name terms with him.

'Oswy, is it?' he asked in English.

The boy moaned, sweat was beading his upper lip. One of the watching women shifted, echoing the boy's moan. Yes, that woman had to be his mother.

'Oswy, you will be all right,' Hugh said, in the calmest of voices.

'Broken, broken,' the mother said, wringing her hands. The boy writhed.

Hugh shot the woman a glance; she was not helping. 'No,' he said firmly. 'I do not believe it is broken, and neither does Lady Aude. May I see for myself?'

Oswy's mother nodded and Hugh ran his hands carefully over the boy's shoulder.

Large amber eyes met his. 'Hugh, am I right?' Aude reverted to French. 'I was afraid that if it was a break, we might cripple him for life.'

'It is a dislocation,' he murmured, looking meaningfully at her. 'Hold hard, Aude. On the count of three…'

She nodded.

Casually, Hugh kept his hands in place and made as if he were looking about the hall. 'So this is Alfold Hall…one, two…oh, look at that…!'

Hugh gazed round-eyed through the doorway and as soon as the boy's eyes shifted to see what he was looking at, he moved.

One deft motion, a dull click and it was done.

The boy squealed like a stuck pig.

'A dislocation.' Aude blew out a breath. 'Thank God.'

Leaning back on her heels, she rose and gestured for the boy's mother.

The woman rushed to the hearth, crooning and smiling through her tears. 'My lady, I thank you.' Despite her words, a certain awkwardness in the woman's manner warned of an inbred mistrust of Normans.

Aude lifted a brow at Hugh, and reached for his hand. 'That much I can understand. Hugh, I should be furious with you.'

He grimaced. 'The ship?'

'Yes.' For a moment her brows drew together in a frown. 'But I have decided to forgive you.'

'I am sorry about that river barge, Aude, I had run out of time.'

'I understand. Anyway, today you have made up for that.' She smiled. 'Oh, Hugh, I was never so glad to see anyone in my life! Sir Olivier and I were trying our best to speak English, but there are times when it is hard. After Oswy fell off the roof I am afraid that I panicked, and what words I know abandoned me.'

Raising her fingers to his lips, Hugh smiled. 'You seemed to be doing very well.' It was a pleasure to actually see her—no, it was more than a pleasure, it was a joy. Those large eyes were smiling up at him, more warm and friendly than they ought to be given that he should not have come in. He must remember, he could not stay long…

Realising he still had her hand, Hugh released it and eased back. He had come to Alfold to learn if Edouard de Corbeil had arrived, not to renew his friendship with Aude. The less involvement Aude had with him, the better for her.

'That may be,' she was saying, 'but Oswy didn't

understand what we were trying to do. He was fighting us and…oh, well, it is done now.' She looked down at Oswy, who was already sitting up, tentatively moving his shoulder. 'For his own good, that lad had better be strapped up for a few days.' Her lips quirked upwards. 'If this accident keeps him off that roof for a couple of days, I shall be best pleased. Oswy is the thatcher's son,' she added, taking Hugh's hand again.

Hugh allowed himself to be drawn towards a table under the eaves. 'I must leave shortly.'

'You will at least let me take your cloak, you must be half-stewed in it! And then you must tell me what you are doing here. Did you—' when her smile enlarged, Hugh felt it in his belly '—come to see me?'

'Why else?' Hugh murmured lightly as he handed her his cloak. There was no point confessing he had not intended to cross her threshold, and what harm could there be in letting Aude think he had come to see her? Particularly since he was harbouring some guilt on her account. Not for taking her place on that barge, that had been a necessity. It was that meeting he had had with Edouard shortly before leaving Jumièges, the one in which he had warned Edouard that his sister was going to visit her English estate sooner rather than later. He had had Aude's interests at heart, but he hadn't liked himself for doing it. Lucky for him, though, that that conversation with Edouard had taken place, otherwise Alfold might not have come to mind as the most obvious place in England where he might safely contact Edouard.

Aude's estate was close to Winchester, and all the world knew that the King had built a castle there—Winchester Castle—known to be one of his favourite residences. Since 1066, William had been obsessed with strengthening his power base in England. Determined not to lose his crown, it was said that Normandy had been relegated to the back of his mind. Whatever the truth of that, Hugh had come to realise that he would have to travel to Winchester when the time came for him to place his petition before the King. The only certain way to gain a personal audience with William would be to lie low and wait for his next appearance in Wessex.

Soon I will prove my innocence; soon I will offer King William the kiss of peace.

Grimacing, Hugh lowered his voice. 'A friendly face is a rarity these days.'

'Come.' With a familiarity that made his heart ache, Aude pushed him to a bench. 'Sit here while I find some bandages and get Oswy strapped up. Then we will share some wine and you may tell me what you are doing in England. All this time I have been thinking that you must have taken refuge in Brittany.'

Hugh! Hugh had come to see her! Aude could scarcely believe it. In the month since she had come to Alfold, he had entered her thoughts many times. She had found herself wondering how he was faring, she had prayed for him and, yes—she had done more than a little regretting that she was not likely to see him again.

But here he was, despite the dangers of being caught in England, large as life and even more handsome than the images she had stored in her memory. And he had come to see her!

Aude hurried to the chest where the bandages were stored. When she had arrived at Alfold, the chest had been empty, and one of her first tasks had been to re-stock it. Bandages had been made, and because the herb garden behind the hall had run to seed, she had bought herbs and medicaments in the Winchester market. There had been much to busy herself with since landing in England.

First she had had to ride to Winchester to lay her claim to the hall before Sir Guy de Mortain. Sir Guy was commander of the Winchester garrison and he had the King's authority while he was fighting rebels in the fens.

Aude had asked for Sir Guy's assistance in the hiring of a couple of knights who would, along with Sir Olivier, give teeth to her commands at Alfold. The moment she had laid eyes on the men whom Sir Guy had recommended—Sir Ralph d'Auray and Sir William Laval—it had flashed in on her that neither of them looked half as strong or as competent as Hugh Duclair.

The villagers had begun to bring in the harvest, so Aude had one of the barns repaired. After the famine of the previous year, it was essential that all the grain must be properly gathered and carefully stored.

She had begun overseeing the cleaning and repair of the hall itself. If Alfold was to be returned to anything like its former glory, the list of things she must do was never-ending—but somehow, despite being rushed off her feet, Hugh Duclair had kept intruding into her thoughts.

Noticing that Sir Ralph and Sir William were eyeing Hugh curiously from their wall-bench, Aude bit her lip. It might have been best if she had not called Hugh by his first name when he had walked into the Hall, but surprise had torn it from her before she had time to think. What was done was done, but she must take care to make no mention of his county; she would introduce him to her knights simply as Hugh of Jumièges, a family friend.

Reaching into the chest, Aude drew out a strip of fabric that would make a bandage. Yes, while he was here, Hugh would be known as Hugh of Jumièges.

'Eadgytha?' Eadgytha was Oswy's mother. Aude had been told that Eadgytha's husband, the best thatcher in the village, was dead. This might in part explain the marked way she doted on her son.

'My lady?'

'Here, you had best take this.' When all she received was a blank stare, Aude shot a pleading look at Hugh. 'Please to explain to Eadgytha that Oswy must be tightly strapped.'

Aude handed over the bandage fabric while Hugh went back to the ringed hearth with Eadgytha.

How did Alfold Hall look to Hugh's eyes? So much remained to be done—the boards around the shutters were rotting; the door was warped past closing; and even now at summer's end, the greying thatch brought the smell of mouldering reeds right into the hall. In its finest hour, Alfold Hall could not compare with the meanest of Hugh's confiscated holdings in Normandy.

Aude could hear Hugh's opinion of the hall as though he were muttering in her ear. *Unsophisticated. Draughty. Falling apart. Scarcely better than a hovel...*

Aude gave the hall a quick glance herself, only too conscious of how it must look. Indeed, her thoughts on her arrival had been much the same. It hadn't been easy, but she had set to work, meeting the village priest, the miller, the smith. Somehow she had managed to convey her ambition to restore the hall to its proper state. Work parties had been set up, perhaps too hastily, for young

Oswy should not have been up on the roof unsuper-
vised.

Hugh was holding Eadgytha's gaze, indicating the
bandages. 'For your son.' He smiled, speaking so slowly
that Aude could follow his English without any difficulty. 'Bind him securely to ensure that his shoulder
stays in place. And—' a meaningful frown was directed
at Oswy '—no more climbing ladders for a day or two.
It is possible that you are too young to be on that roof,
in any case.'

'No, sir, I am not!' Oswy blurted, tipping up his chin.
'I am good on the roof.'

Hugh glanced at Aude and lifted a brow. 'Aude, is
that true?'

As she looked at him, her heart bumped about in her
breast. He was so handsome. It was unsettling seeing
him again. It was unnerving, and she didn't want to be
unnerved. Why couldn't Hugh be more…ordinary, like
Sir Olivier?

'Aude?'

'Yes, it is true. Or so I thought until he fell. I left it
to Eadgytha to decide how much he could do.'

'It wasn't my fault,' Oswy interrupted. Unlike his
mother, he did not appear the least bit wary of Normans.
'It was just that they startled me, that's why I fell off the
roof.'

Hugh frowned. '*They*? And who might they be?'

'The thieves, sir, they are back.'

Oswy's mother started, panic flashing in her eyes.
'They are back? Saint Swithun help us!' She made a
swift sign of the cross on her breast. 'Oswy, are you
sure?'

Aude blinked. Something about Eadgytha's reaction

did not ring true. But Oswy was nodding, and Hugh was looking to her for an explanation, so she let it slide by.

'Aude?'

'Apparently, earlier in the summer a gang of thieves was terrorising the area. Villagers were robbed and one poor girl has vanished.'

'A girl has vanished?'

'Yes.'

'Who are these thieves—does anyone know?'

Shaking her head, Aude went back with him to the table under the eaves and gestured for wine to be brought. 'You will know that the King's rule in England is not...' she hesitated '...universally accepted. It may be that the thieves are dispossessed Saxons, but whoever they are, neither hide nor hair of them has been seen since my arrival. I had hoped that word would get about that this hall was no longer untenanted.' She waved at her knights. 'I did not come unprotected and since there has been no trouble, I assumed the thieves had gone elsewhere in search of easier pickings.'

'Did you arrange for guards to be posted?' When she looked blankly at him, Hugh sighed. 'That would be my first suggestion. They will have been watching you and you need to be seen taking charge.'

'I do not recall asking you for advice. Anyway, I am taking charge!'

The hint of anger darkening her face had Hugh touching her hand. 'I meant militarily speaking. You are not a soldier, Aude.'

A serving girl had brought a jug of wine to the table, Aude poured some into a cup and offered it to him. 'No, but I should have thought of this, Heaven knows I spent long enough with my father.'

'You are not at fault, although I do think Sir Olivier might have suggested it.' He grinned. 'I dare say the man has other things on his mind.'

Her eyes flashed. 'What do you mean?' Her own wine poured, she thumped the jug back on to the trestle.

Yes, she was becoming angry. Most likely she viewed his comments as interference. Couldn't she see he was trying to help her? He wanted her to be safe!

The sun was streaming in through a shutter, falling on a coppery curl of hair. Conscious of an impulse to wind the curl round his finger, Hugh clenched his wine-cup. 'If I might suggest, get your men to set up a watch-point at the top of the rise. It would give a commanding view of the road. They should post guards at night too, both in the hall and in the stables—you can't afford to lose your horses.'

'You take a lot on your shoulders, Hugh.' Her voice was dry. 'You breeze in, you say you will not stay and yet here you are criticising my knights.'

'What about the storerooms, are they secure, or are they...' he waved at the shutter, indicating the rotting sill '...in the same state as this?'

She flinched. 'I think you may guess the answer to that. Although we have seen to the repair of one of the barns.'

'Aude, if there are felons in this part of Wessex, they will be on the look-out for the first sign of weakness.'

'I know that!'

'Good, but the repairs you have organised, while important, are only a part of what needs to be done.'

She looked frowningly at him. 'I see that. Hugh, be assured, I will consider your suggestions.'

Yes, she resented him giving her advice, but thankfully she seemed to be listening to him.

By the evening, Hugh should have long gone, but first Louise and Gil had to be fetched from the smithy, and from there it was an easy step, far too easy a step, for Aude to persuade them to stay for the evening meal.

And why not? Oswy's cry had lured him in, and now the damage was done, everyone here at Alfold had already seen him.

And the thought of one night, just one night, in Aude's hall where they had some friends was tempting indeed. Too many had been passed in places that were alien to them. Hugh was tired of struggling to find sleep because he must at all times be braced for discovery. His longing to stay had nothing to do with the Lady of Alfold—no, he simply wanted a good night's sleep.

Neither had he been able to withstand a combined assault, with both his sister and Aude pleading for him to stay. Which was how, before he knew it, Hugh had agreed to stay for one night.

Two things remained for him to do before he left. First he must ask Aude about the possibility of Louise remaining on at Alfold, and then he must discover when Edouard was due to arrive.

They were seated at table and the warm glow of fire coloured the hall. It was reflected in the polished surfaces of the bronze bowls hanging on chains from the rafters, in the lanterns hanging from hooks on the walls, in the candles dripping wax on to the table. The air was fragrant with the homely smells of roasted meat and ale. Hugh's belly was pleasantly full, he had been served the tenderest lamb and the best wheaten bread this side of the Narrow Sea. He pushed his platter back with a satisfied smile.

His smile wasn't wholly due to the food. Aude had taken his advice to heart. The hall door had been re-hung for their security as much as to keep out the draughts. Work had been suspended on the roof and the tools locked safely away. A party had been sent up the road to discover the best place to set up a look-out post and a couple of men had been selected as night watchmen. They would guard the hall entrance while everyone else slept.

For the meal, Aude had attired herself with elegant formality in a silk veil and a fresh green gown that put his old black tunic and plain grey chausses in the shade. She sat on his right hand, Louise and Gil on his left. The maid Hugh had met on the banks of the Seine, Edwige, was talking non-stop to a taciturn Norman named Médard. Hugh presumed he was her husband.

Down the board, Olivier de Fougères was seated with two other knights who had been introduced as Sir Ralph d'Auray and Sir William Laval. And he was plain Hugh of Jumièges, may he never forget it.

Hugh's smile faded. *Diable*! What kind of a fool was he to be staying here tonight? It went against his better judgement. Some of Aude's knights were unknowns—what might they do if they realised his true identity?

He glanced uneasily at Sir Olivier. Hugh knew him, having met him at the Christmas revels at Rouen, and he knew that Sir Olivier had formed part of Aude's escort from Normandy.

Hugh was at a loss as to why he felt so put out by Sir Olivier's presence in Alfold. Aude seemed to trust the man, who must be nursing hopes to marry her. But as far as he was concerned, and Hugh was under no illusions over this, Sir Olivier knew Hugh's real identity.

Was he trustworthy? Until Hugh had met with the King and reaffirmed his loyalty, it was not just his own life that was in the balance—Louise's and Gil's were too. And Aude would certainly be questioned if she were caught harbouring the Count of Freyncourt before he had cleared his name. At dawn, he must be gone.

Sir Olivier's dark eyes were resting on Aude. The knight was always watching her, and it was clear he was more than half in love with her. Was that enough to ensure that he kept Hugh's identity to himself? It was impossible to judge.

But Sir Olivier was not the only person at this table who knew Hugh was the Count of Freyncourt. The maid Edwige knew and likely her husband did too. Hugh was more certain of them. Edwige had been with Aude for years—surely she would honour the wishes of her mistress?

Which left the unknowns, Sir William and Sir Ralph. Hugh rubbed his chin. They had been quick to back up his suggestions regarding the watchpoint and night guard, but was it his imagination or were their eyes full of suspicion? Hugh caught Aude's attention and jerked his head at them. 'When did those two join you?'

'Winchester. Sir Guy—he commands the garrison there—put their names forward.'

'Sir Guy was aware thieves were causing havoc here?'

'I am not sure. I think he was concerned that some of the villagers might be troublesome.'

'And were they?'

'There has been nothing overt, not so far. I gather the

priest was relieved to see someone take charge, the smith too. And Oswy is fine, or he was until he fell. Most of the younger ones are. Oswy's mother Eadgytha can be difficult. Her husband died at Hastings alongside Thane Frideric, so that is no surprise. The rest of the people seem, if not exactly welcoming, willing to let me take the reins. But there is a marked hostility when I have to resort to speaking French and sadly, that is quite often. And there is a noticeable unwillingness to try to understand me when my tongue trips up on their English.'

Hugh couldn't tear his gaze from hers. He did not know how it was, but his own concerns seemed to diminish when he was talking to Aude. It made a pleasant change. 'It is only to be expected, you were not born here, you are one of their conquerors.'

'I see that.' Aude was studying the faces ranged round the board. 'Back in Jumièges my expectations were somewhat naïve, I see that now.' She squared her shoulders. 'But I tell myself I am making progress. We will repair the hall. As you have already noticed it has been languishing, but I am in hopes that we will have a new roof on before winter sets in.'

Hugh nodded, although once again it crossed his mind that perhaps it was not the best use of her manpower to put too much effort into repairing a wooden hall that would, militarily speaking, be less than useless in the event of an attack. He was trying to find the most tactful way of telling her this when it dawned on him what she was doing. He leaned closer, and an elusive fragrance wound into his thoughts. The light scent of summer flowers was mingled with something far more heady, a rich, musky scent that tugged at his senses and conjured images of glittering palaces in some far-distant empire.

It was rather unsettling to discover that little Aude wore such a scent. 'You are moulding your people, testing them to see how well they work together?'

Her smile was warm. 'Of course. I want to give them a new sense of purpose.' She leaned fractionally towards him, her breast brushing the sleeve of his tunic. Hugh's mind emptied of rational thought. Suddenly he could think of nothing else but of cupping that breast in his palm, of gently stroking, of…

Hell and damnation! That intrusive image had jumped into his mind, clear as day. *Aude in bed.* And this time there was no question but that she was naked. And this time—Lord—Hugh was the person in bed with her. He too was naked and…

'I thought…' Hugh's tongue tied itself in knots, his breathing was constricted. It was impossible to focus on mere words when the heat from her thigh was warming his, and that compelling image of being in Aude's bed was burning itself into his brain and…

She was speaking rapidly in French. 'I appreciate that militarily Alfold leaves much to be desired. And I know that the hall is disastrously run down, but I thought it best that it was repaired. I wanted to show the villagers the sort of mistress I plan to be. It will not stop me from building something more…substantial later. In the meantime, it is important they know I intend to honour their traditions, not bury them.' Her expression sobered. 'They lost enough when they lost their Saxon lord. Thane Frideric was, as I understand it, much loved.' She leaned back and her amber eyes looked earnestly up at him. 'Hugh, are you listening?'

Hugh cleared his throat. 'Indeed, and I applaud your

aims.' Further down the table, Sir Olivier was observing them so closely Hugh's cheeks heated. The man was looking at him as though he could read his mind and was envious of those secret fantasies that had been flitting through his brain. Lord, this was madness! Hugh struggled to order his thoughts, even while Aude's scent, heady as any perfume from Araby, lingered in his nostrils. He should not be thinking of her in this way. *Edouard's sister, this was Edouard's little sister.* God save him, he should be pondering on his next move, not lusting after Edouard's sister. 'You have made a good beginning here.'

'What, despite my military shortcomings?'

'Yes, in time I am certain the people will come to accept you.'

'I hope so.' Noticing his cup was empty, she gestured at the wine-jar. 'Please help yourself.'

Hugh was refilling their wine-cups when her smile vanished. 'Aude, what's amiss?'

'I should have talked of this earlier, but what with Oswy's hurt I was somewhat distracted, and then your arrival discomposed me.' She directed her gaze at Sir William and Sir Ralph and lowered her voice. 'Surely it is dangerous for you in England?'

Taking her hand, Hugh kissed it. *Mistake*, he thought, as in a trice that tantalising scent had muddled his thoughts. She seemed to do that to him. His gut clenched. 'You would rather I had stayed away?'

'No, *no*. But...' she kept her voice to a murmur '...since the Duke of Normandy is King here, you have not left his territory as you should. The King does not take it well when his vassals flout his orders.'

'I need a little time.'

'What if you are discovered?'

'You are concerned Sir Olivier will betray me?'

She shook her head and her veil shifted, an escaped curl caught the light. For a moment her eyes would not meet his. 'No, he is no longer Abbot Bertram's man, Sir Olivier is my knight now. It is Sir Ralph and Sir William I am thinking about. They may be breaking bread at my table, but they are first and foremost loyal to the King. The only reason that they have not attempted to arrest you is because they have no idea of your identity. I was wrong to persuade you to stay.'

Hugh shrugged. She was right and they both knew it. The presence of these knights made Alfold more dangerous for him. But perversely, Hugh wanted to stay more than ever.

One thought had him in its grip. *Sir Olivier. She said Sir Olivier was hers. He swallowed bile. Was she considering marrying the man? Hugh had heard that Sir Olivier had her brother's blessing.* Until now he hadn't given it a moment's thought, but seeing the way the man's eyes never left her….

He forced a smile to his lips. *Lord, this woman was a danger to his sanity, she really muddled his thoughts.* 'They know who I am, you introduced me as Hugh of Jumièges.'

'That may be, but—'

'Aude, I am in England to prove my innocence, not to work against the King.'

'You should not be here. If they realise…what if I inadvertently betray you?'

'You won't.' He squeezed her hand. It occurred to him he had been holding it for some minutes. Experimentally, he twined his fingers with hers. She made no objection but, down the board, Sir Olivier's brow had darkened. Hugh suppressed a smile. 'I would like to ask a favour of you.'

began crumbling a piece of bread. 'Indeed, I may have to...'

A shiver ran down Hugh's back, like the touch of cold steel. 'How so? I thought you were set against him?'

She shot him a startled look and dropped the bread. 'Who told you that?'

Damn, that was a slip. 'I...Edouard must have mentioned it.'

A line formed between her brows. 'When?'

'I...I cannot recall.'

Aude leaned confidentially towards him and again he was inhaling that heady scent. 'In truth, I told Sir Olivier as much, back in Jumièges. But it would seem that the Church here in England is just as—interested—in my entering one of their houses, as Abbot Bertram was in Normandy. Sir Olivier may be the lesser of many evils.'

'Oh?'

Her lips curved, but her smile seemed sad, resigned. 'He is malleable, you see.'

Malleable?

Her veil fell forwards; impatiently she pushed it back. 'I thought to find a refuge in Alfold—instead, I find myself under siege here. And I am not speaking of the thieves. A few days after my arrival the Abbot of New Minster sent an envoy asking if I required an introduction to the Prioress of St Anne's Convent. A week after that the Abbess of Nunnaminster honoured me with a visit.'

Hugh picked up his wine-cup. 'Word certainly spread fast.'

She shrugged. 'I made no secret of my arrival, why should I? In any case, Edouard had suggested I should apply to the garrison commander in Winchester for men who would support me and once I had done that, well, I suppose the entire district is talking about the Norman lady who has come to Alfold.'

'Not just any lady, an heiress,' he murmured.

Her mouth curved. 'Hardly. The revenues of my manor in Normandy are meagre and entirely dependent on Edouard's goodwill. And you have seen this place—it is so run down it is practically a wasteland.'

'Not for long, I am sure, with you setting things to rights.' His gaze wandered to Sir Ralph and Sir William. 'I take it they have transferred their loyalty to you.'

'Yes, they are both landless like Sir Olivier.'

'So they, too, are likely to be interested in your person.'

'If they are,' her voice was dry, 'it is my lands they are interested in, not my person.'

Aude sat at the head of her board, eyes glowing with inner fire. There were tiny silver threads in her veil, which shimmered when she moved. She had an otherworldly beauty tonight—no, not just tonight, she had always had it, even as a child. Hugh's gaze skimmed her face, moving lower so it rested for a moment on the breasts that proclaimed her very much a woman. Her waist was tiny. There was no doubt about it, Aude was beautiful. Dignified.

Yet an air of *tristesse* hung about her. It had been with her since Martin's death and it made her appear untouchable. Distant, somehow. Hugh wondered if her knights felt the same. *She wanted a malleable man?*

'They are fools if they cannot see your beauty,' he found himself saying.

She exhaled sharply. 'Beauty? Oh, yes,' her voice

dropped to a whisper, 'I am beautiful in their eyes and shall remain so for as long as these lands remain mine. In the eyes of the nuns I also have merit, merit which has little to do with the state of my soul. Put plainly, the good sisters want to join my land with theirs.'

Hugh flinched, but there was truth in what she said. A landless knight would do much to wed a lady with even a small estate such as this. The knights about this board had little chance of acquiring lands unless they married well.

And here sat Aude, aglow with rare beauty, surely the answer to their prayers.

'Under siege at your own table,' he murmured, sipping his wine. 'I see what you mean.'

'At least Martin loved me for myself,' she murmured.

Hugh almost choked. *Did she not know? Was she really innocent of Martin's true nature?* He wondered if he should enlighten her. *It might be better if she lived on in ignorance. Whatever Martin's preferences, there had been real affection between them. She obviously idolised him.* Diable. *It was my fault she became his fiancée, it was I who first put the thought of an alliance between Beaumont and Crèvecoeur into her head by suggesting she became betrothed...*

Hoping to tease her out of the melancholy that took her whenever she thought of Martin, Hugh smiled, but he knew it was crooked. 'I leave you for scarcely a month, dear lady, and here you are beset by admirers.'

She lifted a brow. '*Dear Lady*? Heavens, Hugh, why the sudden formality?' Her eyes danced. 'You had other names for me once. I recall your calling me "Freckles", more often than not, or "Chestnut", or—'

'Brat,' he said, not missing a beat. 'That was my pet one.'

Her brows snapped together. 'Don't, Hugh, I *hate* that one—'

'Brat,' he repeated, smiling when her scowl deepened as he had known it would. Something squeezed in his gut—how odd, it seemed he liked her frown. Testingly, he ran a finger over the scattering of freckles running across one smooth cheekbone. The action startled a delightful blush out of her. A scowl and a blush—how interesting, he liked that too. Squashing the impulse to repeat the gesture on her other cheek, Hugh eased back and shoved his hand under the table.

'Indeed, you were a most ungallant youth.' Aude had ducked her head, she was fiddling with a serving spoon. 'It is such an ugly name.'

'I like it. I had almost forgotten it, but it suited you.'

She gave him a withering look. 'Well, as far as I am concerned the sooner you do forget it, the better. I hoped I had left my childhood behind me.'

Around them the meal was coming to a close. At Aude's nod, a couple of serving girls rose to stack the wooden serving dishes; benches grated as they were pushed back.

'Come, Hugh, we had best secure sleeping places for you and your party.'

Impulsively, ignoring the ever-watchful knights who were repairing to the fire with one of the wine-jugs, Hugh caught her hand. 'A thousand thanks for agreeing to look after Louise.'

Her face softened. 'Really, Hugh, Louise is welcome

for as long as needs be. Although for your sake, I hope
her visit will be a short one.'

He bowed. 'My thanks, Brat.'

'Hugh?'

She was gritting her teeth, she really disliked that
name. 'Mmm?'

'You love baiting me, don't you? Why is that?'

He grinned. 'Why does the sun rise every morning?'

She gave him a blank look.

He shrugged. 'Aude, I have no idea why, it is one of
the simple pleasures in life.'

She jerked her hand free and, before she turned her
shoulder on him, had given him a scowl that would
curdle milk.

Everyone had retired, but Aude lay awake in the curtained box-bed under the eaves. She was listening to
the sounds on the other side of the bed-hangings: the
occasional snore from one of the men; Edwige's soft
murmur as she spoke to her husband.

As lady of the hall, Aude was the only one in a box-
bed, the rest of the household had pallets in screened
bed-spaces at the far end beyond the fire. The various
murmurings were faint and comforting. Familiar. The
box-bed had originally been built for Alfold's Saxon
thane, it was wide and capacious. It was also some distance from the central hearth but since summer had not
quite run its course and the night was warm, heat was
not a problem. In any case, one of the first tasks Aude
had set Edwige on their arrival had been to tear down the
moth-eaten bed-hangings and to burn the musty linens
and mattress. The replacement curtains were embroi-

dered with brightly coloured wools in cheerful swirls and patterns. Edwige had made thick linings for the curtains, so if Aude should chance to be in Wessex when the year turned, she would be cosy. The mattress was springy and smelt faintly of meadowsweet. Fluffy furs were folded at the foot of the bed. However, cold was not likely to be a problem today.

It was Hugh.

As Aude lay in the dusky shadows she couldn't stop thinking about him. What a wretch he was to have taken her boat—twice!—in Jumièges. To be sure he had been under much duress, but even if he had not been under duress, he would probably have stolen her boat, simply to annoy her. He did love teasing her.

Did he dislike her? *Brat.* Such a hideous name. If he started calling her that in public, she would have him in the stocks. *Brat.* It reminded her of a past she was trying to forget, a past Hugh Duclair knew far too much about. *Every time he uses it, he is remembering the time you acted as a squire for your father.* She bit her lip. He had better not start teasing her about that within earshot of anyone else. Her shameful background was not known about in England, which was one more reason Aude had been so anxious to get here. She wanted independence, but she was also trying to leave her past behind.

And then Hugh turned up. She heaved a breath. Given how irritating he was, she should not have been so pleased to see him. But pleased she was, even though the man had barely walked through the door before he was interfering with her command, pointing out that she was concentrating her energies on domestic matters when there were military ones to consider. The realisation that his criticism was justified had made it doubly irritating.

She sighed. It was flattering that Hugh had remembered their brief conversation by the Seine and had found his way to Alfold. Of course, Hugh wanted a refuge for Louise…but did that mean he was about to embark on a particularly perilous course? Despite the warmth, Aude shivered.

William of Normandy was not known for his clemency towards those he believed were his enemies.

Some of the men were talking softly to one another; their mutterings rose and fell like waves on the sea. Her knights? Hugh and Gil?

Hugh had informed her that he and Gil would be leaving at first light. He had said he did not wish to put her in danger by remaining at Alfold. He had mumbled something about 'all roads leading to Winchester' and when Aude had questioned him as to his meaning he had refused to enlarge. Aude's stomach knotted. Undoubtedly Hugh hoped to gain an audience with the King in Winchester. But King William was somewhere in the fens in a place called East Anglia; no one knew when he might return.

Whatever Hugh planned, it was likely to be dangerous. What was he up to?

If only she could do more to help him. Looking after Louise was such a small thing.

What else might she do, save pray that Hugh might take care? It was wrong that Hugh was living the life of an outlaw. It must be a nightmare; until his name was cleared England was enemy territory for him. He was way out of bounds.

The bed-curtain was fringed with yellow light.

Surreptitiously, Aude shifted it aside and peered past the fire towards Hugh's pallet. There was nothing much to see at the far end though, dim shapes, grey shadows, dark patches. On this side of the screen, there were several bumps on the floor, any one of which might be Hugh.

Cedric, his bearded face lit by the fire, was hunched on the wall-bench nearest the door, arms on his thighs. He was taking the first watch. Not all the villagers were antagonistic towards their new lady and Cedric, whose cousin Goda had been the girl to have gone missing, had been delighted to be involved in any enterprise that might thwart the thieves. When Sir Ralph had followed Hugh's advice and asked for volunteers, Cedric had been the first to speak up.

Aude's gaze returned to the sleeping men; she could still hear the low rumble of friends talking into the night and, from outside, the sharp bark of a fox.

It was a shame Hugh had to leave; despite his interfering it was good to have him here, and not just for his military advice. It felt like old times. She might almost imagine he was reassuring himself that she was well.

The thought was warming. How odd, how *very* odd…

'Farewell, Hugh,' Aude said, reaching up to give him her hand to kiss. A bright morning had dawned, and Hugh and Gil were cloaked and mounted and ready to ride out. She had loaded them with supplies, food, blankets, wine-skins, even a bucket. She was certain they had a camp nearby, but Hugh would tell her nothing. She asked him one more time. 'I don't suppose you will tell me where you are going, or when we might hear from you again?'

Hugh kissed the tips of her fingers, lingering a little as a knight would over his lady's hand. She even imagined she could feel him take a gentle nibble, as though he were tasting her. Aude willed herself not to blush, he was only doing it to annoy her, as she could tell from that teasing smile at the corner of his mouth. 'Sorry, Brat.' He lowered his voice. 'And it is no use trying to wheedle anything out of Louise. She does not know everything and what she does know—'

'You have forbidden her to tell me.'

His eyes danced. 'Exactly.'

Shaking her head at him in mock anger, she withdrew her hand and stepped back so Louise could make her farewell. Aude wrapped her arms about her middle. They looked like a couple of pedlars and she felt hollow inside.

Hugh, be careful, please be careful.

The thought of him being caught and shut up in a dank dungeon…or worse, being executed for breaking the terms of his banishment sent shivers down her spine. The dangers for Hugh were as great in England as they had been in Normandy. Greater, perhaps, because Wessex was uncharted territory for Hugh.

Except, thank God for small mercies, surely there were not many people in England who recognised him by sight?

'Take care, Hugh,' Louise said.

Amen to that.

'And you too, Gil. God go with you.'

Louise at her side, Aude emerged from Eadgytha's cottage, and blinked into the setting sun. The two days since Hugh and Gil had left to pursue some mysterious course in Winchester had been the hottest that she could remember.

Large white clouds had been sailing across the sky for most of the day and the atmosphere was thick and heavy. The wheat was ripe and most of the villagers were bringing the harvest in from the field strips. Scythes and bill hooks flashed in the dying sun. The stalks were being snatched up almost before they fell, they were quickly bundled and carted into the barns. Wheels rattled over ruts, villagers shouted, a child was wailing. 'Mother! Mother! *Mother*!'

Outside Eadgytha's cottage, the bees were humming over a clump of lavender. A yellow butterfly was fluttering up the path to the hall, its flight so ragged it must be dizzy with the heat.

'I can feel that storm.' Louise was looking at an ominous band of grey that was darkening the horizon. It was moving steadily towards them. 'It is going to be bad.'

'Yes, the sky is getting very dark. Last year's harvest was poor; we can only pray they get the rest of the wheat in before the storm breaks. It wouldn't do for the crops to be ruined at this late stage.'

'No.'

In the two days since Hugh's departure, Aude had done her best to ensure that Louise felt welcome at Alfold. To that end, she had taken Louise with her when she did the rounds of the village; they had just been examining Oswy's shoulder.

'Do you think Oswy will heed your advice?' Louise asked as they took the path towards the Church.

'I doubt it, that lad was born to climb. He has done well to accept the restrictions of the bandages so far.'

'It was a good thought to make him help his mother with the herbs.'

'I doubt that Oswy would agree.' Aude grinned. 'Tying up herbs for drying is hardly how that boy wishes to spend his time.'

'Yes, but he is doing it.'

'Only because I reminded him of the importance of the village building up stores; he can remember last year's famine. Also, I have promised to think about unbinding him tomorrow evening. I doubt that Oswy would be so keen to help his mother on her own account. As soon as he is able I'll warrant he will be back on that roof, that or he will be volunteering to act as look-out against the thieves. I overheard him talking to Sir Ralph about them yesterday; for some reason the thieves fascinate him.'

A rook was flying towards a line of trees that marked the village boundary and the beginnings of the tangled forest known as Crabbe Wood. Aude had yet to explore it.

The sky was dramatic—half-dark, half-light. In the east, the black clouds were continuing to pile up, huge iron-grey clouds tinged yellow at the edges by the lowering sun, a sun which cast an evening glow on the weathered boards of the church.

The church roof, Aude noted with a sigh, was yet another building where the thatch was in dire need of repair. She rolled her shoulders. Her veil was hot and she longed to remove it, but it was too soon to relax, she had one more visit to make…

Father Ambrose was in the field strip adjoining the churchyard. His sleeves were rolled up and he was bent over his hoe, working between two lines of cabbages. Onions gleamed in a wicker basket at one end of the line.

'Good evening, Father.'

'Good evening, Lady Aude.' The priest paused in his work to smile at them. 'And Mademoiselle Louise.'

Louise had been introduced as a distant relative of Aude's, with no mention made of her family or title. As far as the villagers were concerned, Louise Duclair was Louise of Jumièges, exactly as Hugh had been made known as Hugh of Jumièges.

'We won't escape that storm, I fear,' Father Ambrose observed.

Aude grimaced at the darkening sky. 'It certainly looks that way; I shall pray that it is short-lived, it won't help the harvest.'

'That's true. After such a dry summer, to have a downpour now, just as…' He leaned on his hoe, expression sharpening as he tipped his head to one side. 'Do you hear that? Listen…'

Dogs were barking some way off, sounding as though they were on the Winchester road. Behind a clump of trees a cloud of dust was rising. And there, again, borne on the evening breeze, more barking. A horn blared, a dust cloud rolled up the slope towards Alfold.

'What is that?' Louise asked, a pleat forming in her brow. 'A pack of dogs?'

'Hounds in full cry.' Father Ambrose crossed himself. 'Manhunt.'

Aude's scalp prickled. Louise went white and Aude wished the priest had held his tongue.

'M…manhunt?' Louise said.

The priest's face was tight with anxiety. 'I am afraid so. There have been rather too many of those lately.'

Aude felt the colour drain from her own cheeks. *Hugh! Was Hugh all right*? Avoiding Louise's eyes, Aude strove for a neutral tone. 'Who would they be hunting, Father?'

'Some felon or other, I expect.'

'The band of thieves?'

'Aye, or maybe some rebels.'

'Saxon rebels?'

'Could be.'

'And would it be the King's men who are doing the hunting?'

Father Ambrose gave a heavy sigh. 'Yes, it is likely to be soldiers from the Winchester garrison.'

The horn blared, the hounds bayed, the dust had reached the ridge.

'They are heading for the giant's road.' Father Ambrose looked thoughtful. 'If the fugitives reach the wood, there is a chance they might escape.' He glanced at Louise's pale cheeks and gave her a kind smile. 'I am sure it will not be anyone you know, *mademoiselle*.'

'How could it be?' Aude said. Taking Louise firmly by the hand, she turned away. 'Good evening, Father.'

'Good evening, ladies.'

Louise pulled back when they reached the hall and looked towards Crabbe Wood. The fringes of the forest were blurred by a fog of dust. 'It will not be Hugh,' she said. 'It will not.'

Aude had to swallow before she found her voice. 'Of course not.' Even to her own ears, her reply was unconvincing.

Sir Ralph rounded the corner from the direction of the cookhouse. 'Good evening, my lady.'

'Good evening. Sir Ralph?'

'My lady?'

'Father Ambrose mentioned something called the giant's road—what did he mean?'

'That's the peasant's name for the old Roman road.'

'Yes, that must be it.' Aude hovered on the threshold. 'Is it used nowadays?'

'Yes, my lady.'

'Where does it go?'

'To the east it runs towards Winchester.'

'And the other direction?'

'It runs just below the ridge and leads eventually to the Narrow Sea.'

'Thank you, Sir Ralph, that is all.'

The sun dipped below the horizon and as though it had been a signal, the rain began, making small puffs of dust in the path. Some of the villagers scurried for shelter; others, determined to finish that last stand of corn, pulled scraps of sacking over their heads and renewed their grip on their scythes. In the distance, there was a faint rumble of thunder.

Sir Ralph shut the door with a bang and the field-strips, the ridge and the dust-fogged margins of Crabbe Wood were lost to sight.

Aude ushered Louise to the fire. It was not cold, but Louise's pallor concerned her.

'Louise, I shall have Edwige warm you a cup of milk.'

Louise sent her an intent look. 'He will be all right, won't he?'

Giving Louise's hand a final squeeze, hoping that she looked more certain than she felt, Aude nodded and beckoned for her maid.

* * *

The thunder did not begin in earnest until later, when the evening meal was over and the boards were being put up for the night.

A dazzling white flash revealed a split in the wall in front of Aude. The flash should have warned her, but the following crash had her leaping out of her skin. She was edgy tonight and no wonder, Louise was not the only one to be worrying about Hugh.

'I can see myself to bed, thank you,' Aude said, dismissing Edwige with a smile. She looked significantly at Hugh's sister who was drifting about like a lost soul at the other end of the hall. 'Keep an eye on Louise, would you? She is in need of your friendship tonight.'

'Yes, my lady.'

Taking up a lantern, Aude retired to the box-bed and drew the bed-curtains. She had loosed her hair and was sitting cross-legged on the mattress reaching for her comb, when she heard a sharp whisper.

'Aude, are you there? Can you hear me?'

Aude thrust aside the bed-hanging. There was no one there. People were organising their pallets beyond the fire, jostling for the best spaces. But that whisper had been so near…

The curtain dropped back into place; the rain pattered onto the thatch.

'Aude!'

The voice was urgent and closer than before. Rather mysteriously, it appeared to be coming from the other side of the wall, from *outside*. Her heart thumped, the thunder rolled. Could someone be standing under the eaves, trying to catch her attention?

Just to make sure, she lifted the curtain a second time, but no one was anywhere near the box-bed.

Outside, something thumped against the wall. The tapestry wall-hanging quivered, the embroidered horses trembled.

'*Aude*!'

She dropped the comb. Hugh! He sounded desperate. Heart in her mouth, she made certain the bed-curtain was firmly closed and scrambled across the mattress to the outside wall. Scooping the wall-hanging to one side, she grabbed the lantern, angling it so the light fell on the limewash. There was a small crack running across it—a wall plank must have shrunk in the heat of the summer, the plaster was working loose.

Hugh was outside, she would stake her life on it.

Chapter Eight

Hugh was outside! In her mind's eye, Aude could picture him in the thick shadows under the eaves.

She put her mouth to the break in the limewash. '*Hold on,*' she hissed. '*I'm coming.*'

Twisting her hair into a knot at the base of her neck, Aude snatched up her cloak and boots. Moments later she was hurrying through the hall.

Dynne was acting as guard tonight, he was already at the bench by the door, hugging a clay goblet to his chest. He nodded at Aude as she passed. Closing the lantern shutter so that the wind would not extinguish the flame, she reached for the latch. The latrines were in a small hut around the back of the hall; no one would give it a moment's thought if she headed outside. *I must not be long, Dynne will notice if I don't return soon.*

Several drops of warm rain landed on her face. Drawing her hood up, she crept along the walls and went straight to the latrine where she made a show of banging the door, in case Dynne should be listening out for her. Her light flickered. She held the lantern steady, protecting the flame as best she could. Its light was weak, but necessary. She didn't want to fall flat on her face in mud.

The stars were lost behind cloud. She was rounding the corner by the gable end when a shadowy figure separated itself from the night.

'*Hugh*?'

'Aude, thank God!' He caught her hands and drew her into deep darkness. Taking the lantern, he opened the shutter and blew out the flame.

'I need that!'

'Sorry, Brat, but we can't be too careful.'

Stretching up, she found his face and slid her arm about his neck to give him a hug. '*Don't call me Brat*! Hugh, I heard dogs earlier, the priest said it was a manhunt. Was that you?'

Hugh's arms had gone round her waist. He returned her hug. He felt warm and solid—if a little rain dampened. It hit her that if anything happened to him, she would be hurt beyond bearing. She tipped her head back. Hugh's face was taking shape as a pale blur in front of her.

'Yes, that was us.'

'What happened?'

Easing back, Hugh took her hands. A flash of lightning lit his handsome features. 'Gil is hurt. I am sorry to bring trouble to your door, but he needs your help.'

'Don't be ridiculous, Hugh, where else should you come? How badly is he hurt?'

Thunder rumbled, the storm was moving away. Hugh shifted, shaking his head. 'I do not know precisely, there was an…incident in Winchester yesterday afternoon. Gil took a knife wound in the leg before we got away. He said it was nothing, wouldn't let me look at it, the fool.'

'He was afraid you might leave him behind.'

Hugh swore. 'You are probably right, he is loyal to the point of stupidity. But hang it, Aude, Gil cannot do anyone any good if he is dead, even he must realise that.' He gave a deep sigh. 'I couldn't see any sign of bleeding, so I assumed he was fine, that it was indeed a scratch, but…'

'Did someone recognise you?'

'We were careful, but they may have done. I had been making enquiries in a tavern—it is possible I was over-heard. We were leaving and had reached the city gates. No sooner were we through when someone bawled out that they had been robbed and before you could blink half the Winchester garrison was on our tail.'

Aude gripped the front of his tunic. 'The manhunt—yes, I was afraid it might be you.' Briefly she rested her head against his chest, for a moment reluctant to move away.

He stroked her hair and said, 'We got clear of them, but Gil's wound… By the time we stopped he had lost much blood.'

She looked up. His hand on her hair was in some indefinable way unsettling, but this was not the time to dwell on that. 'Where is he?'

'In the forest that starts just beyond the village.'

'Crabbe Wood?'

'That's it. The place is a network of trackways; we found a ruined building about a mile in, he's there.'

'Hugh, I must go back inside, Dynne saw me leave.

If I don't reappear he will send someone to look for me. But I will help you. Stay here and await my signal.'

Taking his hand, Aude placed it against the wall. 'As you have already realised, the box-bed is on the other side of this wall, about here. I shall collect medicines and bandages—'

'I'd like to raid your cookhouse.'

'Help yourself. And see what you can do to prise one or two of these boards loose.'

There was a moment's quiet while Hugh felt along the wooden planking.

'The boards are fairly wide,' he said thoughtfully.

'Exactly. And more than one of them is in need of repair, so your part should be easy.' She gave a soft laugh and stooped for the lantern. 'Just make sure that the planks you loosen make a space large enough for me to squeeze out.'

Back in the hall, Aude moved quickly and quietly, taking several things from the linen press as she passed it. If anyone questioned her, and she did not think it likely, she would embarrass them into silence by muttering about her courses and the need for fresh linen cloths. It was an easy matter to take a pouch of herbs and medicaments out of the press and stuff a few bandages into it.

She turned back to the general sleeping area, but the curtains were down for the night and Edwige and her husband had already retired. Aude hesitated, uncertain which was their curtain.

'Edwige?'

A curtain shifted and Edwige looked out, sleepy-eyed. 'Here, my lady.'

Aude went over and leaned close. 'It is my woman's time,' she murmured, praying that Edwige would forget it was two weeks early.

Immediately, Edwige flung back her blanket. 'But, my lady, I thought—'

'I am all right, Edwige, really.' She pressed her back onto the pallet. 'There is no need for you to disturb yourself. I am only telling you now, lest I shall be late rising in the morning.'

Edwige looked thoroughly confused. She knew Aude too well, it was rare for her to rise late. 'My lady?'

'If I am, please let me sleep. I…I have had some difficulty in that regard since arriving in England, it must be the unfamiliar climate.'

Edwige's mouth opened and again Aude leaned close. It was easy enough to feign embarrassment to be discussing such matters in a place where anyone might hear them. 'If you could put it about that Lady Aude finds her courses something of a trial, I would be grateful. Say that she often takes to her bed for a few hours at such times, no one will know that I rarely have such trouble.'

'I am not to wake you, my lady?' Edwige whispered.

Aude shook her head. 'No, and forget about me breaking my fast. There won't be any need to bring me anything. I will come out when I—'

'When you are feeling more yourself,' Edwige said. 'Just so.'

Edwige gave her an intent look. 'Will you not tell me what is wrong?'

Aude swallowed. 'Do as I ask, Edwige, and all will be well.'

'Yes, my lady.'

Aude returned to the box-bed, clutching the pouch. Once she was sitting cross-legged on the blankets, she drew the bed-curtain tightly shut. In the dim light of the lantern she took stock of what she had gathered and waited for a sign that Hugh was ready to break into her bed.

She did not have to wait long.

A soft clunk had her lifting the tapestry on the end wall and hooking it out of the way. A loud scratching was immediately followed by the creak and groan of straining wood. She shot a guilty glance over her shoulder at the main body of the hall, praying no one could hear. Thunder, thank goodness. It was moving steadily off, but it made enough noise to mask what Hugh was doing.

'*Aude*?' Hugh hissed through the crack. '*Are you there*?'

Softly, she rapped on the wall. '*Yes*!'

'*Shift aside*!'

She edged back until the bed-curtain brushed the hood of her cloak—any further and she would fall out into the hall. She gripped the lantern. The blade of a knife winked silver, lumps of plaster and daub plopped on to the bedding. Sensing that this was the moment, she coughed to cover the noise; even as she did so, there was a creak and another flash of the knife. With a crack more plaster broke away.

Dust showered down. The night air rushed in. Aude coughed as though her life depended on it and a board was wrenched aside, shrieking in protest.

Hugh's face appeared. Pushing his shoulders through the gap, his lips curved.

'What's the matter? Hugh?'

His grin deepened and a wicked light gleamed in his eyes. He shouldered his way through the opening and crawled beside her on to the mattress.

'Hugh, what are you doing?' She thumped her fist on his chest, scandalised. She knew Hugh liked baiting her, but this was ridiculous. *This is my bed! Get off!*'

A large hand reached for her, it whispered across her cheek. Her hood was pushed back. They were kneeling facing each other. On her bed. Because of the lack of height, Hugh had to stoop his head to avoid touching the planks above them; it brought his lips very close to hers.

'*Hugh*!' Despite the poor light, everything snapped into sharp focus. Hugh's eyes were very dark, his expression arrested, as though he had just come to a realisation and was not certain that he liked it. Flakes of limewash and plaster were stuck in his hair. Hanging the lantern on a nail in the headboard—her hand had for some reason begun to shake—Aude reached up to brush them away. When she realised what she was doing, she snatched her hand back. Hugh seemed to be waiting for something. 'Hugh?'

Her mouth was dry, it must be the plaster dust. She could hear their breathing, the mutter of voices in the hall, and the soft hiss of rain in the mud outside. Time seemed to slow.

His hand slid round the back of her neck and carefully, eyes never leaving hers, he brought her closer. When his breath warmed her cheek, her heart began to pound.

His mouth went up at the corner and he cleared his throat. 'Everything is ready?' he murmured.

She waved at where she thought she had put the pouch and bundled-up blanket but, truth to tell, she could think of nothing but…Hugh. She was transfixed, unable to look away. 'I…I got as much as I could without raising suspicion.'

He didn't so much as glance at the bundle. He was examining her face as though he had never seen it before, eyes lingering on her mouth, her eyes. Aude couldn't breathe, she felt absurdly self-conscious. He was rubbing the tips of his fingers up and down in the nape of her neck—setting off little tingles that created disturbing echoes in her breasts and belly, starry little tingles…

'Hugh, why are you staring at me like that?'

'Don't you like it?'

'No…yes…I…I am not sure. It makes me feel… strange.'

He gave a soft laugh. 'Not as strange as I feel, I am sure. Little Aude…Brat…' He shook his head. 'Lord—'

'Hugh, you really should not have climbed in here.' Aude's thoughts raced. She was an unmarried lady and her reputation here in England was unsullied. It simply was not done for a lady to have a man in her bed, even though he was her brother's friend and it was perfectly innocent.

Hugh's smile twisted.

Innocent? Sweet Mother, save her.

'I dare say you are right,' he muttered, 'but I couldn't resist…you smiled so invitingly, it seemed you were welcoming me to your bed.'

'But I was not!'

'Pity, it is delightfully cosy in here.' He heaved a sigh.

'Aude, it was simply too tempting, I have imagined you in bed many times…'

Her mouth fell open.

'But I confess I never saw you in so many clothes.'

Her cheeks took fire and for a moment she was unable to draw breath. There was a hall full of people on the other side of the bed-curtain. She was conscious of the cool night air flowing through the gap he had torn in the wall, but most of all she was conscious of Hugh. Of that beguiling masculine scent that she had first noticed in Jumièges.

His hair was white with limewash. She brushed it away and immediately regretted it, for he leaned his head into the palm of her hand as though she had offered him a caress. Which she most certainly had not.

'Limewash,' she muttered. 'You have bits of lime-wash on your head.'

His smile was his old teasing smile, so why did it make her feel so hot? His gaze was dark and watch-ful; and his fingers, tangling in her unbound hair, were making tiny stroking movements. She sensed that he was waiting for something—but what could he be wait-ing for, when they ought to getting to Gil as quickly as possible?

'Gil,' she muttered, 'we must get to Gil.'

'This will take but a moment.' His fingers tightened on her scalp, his other hand dived beneath her cloak and wound round her waist. He tugged and she fell against that broad chest. Smiling crookedly, Hugh lowered his head.

A kiss? With Hugh? Her heartbeat went wild. This was a kiss that she was going to enjoy, this was…

Their lips came together. There was a rush of starry

tingles, *everywhere*. Aude had no sooner sighed into his mouth than he drew back…leaving her with no choice but to frown and tug at his hair…

Another kiss? More?

His mouth was gentle, and again he was smiling as he pressed one, two, three, small teasing kisses against her lips. Her bones were melting, the tiny stars were shooting everywhere. Her muscles went lax.

'Hugh.'

More tiny kisses, tantalising kisses, kisses which made her crave more… She pressed against him, held him against her, chest to breast. Her nipples tightened, the stubble of his growing beard grazed her cheek. She moaned.

'Brat.'

He nibbled at her lips, he licked them. She opened her mouth and then his tongue was inside, touching hers, playing. They fell back on to the blankets, a startled, messy tangle of limbs, cloaks and flurried breathing. Those stars, she could feel them *everywhere*.

'Aude, we must stop.' He lifted his head.

Stop? One hand was draped possessively over her breast. Aude had no recollection of him placing it there, but since it was there, she let it be. His thumb moved, her nipples ached in a reaction that was both pleasure and pain. Instinctively, she shifted against his hand, trying to intensify the contact.

Stop?

The mattress rustled, Hugh's thumb went still and lifted away. '*Diable*, what are we doing? We must go.' He rolled away from her. Picking up the blanket, he narrowly missed banging his head on the planked ceiling and squeezed through the gap.

Hugh had not been on her bed for more than a minute, but in that time he had wreaked havoc with her, mind and body.

Shocked at herself, wondering how on earth kissing Hugh could have driven poor Gil from her mind, Aude straightened her bodice. Her fingers had turned into thumbs. Snatching up the pouch and lantern, she scrambled into the night.

Outside, Hugh jammed the boards back in place, bracing them with a bundle of reeds he dragged from the pile under the eaves. Taking her hand, he crept to the corner and peered through the gloom towards the main door. The pouch was heavy on Aude's shoulder. Alfold Hall was quiet, the rain was easing.

Hugh's kiss lingered in the back of Aude's mind. It lay in her mind even as she wondered whether someone in Winchester had recognised him as the exiled Count de Freyncourt. If so, it was imperative he was not caught. Her heart hammered.

The kiss lay in her mind while she prayed that Dynne stayed put on the bench by the door; they would be very unlucky if he chose this moment to beat the bounds. Reminding herself that that would not happen until the second watch took over, she willed herself to remain calm.

Hugh was carrying a sackcloth bundle. 'You found food?' she whispered. She would think about that kiss later…

'Yes. Are there dogs at Alfold?'

'In the stables, they must be asleep.'

'Thank God.'

Hugh closed the lantern shutter and they crept across the yard. It had never seemed so large. A dark mass that could only be the church was visible on their right, which meant that Crabbe Wood lay straight ahead, across the fields.

'Horses?' Aude breathed. They were wrapped in darkness and with the clouds blocking out both moon and starlight, it was a strain to see the ground. Ridge, furrow, wheat stubble; ridge, furrow, wheat stubble…

'A little further.'

They stumbled on in silence. It couldn't have taken long, but it felt like an age. Finally the farmer's strips lay at their backs and the trees began to close in behind them. The lantern shutter squeaked and a pale beam of light illuminated their path.

'You can ride Gil's horse,' Hugh said.

Lifting her hand, he kissed it before forging his way along a slender trackway, half-pulling, half-leading her to where the horses were tethered; warm, friendly shapes in the dark that snuffled at their approach.

Once Aude was mounted, Hugh produced a leading rein and put out the lantern. 'It would most likely blow out on the ride, in any case.'

There was even less light in the wood than out in the fields, but Hugh plunged confidently on. A million half-seen trees and shrubs crowded close. Rain-sodden branches brushed Aude's shoulders and thighs; her skirts clung damply to her skin. How Hugh knew where he was going was a mystery, but Aude had already discovered that this corner of Wessex was criss-crossed with paths and trackways. It would seem that Hugh had found one of the most ancient, and since Gil's horse never faltered, he must have learned the way so he could ride it blindfold.

Bracken rustled, the horses' hoofs sounded hollow on last year's beech mast. An owl hooted. More rustling.

'Here we are.'

If Aude's eyes had been slow to adjusting to the night, her ears were faster. The jingle of a bit-chain and a dull thump told her that Hugh had dismounted. His footsteps drew near and an indistinct form materialised at her side. A pale face turned up to hers, and a warm hand touched her thigh.

'Come, Aude.'

It was then that she had a most worrying impulse. She wanted to reach for Hugh's shoulders and allow him to help her dismount. She, who had been riding almost as long as she could walk. She, who wanted nothing more than to be independent, wanted Hugh Duclair to help her down. And not because she needed his help, but simply for an excuse to touch him again.

Those kisses had addled her brain.

'I can manage, thank you.'

But his hands found her unerringly in the dark, steadying her. Briefly, he stroked her cheek, eliciting a burst of starry tingles before he released her. 'I thank you for coming with me,' he murmured. 'I was loath to involve you over this, Brat, but I am glad for Gil's sake that you are my friend.'

Brat. He moved away, leaving Aude staring blindly into the shadowy wood. *She was his friend, was she? Did friends kiss each other with such devastating intimacy? She had felt his tongue play with hers, and it had neither shocked nor repelled her. Friends?*

There came the familiar click of a flint being struck. Sparks flew. As the lantern flared into life, the beech trees and bracken around them took form. Narrow paths were running off in all directions.

Gil's horse shifted, stamping its foot. Returning to

her side, Hugh flung the reins over a branch and took her hand. Adjusting the strap of the pouch, Aude tipped her head up. 'But where are we? There's nothing here.'

He struck out down one of the paths. 'It is true there is nothing now, which is why I hope we shall remain undiscovered, but once…' His voice trailed off as he came to a halt and drew her to his side.

They had left the main path a few yards back and appeared to be on the edge of a small clearing, but, no, it was not a clearing. The light was falling on chunks of fallen masonry, the sharp edges had been blurred by time. It might once have been an ancient building, but only spirits or ghosts walked here now.

Ice ran down Aude's spine as she looked at a crumbling wall festooned with ivy. 'What is this place?'

'The Saxons call it the giant's ruin.'

'It is Roman?'

'Yes, it is Roman.' Towing her after him, he picked his way across the rubble. 'Most of the people hereabouts seem to have forgotten its existence; at least I hope they have.'

Aude sent him a swift glance, almost tripping over a chunk of broken masonry. She prayed he was right. Father Ambrose had mentioned a Roman road and if he and the villagers knew of the road, the chances were they knew about this place too. But, responding to another sharp tug on her hand—Hugh's mind was fixed on Gil—she said nothing and concentrated on staying upright.

'Here, let me take that.' Hugh relieved her of the pouch as they reached a low wall. Putting the lantern on the wall, he vanished behind what looked like a curtain of ivy. Moments later he was back to retrieve the lantern and lead her through.

They were in a square room, or what was left of one. A small fire crackled in the middle, flames and smoke rose into the blackness. Most of the roof was gone.

Gil was asleep, swathed in cloak and blankets under a makeshift awning. A rusty iron lantern glowed softly by the boy's head.

'Aren't you afraid someone will see the light?' Aude asked, shrugging off her cloak and dropping to her knees at Gil's side.

Apart from the cleared area where Gil and their belongings had been placed, the rest of the floor was lost beneath a covering of worm-eaten timber and dead leaves.

'Not here, not this deep in the wood. Just look at this place.' Hugh gestured at what might once have been a window, but which now, like the door, was choked with roots and ivy.

'Gil?' Gently, Aude touched the squire's shoulder. There was no response, not so much as a flickering of his eyelids. Guilt was a cold knife in her innards. They had delayed too long. '*Gil*!'

Chapter Nine

Gil lay unmoving. Hugh was at her side, his eyes grey and intent. Gently, Aude laid her fingers at Gil's throat and let out her breath on a sigh. 'Merci à Dieu. His pulse is weak, but steady.'

'Yes, thank God.' Hugh looked earnestly at her. 'He lost much blood.'

'A leg wound, you said?'

'Fool of a boy should have told me how bad it was. The first I knew that it was a real hurt was when he slid off his horse.'

'He was lucky he didn't crack his skull open,' she murmured, frowning at some bruising on the side of his head.

'Yes.'

Briskly, she peeled back the blankets. 'Pass me your knife, I need to examine the wound. His chausses will have to come off and it sounds as though he may need stitching. I hope he doesn't need cauterising.'

'You can do that?' Hugh asked as he hunkered down at her side and handed her his knife.

'I often used to assist at Beaumont, and before that my father needed mending from time to time.'

Hugh grunted; he knew about Aude's past life with her father, acting as Sir Hamon's squire because that was the only way they could stay together after her mother had died. 'Lord, what a world.'

'Hmm?' She bent over Gil, the knife blade glinting.

'I never thought to be pleased that your father dragged you round half of Normandy with him.'

Looking at the dark wetness on Gil's leg, she sucked in a breath.

'Aude?'

'As you said, there has been much blood loss. Did you put this binding on?'

'Yes.'

'I shall be needing water.'

'Of course.'

Warm fingers squeezed Aude's shoulder as, with infinite care, she began peeling back fabric from Gil's thigh. It was soaked. 'Hugh, I am honoured by your trust in me. Now be silent, if you please, while I see to poor Gil. You bound this cloth so tight it is a wonder you didn't stop his blood-flow altogether.'

'You see how he was bleeding—I had to.' Hugh's voice was tight with anxiety. 'Did I make it worse?'

'Most likely you saved him. But if you do not let me work in peace, you might very well make it worse.'

Hugh pushed to his feet. 'There's a spring nearby, I'll fetch water.'

'My thanks.'

'And then I'll get the horses into shelter, we can't leave them where they are. I won't be long.'

Aude murmured in response, but Hugh could see that her thoughts were all for Gil. Leaving her to it, he spread her cloak out to dry and went to find the brook.

Another tumbledown building was set at right angles to their hideaway, perfect for a stable, and Hugh had earmarked it as such some days ago. The entire roof had collapsed as well as a wall, but enough remained to keep the horses from sight of the path. Hugh thought it was highly unlikely that anyone would come this way, but if they did, he was determined they would see nothing. Doubtless, these ruins had once formed part of a prosperous Roman villa and the room in which Aude was tending Gil was all that was left of the main residence.

The wooden bucket made a hollow *thunk* as he went back to deposit it on the floor by Aude. She was busy with clean bandages and barely glanced at him. He returned to the horses and led them into the makeshift stable. Loosening their girths, he set about heaving off their saddles and making them comfortable.

Later, when he was back in the ivy-hung room again, Hugh fed the fire. Yellow tongues flared upwards, the shadows fell back.

Briefly, Aude tore her attention from Gil. 'Are you certain that fire cannot be seen?'

'Quite certain. When we stumbled on this place that was one of the first things I made sure of.'

Satisfied, she returned to her bandages.

Sinking back on his heels, Hugh rested his back against a wall and closed his eyes. He was exhausted. With Gil in as safe a pair of hands as he could find, he would snatch a few moments' rest. The weeks since his banishment had taken their toll and a deep fatigue had taken hold of him. It must be the constant tension, he supposed, the fact that he was at all times braced for the moment when he might be recognised, the moment he might be arrested.

Aude was murmuring to Gil, her voice low and soothing. Half-opening his eyes, he saw that Gil had come round. She was lifting his head to offer him a drink. Mouth curving, he let his eyelids droop. Of course Aude would know what to do. With Sir Hamon dragging her round every castle and tourney field in the Duchy, she had likely seen far worse.

He sighed and rubbed his face. When he had handed Louise over to Aude he hoped his cares might ease. Well, so they had. For less than a day. Before leaving his sister at Alfold, Hugh had worried about her constantly. He had questioned the wisdom of bringing her with him. And once she was at Alfold, where she was sure to be safe, he found himself wondering how she was doing. How Aude was doing. Whether they were missing him as much as he was missing them.

But then Gil had got himself wounded, with the result that Aude had been dragged back into his affairs. Lord. If only he could have done otherwise, but Gil was a loyal friend and he had to do his best for him. It had never been his intention to involve Aude further; the dangers for her were too great, but at this moment he could not regret it.

Stretching out his legs, Hugh's boots scuffed the floor, his heels scoring tracks in the leaf litter. He blinked, just able to make out the trace of a pattern.

Curious, he leaned forwards. Brushing more debris aside, he was able to make sense of it. This floor had been laid with tiny tiles, hundreds of them—the Romans who had lived here had walked across a mosaic floor. The winding design remained clear, surprisingly bright under its centuries-old covering of dead leaves. Three coloured strands were braided together like a plait— cream, ochre, green.

What riches these Romans must have had. Hugh hadn't seen a design to match it, not even in Rouen. He had heard that many Roman villas had hypocausts beneath the flooring to heat them in winter. Likely there was one beneath this floor—he and Gil had been discussing this possibility only yesterday. Tomorrow he would investigate.

Yawning, he slumped back and glanced at Aude. Her hair was not plaited tonight, instead a thick twist hung down her back, burnished and gleaming like copper. No veil. She had been undressing when he had disturbed her.

His lips twitched. Aude in bed. That kiss. He had enjoyed it far too much. Lord.

He kept his gaze on her back, admiring the narrowness of her waist and the gentle flare of her hips. She was handling Gil most delicately. Think on that, Hugh, he told himself, think on her skills as a healer. He did not want his thoughts to return as they had often done in these past months, to the Aude of his dreams.

That fantasy where Aude had greeted him each night in her bed, wearing progressively less and less as the days of his banishment had stretched into weeks. He had, he realised with something of a jolt, been using Aude's image as a distraction from the unpleasant realities of life as an outlaw. What would she think if she knew? The Aude of his dreams bore no relation to the real Aude, he must remember that. He could not permit his dreams to affect his relationship with the real Aude.

'There,' the real Aude said, satisfaction in her tone as she arranged blankets over Gil's chest. 'He is asleep, properly asleep instead of lying dead to the world. It is fortunate that it is a warm night, he does not feel cold.'

'I thank you.' When she rose, Hugh found himself holding his hand out to her. It was the real Aude he had kissed, after all.

Smiling easily, she came to sit next to him by the wall.

Would she look so calmly at him if she knew the nature of his dreams? *Brat.*

His thoughts ran on. In truth the grubby hoyden who had followed Sir Hamon in his wandering life as a landless knight was long gone; at some point she had been transformed into a vision of loveliness. Hugh wasn't about to admit as much to her though. As he sat there dreamily watching Aude settle at his side, he was struck by a realisation. *Aude had come to England to escape her past.* He frowned. How ironic, Aude was attempting to escape her past, while he was fighting to regain his.

Still, he wasn't about to stop calling her Brat, not when it made her eyes spark challenges at him and her cheeks flush in such an enlivening way...

Aude let her head fall against his shoulder. 'Gil ought to recover well. He needs sleep, and plenty of it, it is very healing.'

Hugh grimaced. 'I hope that he may get it—we *are* hunted men.'

Sliding his arm about her, he dropped a kiss on her

forehead. 'Get some rest yourself, Aude. I can let Gil sleep till dawn and then we must be on the move.'

Against his shoulder, her head shook. 'That wound was deep, Hugh. He will recover, but you must give him chance to heal. If he rides too soon, the bleeding will begin again.'

'Then I shall have to go alone, it will probably be better for Gil in any case. If I am caught, anyone with me will be considered guilty by association.'

'But, Hugh—'

He cut her off with a yawn. '*Mon Dieu*, I am tired. No arguments tonight, Aude, for pity's sake.'

That bright head lifted from his shoulder and large amber eyes frowned into his. Then she nodded and her head fell back. A log shifted on the fire. Overhead, Hugh could hear the wind in the beech trees. In his nostrils he caught the faint scent of summer and musk.

'Sleep, Hugh,' she murmured. 'You look as though you have not rested in weeks.'

'Yes, that is about the sum of it.'

'Tomorrow you can tell me what happened, I would like to know what you were doing when Gil came by his hurt and whether you learned anything to your advantage.'

'I will tell you everything, later.' Hugh closed his eyes, the better to enjoy that elusive fragrance that was beguiling him, heart and mind.

Heart pounding, Hugh jolted awake, reaching for his sword. But all was quiet, there was no need for alarm. There was just the firelight flickering over Aude as she leaned over Gil on the other side of the room. Slender fingers rested briefly on Gil's forehead, as with her other hand she straightened his cloak. His heartbeat slowed.

Through the ruined rafters a slight brightness in an otherwise black sky told him the moon had risen.

'Gil is sleeping, thank the Lord,' Aude murmured, returning to sit at his side. She wound her arms round her knees.

Light from the fire was playing over the curve of her cheek, emphasising a slight pout to her mouth that made him want to kiss her again. Hugh loved Aude's mouth, he could look at it till the end of time. He curled his fingers into his palms. Aude had grown into a beautiful, tempting woman.

Despite the fact that he had dragged her from her bed in the dead of night and brought her to this ruin in the wilds, she remained composed. A strand of auburn hair fell forwards, one glossy russet curl among many. Reaching out, he tucked it behind her ear.

She smiled. It was a gentle smile, the sort of smile she had given him many times in the years he had known her. Loving. Understanding. Accepting. A stab of longing shot through him. He frowned.

'Hugh? What's the matter? I am sure Gil will be well.' Her hand had come up to cover his, so it was an easy thing to wind his fingers—still lingering on her hair—with hers.

'I certainly pray so.' Hugh leaned towards her and brought her close. Carefully, he inhaled. Summer flowers, musk. Aude. Her eyes were wide, full of trust and… affection…yes, he was sure it was affection. He swallowed hard. 'I find I want to kiss you again.'

She made a humming sound in the back of her throat and went very still save that her eyelashes lowered. He had the impression that she was looking at his mouth. He was certainly fascinated with hers. Her tongue peeped out and moistened her lips. Long lashes lifted and bright colour washed through her cheeks. She made no other movement. Their fingers were still entwined, half-tangled in the luxuriant softness of her hair. The ruined villa was very quiet, there was just the reassuring crackle of the fire, the sigh of their breathing…

Closer, he thought. And then with a murmur—Hugh had no idea what he actually said—he moved to her and cupped her head with both hands, ready to turn her face to his. But it wasn't necessary. She had shifted and was already facing him and then they were kissing again. Small tiny kisses. Chaste kisses, as before. Hugh found her mouth, kissed it softly and drew back to observe her reaction. She leaned closer and, because he had moved back, her next kiss landed on his chin. Helpfully, not wishing to waste another should she offer it, he eased in again.

Immediately he was rewarded with another kiss, rather shy and all too brief, but this time it landed on his mouth. Hugh groaned at the catch in his gut. Holding her in place, he increased the pressure, pausing only to drop kisses on her fingers before they made their way round the back of his neck.

She twisted her body and clung, fingers tugging on his hair, the other hand at his waist. And her breasts, the mind-emptying reality of her breasts, was pressing into his chest, weakening his limbs.

'Aude.' Hugh dragged in a breath, he could barely speak.

'Hugh.' She drew back, smiled into his eyes, and

brought his head down for a searing kiss that had lost all traces of shyness.

He held her to him, tracing the line of her lips with his tongue, wanting, no, needing to take this deeper. But she was running ahead of him; she nipped his lower lip and opened her mouth. The tentative touch of her tongue on his was headier than the strongest wine. Heat was building in his loins. When she moaned, Hugh was slightly surprised to discover that his hands were exploring the shape of her buttocks, and he was turning his head this way and that to grant access to his chin, his throat, his ear...

He cupped her breast, feeling the weight of it in his palm.

'Hugh.'

The throaty murmur encouraged him. Gripping her skirts, he tugged, but she was kneeling on them and he could get no purchase. He pulled back, throbbing painfully, all urgent need. Long lashes lifted, amber eyes gazed trustfully into his.

It was the trust that did it.

It was like falling into an icy stream. *What was he doing?* He had been about to tumble Edouard's sister in an out-of-the-way Roman ruin on the edge of her land. And his squire was asleep barely three yards away.

Framing her cheek with his hand, he smiled. 'Aude.' It was something of a shock to find that his voice was not entirely under his control. Shakily, he leaned his forehead against hers and tried to smooth some sort of order back into her hair.

She released a shuddering breath. Thank God, he was not the only one here who needed a few moments to find calm. Aude's cheeks were a delightful pink and her eyes were shining. She looked so adorable and so beddable, it hurt.

But he must be realistic. A man on the run should not be thinking of tumbling his best friend's sister, however much she tempted him. Aude was innocent and must remain so. *He had nothing to offer her.*

He cleared his throat. 'Lord, this will not do, we should sleep while we can. In the morning we shall decide what to do with Gil.'

Her hands fell from his waist. 'Yes, of course.' She glanced at Gil, a slight crease between her brows, as though she had for a moment forgotten his existence. 'It really would be best not to move him for a few days.'

'In the morning, Aude, we can discuss it in the morning.'

Putting space between them, Hugh tossed her a blanket and set about using his cloak to make his bed. She watched him, biting her lips, but said nothing until he had stretched out full length on his makeshift bed on the floor.

'Hugh?'

'Mmm?'

'I would like to be close.'

Hell. One look at her, tentatively stretching a slender hand towards him, and Hugh changed his mind about sleeping apart. Closing his fingers on hers, he opened his cloak. In moments that disturbing body of hers was settling against him. That innocent body, he reminded himself. And she fitted so neatly. Even the hard mosaic floor could not disguise the fact that it felt right to have Aude lying next to him. It flashed in on him that they might have been made for each other.

Merde. The aching and throbbing went on, most painfully. But the knowledge that Aude trusted him enough to lie so close invested him with the strength to resist her.

Odd that… Hugh's thoughts began to drift as exhaustion drew him towards the edge of sleep. *Her trust in me helps keep her chaste. How utterly ridiculous.*

Ridiculous or not, minutes later, he slid into sleep.

Well! Aude thought, smiling into the flickering gloom. She wriggled into a more comfortable position against him. *Finally, she had kissed him! Twice in a day.*

With a dreamy sigh she cuddled closer. Kissing Hugh had been something of an eye-opener. Hugh's kisses were a world away from the cool formality of Martin's kisses; they were a thing apart from Richard of Beaumont's rather abstracted salutes and Olivier de Fougères's too-eager ones. Hugh's kisses were…perfect. If perfection was indeed the correct word for kisses that made her burn to do all manner of unseemly, unladylike things…

She had wanted to kiss Hugh for years. Perhaps not quite years; it was true that she had idolised him when she had had to play at being her father's squire, but in those years she had never thought of kissing him. She had idolised Hugh all her life, but the desire to kiss him had come later.

Turning her face into his broad chest, she pressed one last kiss into his tunic and let her limbs go lax. Shockingly, the first time she had thought seriously about kissing Hugh had been shortly after Richard of Beaumont had married his mistress. It had been an impulse that had taken her by surprise. What kind of a woman was she, to have had such thoughts when she should have been grieving for Martin?

It had been just over a year ago, in the spring of 1070. Before Hugh's banishment. With Count Richard married, Aude had realised that two ladies at Beaumont was one lady too many. She had returned to her brother's holding at Crèvecoeur.

Crèvecoeur couldn't have been more different from Beaumont. Beaumont Castle was a vast stone city, perched on a rocky outcrop overlooking the valley. It had a large bailey and thick turreted walls that contained stables and outbuildings by the dozen. Crèvecoeur, on the other hand, was little more than a wooden tower built on top of a man-made mound. The bailey at Crèvecoeur was so small most of the space was occupied by an ancient stable, a tiny wooden chapel and some tottering outbuildings which looked as though a stray puff of wind would complete their demolition.

On the day that Aude had returned to Crèvecoeur, matters there had reached a low point.

A herd of goats had been running wild in the bailey. As Aude fought her way through them, it was apparent that her brother had more need of her in Crèvecoeur than Martin or Richard had ever done in Beaumont.

The state of neglect in Crèvecoeur had nothing to do with Edouard, the blame for that could be laid squarely at the steward's door. For the duration of her grandfather's disgrace, right up until the moment the family lands were returned to Edouard as a reward for his service in England in 1066, Thierri Pointel had acted as steward. No less a person than Duke William had appointed Pointel, but his stewardship had been disastrous—he had milked the estate dry.

Undaunted, Aude had set to work with a will.

By late morning, the goats had been securely penned, several cartloads of seasoned oak had been ordered, and some major rebuilding work had begun.

Noon found her stationed outside at one of the southern watch points up on the wooden palisade. She was overseeing the dredging of the moat and because of the breeze, she had twisted her veil back over her shoulders to keep it from blowing in her eyes. The sun was warm on her head. Below in the village, white butterflies were dancing over the cabbages in one of the field strips.

The sound of hoofbeats rose over the hammering in the bailey, pulling her gaze in an easterly direction, to the wooden drawbridge. She leaned out to look. A group of horsemen had reined in at the gatehouse. One glance at the lead rider knocked the afternoon's work from her mind.

'Hugh!' Setting her hand to the ladder, she hurried down as quickly as her long skirts would allow. By the time she was back in the bailey, the Count of Freyncourt and his party were clattering through the gate.

Grinning, Hugh swung himself from the saddle. Aude had the impression that he was about to fling his arms about her when he checked himself and bowed, most formally, over her hand.

'Lady Aude, I trust that you are well?' He tossed his reins to his squire.

'Very well, indeed, Lord Hugh,' she said. Though she had replied with equal formality, she could not resist adding, 'It is so good to see you!'

Hugh offered her his arm, the light in his eyes warming her to her toes. As he covered her fingers with his, a blue gem on the pommel of his sword winked in the sunlight. He lifted a brow at the men wading about in the moat. 'Upsetting the ducks, are we, Brat?'

Briefly, she had scowled at him, the only sign that she had noticed his use of the hated name from her disreputable childhood. She had been so happy to see him.

'Hugh, the state of it! So much rubbish has been thrown in you could practically walk across. My knowledge of military matters leaves much to be desired, but even I can see that as defences go, it is pretty poor!'

He had escorted her to the bottom of the tower stairs, where he paused for a moment, smiling down at her. His eyes had been very blue. Sometimes Hugh's eyes were the colour of storm clouds, but that day they had been as blue as cornflowers.

'I am glad my worries were groundless,' he said, resting a boot on the first stair.

Her heart had given a small lurch and she had blinked up at him. 'You were worried about me?'

'I heard Richard of Beaumont had married that Saxon woman—'

'Emma, her name is Lady Emma of Fulford.'

'I was concerned when I heard. I care about you, Aude, always have.'

The sincerity in his voice made her eyes sting. Count Hugh de Freyncourt was concerned for her well-being. Aude knew she ought not set much store by such a light remark, but nevertheless for a moment his face was lost behind a mist of tears. When her eyes cleared she saw that his mouth had gone up at the corner. He reached out and briefly—too briefly—ran the back of his fingers down her cheek. She had stopped breathing.

Hugh turned away and started up the stairs. Hastily,

Aude gathered up her skirts to keep pace with him. That was the moment her feelings for him had begun to shift. Her fingers had tightened on his sleeve. A silk sleeve, the hem of which was embroidered most artfully in gold thread.

'Do you have business with Edouard today, Hugh?'

'Yes, but I also wanted to make certain he was not about to bully you into making an unsuitable alliance.'

Aude's heart squeezed; her thoughts had become tangled up one with another, but one strand had stood out from the rest. Hugh cared.

'Edouard is not about to force me into anything, he knows I am grieving for Martin.'

Hugh shot her an impenetrable look. 'Really?'

'Hugh, you know this. I only agreed to marry Richard because Edouard asked it of me and I felt duty-bound to do so. But Richard has married Emma of Fulford and I have had enough of duty.'

'So, no more betrothals?'

'Not for me. Edouard has promised to give me time and then—who knows?' *They had reached the top of the stairs and Aude paused with her hand on the door. Keeping her face straight, she added,* 'I may even become a nun.'

'A nun? You?'

Taken aback by the shock on his face—it was not entirely flattering—she had hastened to reassure him. 'You must know I am teasing! I do not think the cloisters are for me.'

Smiling, he had expelled a breath. 'I should think not! Lord, I actually believed you for a moment.'

Laughing, Aude let him hold open the door for her and stepped over the threshold.

That had been the first time Aude had wanted Hugh to kiss her. In point of fact, she had wanted to kiss him. But Hugh had simply looked at her, nothing on his face save amusement at the thought of the appalling nun she would make.

Grimly aware that no unmarried lady had any business yearning for kisses from Count Hugh de Freyncourt unless she were betrothed to him, Aude had tried to dismiss the thought. It had been far too unsettling. She had failed miserably, because last spring when she had ostensibly been grieving for Martin, she had found herself longing for Hugh. If she were honest with herself, she had wanted to cuddle him as she was now cuddling him; she had wanted the right to stroke that large body, so dear, so familiar and yet at the same time so utterly unknown. It had been most confusing.

How could she have had such thoughts so soon after Martin's death?

She had longed to run her fingers through Hugh's gold-tipped hair, to test its softness. She had been curious as to how it would feel to have the hardness of his thighs pressing against hers...but most of all she had wondered what it might be like to hear him say her name in that breathy, startled way such as he had done in this villa, only a few short minutes ago.

Yes, even a year ago, when there had been nothing to suggest there could ever be anything between them but friendship, she had longed for Hugh's kisses.

And now they were lying together on an antique mosaic floor in a Roman villa. Hugh has been stripped of his title and lands. *Everything* has changed. But not quite everything, Aude thought, hugging Hugh's large body to her. She still craved his kisses, she still craved… him.

The fire hissed, drawing Aude out of her abstraction. Gil was muttering and shifting in his sleep. And fast in her arms, Hugh slept the sleep of the exhausted.

Sweet Mother, but she was angry on Hugh's behalf. Angry that he had lost his county and was forced to hided out in Crabbe Wood, worrying whether his squire would survive a life on the run. At least she could offer him some comfort.

For as long as he needed her. Her stomach gave a hollow lurch. *For as long as he needed her.* It was good to be needed, but it might not be for long. The howls of those hounds echoed through her mind. Would the manhunt return?

And if Hugh were reinstated? He would certainly not need her then. Hugh Duclair, Count de Freyncourt, was the most self-sufficient man in the Duchy. He *never* needed anyone.

Whatever the future held, tonight was likely to be their only night together.

Chapter Ten

Aude was drowsy when she woke. Birdsong. She lay there, half in a dream world, reluctant even to open her eyes. A woodpigeon was murmuring, a woodpecker drumming and...she smiled, sleepily content. The dawn chorus in Alfold sounded much the same as it did in Crèvecoeur.

Saints, it is hot this morning, this box-bed really keeps the heat in.

Next to her, someone stirred.

Next to her? Her eyes snapped open.

Hugh!

The events of yesterday rushed back to her. She was not safely ensconced in the box-bed at Alfold, she and Hugh had passed the night in Crabbe Wood! His long body lay close to hers, so close that their legs were entangled. Hugh's arm was warm and heavy on her waist. His head lay beside hers in the nest he had made for them on the mosaic floor. It had been the heat from his body that had woken her.

So much for Aude coming to England to escape her unladylike past! This made her past life seem tame indeed. In Normandy, she had been but a child when she had acted as her father's squire, but if word got about that she had slept like a wild woman in an English forest with a banished man...

She was scowling at Hugh, on the verge of jumping up before he woke and said something to embarrass her, when something extraordinary happened. She felt her face soften.

It was such a novelty to see Hugh in repose like this, never before had she been able to study him without having to face those teasing eyes. She had always liked the way his hair sprang back from his brow, thick and springy and gilded at the tips. Carefully, she slid her fingers into it. Soft. Warm. Inhaling, she drew in the scent of him. Man and Hugh. A male scent that could have been alarming, but for some unfathomable reason eased a tension in her, body and mind. The urge to cuddle into him was overwhelming.

Drawing her head back, to stop his scent from befuddling her, she continued with her study of Hugh in repose.

His beard, beginning to show, was a couple of shades darker than his hair. His eyelashes were dark, too; he had thick eyelashes with a definite curl to them. Her fingertips ran lightly over his cheekbones, noting how his skin had been bronzed by the sun. She felt his stubble. Smiled at the prickliness. Never had she seen Hugh Duclair looking half so unkempt. If she, lying with him in the forest like this, was a wild woman, he was a wild man.

Even in his dishevelment Hugh remained handsome. There was no disguising the strength of his jaw, it warned anyone with eyes to see that this man had a will of iron. A will that refused to accept the terms of his banishment, a will that was fully engaged on attaining his goal. Hugh would, Aude was certain, prove that the charges against him were false. He would once again be the Count de Freyncourt. That, or he would die trying.

Her guts twisted.

He would succeed, he must! At the thought of him failing, her whole body went cold. She would not think of it.

Unable to take her hand away, she smoothed his hair back from his brow. For this small space of time, he was hers.

Such immoderate, immodest feelings he evoked in her! So unladylike.

Her feelings for Martin had never been half as powerful. What she had felt for Martin had been sensible and considered.

Back in 1066 after her father's death, Aude had accepted she needed somewhere to go while Edouard and Hugh went to England to fight at Duke William's side. Count Martin, whom she had liked for giving her father a place among his knights, had seemed the obvious choice. And when Hugh had endorsed the suggestion, Aude's thirteen-year-old self had agreed.

She had thought she loved Martin. But what she felt for Martin had been moderate. Sensible.

What she felt for Hugh on the other hand... Her heart lurched.

No! It was impossible, she would not even think of it! Any feelings for Hugh were impossible. They were ill considered.

Passionate?

No. *No!*

Withdrawing her hand from his hair, sternly reminding herself that unruly thoughts must be controlled, Aude extricated herself from their bed and went outside in search of the brook that Hugh had mentioned the previous night.

Her morning ablutions complete, Aude picked her way back to the shelter.

She was careful to avoid the nettles and briars; the paths were choked with them. Even in daylight, the Roman villa was barely visible unless you stumbled over it. Most of the structure had collapsed centuries ago. Of the walls that remained, including those in the chamber with the mosaic floor, much had been eaten by plants. Tall brackens unfurled next to stonework that was screened by thick curtains of ivy; straggling brambles poked through windows and rooted in crevices; seedlings sprouted from cracks in the crumbling plaster.

It is a good hiding place, but given how close the hounds were yesterday, surely it is not entirely safe? Until yesterday, Aude had not known of the villa's existence, but she was a stranger from Normandy. Those familiar with this corner of Wessex must know of it. Her stomach cramped. Hugh must leave this place, and quickly!

Beech branches stretched out towards her as she approached the hidden room. A blackbird let out an alarm call, twigs snapped underfoot.

'It is me, Aude,' she said, reaching the ivy-hung doorway.

Hugh was standing in front of Gil, his sword drawn, his mouth a thin line. '*Merde*, Aude, we took you for a garrison scout.' His sword slammed back into its sheath.

'I did not know how best to announce myself.'

Hugh grunted and rubbed his face; if anything, he looked more exhausted than he had the night before. Gil was struggling to rise, his face the colour of whey.

'Lie back, Gil,' she said. 'I am sorry I startled you.'

'Told him to lie back myself, but he insists on coming with me,' Hugh said, lifting a brow as he looked at his squire. 'However, since Lady Aude agrees with me, perhaps you will do as you are told for once.'

Aude caught the worn sleeve of Hugh's tunic. 'Might I ask where you are going? A manhunt tore across the boundaries of Crabbe Wood yesterday, I suppose this morning you are going to try and tell me it had nothing to do with you.'

Hugh grinned. 'Actually, Aude, you took the very words out of my mouth.'

Aude put her hands on her hips. 'You will have to do better than that. I remember what you said last night. You were both involved and that is how Gil was hurt.' Going to Gil, she hunkered down and laid her the back of her fingers against his brow. 'No fever, thank God.'

Gil's eyes lit up. 'Does that mean I may accompany Hugh?'

'Not unless you want to undo those stitches and the benefit of last night's sleep.' She longed to tell Hugh to take care of himself, but the words remained unspoken.

They seemed too revealing; in any case, Hugh would do what he must.

'Gil, Aude is in the right, you must stay here.' Hugh was at the doorway, cloak in hand. 'I don't intend to be long. Aude, a word, if I may, before I leave.'

Aude pushed through the ivy curtain and followed Hugh out.

'I don't need to ask you to look after him,' Hugh murmured. A shaft of sunlight brightened his hair. His eyes stared steadily into hers; they were a stormy grey today, not blue as they had been that day in Crèvecoeur when he had ridden in as Count de Freyncourt. A lump rose in her throat.

'I'll take care of him.' She touched his hand. 'Won't you tell me where you are going?'

'St Peter's Priory.'

Aude had heard of it. St Peter's Priory was one of the more humble of the Wessex monasteries. It was sited not five miles from Alfold on the outskirts of Winchester. 'Why? What do you hope to find there?'

'A witness, I hope.' He drew her behind an ivy-clad pillar, so they were out of sight from the track. He looked down at her, mouth turning up into a lop-sided smile, thumbs caressing her knuckles.

Aude's pulse skittered. 'Witness to what?'

'It concerns my father. Shortly before he died he had business with the Bishop of St Aubin.'

'Bishop Osmund? Wasn't he the man who put it about that you had connections with Duke Will—' remembering they were in England, Aude hurried to correct herself '—with *King* William's enemies in Flanders?'

Hugh nodded. His thumb was making small circles on her wrist. Aude frowned; the starry little tingles had started and they were more than a little distracting. She curled her fingers round his.

'Father put a large chest of family silver into the Bishop's hands for safe-keeping,' he said. 'But after Father's death, the bishop denied its existence.'

Aude stared up Hugh. His face was impassive, but she could read him—that impassivity was in truth a mask for anger that went bone-deep. To have one's life snatched away for a chest of silver, and by a man of the church...

'I am sorry, Hugh.'

A muscle clenched in his jaw. 'There is hope. Apparently one of the monks from Jumièges stood as witness to the dealings between my father and Bishop Osmund.'

'Documents were signed?'

'Yes. I have discovered that there were *two* sets of documents and the monk—Brother Baldwin—witnessed them being signed. He is a hard man to find. One rumour I picked up yesterday has it that shortly after acting as witness he went to another house in England, to St Peter's.'

'A rumour? Then you don't know for sure he is there?'

Hugh's expression was rueful. 'Sadly not. Brother Baldwin is the most elusive of men. But I intend to find him, his testimony could be my salvation.' Lifting her hand, Hugh kissed her fingertips. 'So, Brat, if you will excuse me. God willing, I shall be back before the shadows lengthen.'

Giving her a small tug, Hugh brought her to him, chest to breast, and pressed a swift kiss to the top of her head. Before Aude had time to blink, never mind wish him well, he was forging his way through waist-high bracken towards the stable. His use of the hated pet name slid by unremarked.

Noon came and went and Hugh did not return.

Aude's boots tapped across the tiled floor as she walked back and forth. Since Hugh had gone, she had made many crossings of the mosaic floor, each one made with her heart and mind praying for his safe return. It was barely four paces from one broken wall to the other.

Tap, tap, went her feet; it was a hollow sound. No Hugh.

Tap, tap. She was a bundle of nerves. In a moment, she would go and look outside. Again.

Gil was watching her. 'He will return, my lady, he will overcome his difficulties.'

'I wish I had your confidence.' She went on walking, up and down, up and down. 'What if he never finds this monk?'

Gil put his head on one side. 'You doubt him?'

'Not Hugh, of course not, but without proof how does one establish one's innocence? He is contradicting the sworn oath of a bishop!'

'He will regain his title because the accusations against him are unjust,' Gil said. 'He will return to Freyncourt in triumph.'

Aude came to a halt and stared. 'You make it sound so simple.'

'And so it is.'

Shaking her head, Aude resumed her pacing. She wished she had Gil's faith, but she did not. Gil's eyelids were drooping. Selfishly, Aude wanted him awake. She needed him awake so she could talk to him; it would help distract her.

'The floor sounds hollow, Gil, have you noticed?'

Slowly Gil opened his eyes. 'That's because it is hollow, the hypocaust...'

'Oh, I remember. It is how the Romans heated the floor.'

'Yes.'

Talking to Gil was not helping; besides, Aude knew he wanted sleep. *Where was Hugh? Was he safe?* She pushed the curtain of ivy aside and peered out. Nothing. It was embarrassing that Gil should see her so edgy, but his eyes had closed, he was drifting off again.

Unable to help herself, in a fever of anxiety lest Hugh's identity had been discovered, she ducked under the ivy.

Outside, columns of sunlight slanted down through the leaves, lighting up a tangle of moss-clad roots, an ancient creeper with a stem as thick as a man's wrist, a clump of bracken. The woodpigeons were crooning to each other in the green canopy above, and some way to the west she heard the distant mew of a hawk. No hoofbeats. There was little movement other than a flash of red as a pair of young squirrels played in the lower branches of a beech tree.

The moment she stepped back into the shelter, Gil's eyes opened. 'You are worried about him,' he said. 'And in truth so am I. It is not like him to be so late; I should have accompanied him.'

Aude shook her head. 'No, Gil, you most certainly should not. But I confess it, I am very concerned. However, I cannot stay here the whole day, I have to put in an appearance at Alfold. There is nothing for it, I shall have to go back.'

'What will you do?'

Thoughtfully, Aude scuffed at the dirt in a corner, revealing more of the interlocking mosaic pattern. 'First I shall arrange for a litter to be brought to take you back to the hall, I won't abandon you here. And then...' Her voice faded. She forced a smile and continued with more confidence that she felt. 'Don't worry, Gil, I shall think of something, I always do.'

It proved easier than Aude had expected getting Gil to Alfold Hall. Once he was safely there, Edwige threw herself into caring for him, proving herself a staunch and discreet supporter.

In a trice she and Louise had arranged screens around Gil's pallet, declaring him too ill to be pestered with questions. Quickly and quietly, Aude told Louise as much as she could about what had happened and what her brother was doing.

After that, any questions they were asked—such as those coming from Sir Olivier and Sir Ralph—as to what had happened to Gil were warded off with vague mutterings of 'an incident with a pack of wild dogs outside Winchester'. And when asked about the whereabouts of Gil's companion, Hugh of Jumièges, Louise would slide a sidelong glance at Aude, and say that he had most likely left the district.

Time dragged.

Afternoon melted into dusk and the boards were arranged for the evening meal. The torches were lit, their glow was reflected in the bronze hanging bowls that swayed gently above their heads. Finally, the fire in the stone-ringed hearth was banked for the night, and Cedric took his place by the door.

And yet there was no Hugh.

Anxiety was a cold ball in the pit of Aude's stomach when at last she took up her lantern and bade everyone goodnight. Sitting in the box-bed while she drew on her nightshift, the ball grew ever colder.

Hugh! Had he returned to the villa and found them missing? Had he been recognised? Caught? Where was he?

She dragged a linen sheet and a thin blanket over herself—without him at her side the night would be cool and the hours until dawn would be an eternity...

Sweet Mother, what was the matter with her? She was worried about Hugh and...and...

She thumped the mattress and tried to will away her anxiety.

Hugh can look after himself. Hugh will be safe. Hugh...

A scuffling sound broke the chain of her thoughts. Mice in the thatch? Beetles? It really was past time the roof was renewed. Whatever had happened to Hugh— *she must not think of him, she must not*—tomorrow she would see to it that a start was made on the roof.

'*Aude?*'

The harsh whisper had her shooting upright. More scuffling. Not mice or beetles, it was...

The horses on the tapestry wall-hanging shifted; she snatched them aside. The planked board groaned, plaster dust sifted down. And then the night air was playing across her cheeks and strong fingers had appeared round the edge of the plank.

Scrambling to her knees and retreating into a corner to give him space, Aude glanced furtively at the bedcurtain. It was firmly closed, thank God. She made herself small. The lantern light trembled.

Hugh appeared in the opening. The mattress shifted under his weight, straw rustled.

Silently, she mouthed his name and reached for him. 'Hugh!' It was impossible not to give that sun-bleached hair a swift caress before she recollected herself. She had never been so pleased to see anyone in her life, but if Hugh were discovered here in dead of night with her in her bedclothes...

Holy Mother, how would she explain that away?

Her people might know him as Hugh of Jumièges, but she was the Lady of Alfold, and to be discovered with a man in her bed—Heavens! And should it ever be revealed that Hugh was in truth the banished Count de Freyncourt...

Lord. Thin ice indeed.

Hugh crawled on to her bed, yanked the board back and the tapestry fell into place, hiding the wound in the wall. Leaning back against the embroidered horses, he held out his hand. Aude found she had moved to his side like a dove to the roost.

He was happy to take comfort from her because at the moment there was little enough of it in his life. For her part, she was happy to give it, but she could never hope for more. Hugh Duclair might no longer be Count de Freyncourt, but he would always be as far above her as the stars above the earth.

His arms settled round her shoulders and a soft kiss was pressed to her cheek.

'Any success?' she whispered.

His eyes were grey in the fitful light, his face shadowed. His hair had been disordered by the wind on the ride back from St Peter's and he still had not shaved.

He grimaced. 'A little, but not enough, I fear. I could do with finding Brother Baldwin.'

Impulsively, Aude hugged him to her. His head came to rest against hers and he heaved a sigh.

'He had left the Priory?' Aude asked. 'I take it you spoke to the Prior? Surely he would know where Brother Baldwin has gone?'

His shoulders lifted. 'You would have thought so, but I could get no joy of him. I would swear the Prior knows where he is, but he shut up tight as a clam whenever I mentioned Brother Baldwin's name. It was extremely frustrating.'

'How odd.'

Hugh caught her hand and locked his fingers with hers. 'Luck wasn't entirely against me. The prior did tell me that Brother Baldwin had left a document in his keeping.'

'One of the missing documents?'

'The same.'

'But that's wonderful! Do you have it?'

'It is safe.' He gave her a weary smile. 'It proves my father left much of the Freyncourt silver with Bishop Osmund. However, my testimony would be more convincing if I could produce the witness who attested to the signatures on it. Brother Baldwin is such a witness. If only I could persuade him to testify to the truth, Bishop Osmund's honour will be revealed as worthless, he will never be trusted again.'

The light was playing tricks with Aude's eyes; it was shifting over the various planes and angles of Hugh's face in such a way that she felt she was looking at a stranger. At one moment his long eyelashes cast shadowy crescents on his cheekbones, the next his nose was shaped like the beak of a hawk.

'What will you do?'

He ran a hand round the back of his neck and lifted his shoulders, and then he was Hugh again, the Hugh that she knew. 'I shall go back to Winchester to make enquiries there.'

'To the Abbey at New Minster? *No*! It's too close to the garrison.'

Frowning grey eyes clashed with hers. 'I should have gone there at the outset,' he said, softly. 'All roads seem to lead there.' He gave her a twisted smile. 'Aude, you know I have to do this.'

Her fingers clenched convulsively on his; she forced them to relax. She wouldn't dream of trying to prevent Hugh from doing whatever he thought necessary to redeem himself, but equally, she did not want him riding back to Winchester. The snarls and yelps of hunting dogs echoed in her mind.

She was opening her mouth to whisper her objections when, on the other side of the bed-curtain, someone coughed. She clamped her mouth shut and sent Hugh a look, she doubted that he noticed. He was toying with her fingers, measuring her wrist by encircling it with his finger and thumb. Lifting it to his mouth, he kissed the back of her hand.

He eased himself against a wall-post, eyelids drooping. 'No arguments, Brat, I beg you. Tell me about Gil—I take it you brought him here?'

'Yes, Gil is safe and getting more attention than he can cope with. Louise and Edwige are fighting over him. He is already much recovered, he has eaten well, his colour is better and—'

'Gil always did like his food.'

She frowned. 'Yes, but what about you? Have you eaten—shall I fetch you something?'

'Best not, lest you raise suspicions. Anyhow, I managed to persuade a cottager to sell me some bread and meat.' He yawned. 'I'm tired more than anything, I ought to get back to Crabbe Wood.' His eyes opened and he lifted an expressive brow, leaning so close she could feel the heat of his mouth. 'Wouldn't want to cause a scandal by being caught in your bed.'

Biting her lip, Aude nodded, though her heart was squeezing at the thought of him creeping back to that cheerless ruin alone.

'Hugh, I wish—' She bit off the words.

'Hmm?'

Briefly, she touched his cheek. It was warm and she could feel the slight prickle of his growing beard. 'Nothing, except… Oh, Hugh, I really wish you didn't have to go.'

That dark brow shot upwards. 'You want me to stay?'

She nodded.

Eyes dancing, he shook his head, but she couldn't help but notice that for the space of a heartbeat, his gaze had dropped to her mouth. 'I couldn't possibly put the virtue of the Lady Aude in question.'

'You did last night.'

'Last night—' his wave took in the box-bed and the occupants of the hall beyond the curtain '—was different.'

A large hand came to rest on her shoulder, his mouth met hers.

Heat raced through her. Hugh was worn out, he

should not be here and she knew he would not stay. Their tongues met, hers was playing with his and he was smiling against her mouth, making tiny noises, noises which, inexperienced though she was, told her very plainly that he was enjoying the kiss as much as she. Indeed noises of a similar nature were coming from her throat, before she thought to stop them.

Someone might hear!

She eased back. He murmured a protest, a protest that turned into a yawn. The man was exhausted.

'A final kiss to send me on my way,' he said.

Fear engulfed her, a bone-chilling wave of it. *If Hugh left, she might never see him again*. Such dread, but amazingly, it emboldened her. Lifting her mouth, she reached for his shoulders.

Their eyes held, their breath mingled. And then they were kissing again. Desperately, as though they were starving and kisses were their only nourishment. One of Hugh's hands was freeing her hair, the other was warm on her breast, shaping it, making it swell and tighten. Aude smothered a gasp at the connection that fired between her breast and belly.

'Starry tingles.'

'Mmm?'

'Nothing.' Wherever Hugh stroked her, her belly warmed, she was turning to wax, her entire body was molten…

He planted a line of kisses along her jaw.

Her breath caught. A moan was rising in her throat. Casting a guilty look at the bed-curtain, she managed to suppress it. The hangings remained closed, thank God, because Hugh was pushing against her and her muscles had had lost their strength to such an extent that they collapsed on to the mattress with a soft thump.

The bed ropes creaked. A bubble of laughter escaped.

Hugh lifted his head. His eyes were glazed and dark with something that had Aude ache with longing.

'What?' he breathed.

She gestured at the curtain. 'If they knew...'

'I shall go in a moment.' He gave her a lop-sided smile. 'You may banish me at midnight.'

Chapter Eleven

Aude permitted herself the luxury of relaxing in his arms. Hugh was, it would seem, as eager to caress her as she was to caress him. And he had said he would go in a moment, he had promised. He made no protest when she ran her fingers through that wind-swept hair; in truth, he made that tiny sound again, the one that made her want to snatch him to her and kiss him until he begged for mercy.

For her part, she made not a sound when he in turn wound his fingers into her hair, stroking it out, spreading it on the pillow behind her, trailing it down her breasts. He pulled back an inch to look at her. Her cheeks burned.

'What?'

He smiled and she watched, fascinated, as his cheeks darkened. Hugh, blushing? He shook his head, running his fingertips down the length of a tress as though it were the costliest silk from the Eastern Empire. Her breath caught. 'Nothing,' he murmured, 'save that I have longed to do this for an age.'

'You have?'

'Hush.'

He was back to stroking her breast, reaching for the ties at the neck of her nightgown. She clamped her lips together, to hold in the moan. Her breath sounded too loud, but she was unable to quieten it. They were alone on a soft, lantern-lit island in the dark, and there wasn't enough air. Hugh must feel the same, he too was short of breath.

Long fingers skimmed the neck of her night robe, loosening it, sliding the fabric to one side. She twisted to help him.

By now, Hugh was lying half across her, the weight of a leg over hers. She made no protest. His lips were nudging along her collar bone; he was tugging at the linen of her bed gown.

She ought to be shocked.

His sister, his squire and her people lay but a few feet away on the other side of that curtain—but her body simply did not care. Aude might be innocent, but where Hugh was concerned her body seemed to have some secret knowledge. It was arching towards Hugh in such a way that he could not fail to gain access to her breast. Carnal matters were suddenly no mystery, but the most natural thing in the world. One would have thought she wanted his mouth on her—

Oh!

Delight shivered through her.

'All right, Aude?'

'Yes.'

Was that voice hers? She hardly recognised it. Husky, dreamy, abandoned…

Clenching and unclenching her fingers on his scalp, she held down a whimper and strained towards him.

Oh!

Hugh's lips and tongue knew exactly what she wanted, they…

A whimper escaped. '*Oh!* S…sorry.'

Hugh's head came up.

'Again,' she whispered. 'Please.'

His lips curved, his head lowered and the magic began all over again. The starry little tingles. The sensation of melting. She kept on stroking his hair, his ears, his neck. The light wavered.

'Hugh, oh, I never dreamed…I had no idea…'

'Brat, you are such an innocent,' he responded softly and went on kissing her breast.

Frowning, she tugged at his hair. 'Hugh?'

'Mmm?'

Her cheeks were aflame and when their eyes met, Hugh must have noticed for he pulled back, angling his body so they were lying side by side. A gentle finger ran over her cheekbone. His leg rested possessively over hers. She was breathing in his scent, and heaven knew that was dizzying enough, but to feel Hugh's weight pressing her into the mattress…if he but knew the effect he had on her…

She cleared her throat. A warm smile was curving his mouth. Her heart gave a crazy lurch. Hugh knew. Hugh knew exactly the effect he had on her and somehow— this was shaming, though for the life of her she could not see why—he also knew that he was the first man to move her in this way.

He said nothing, simply wound his fingers into her hair before leaning forwards to catch her earlobe gently between his teeth. She shivered and drew in a shaky breath.

'Hugh, no one but you has touched me like this.'

His eyes darkened. 'For that I am very glad.' A warm hand lifted and trailed its sensuous way down the side of her neck, her shoulders, her breast, watching, with some satisfaction she thought, as her breast tightened.

'How did you know?'

Sighing, he drew the edges of her neckline together. 'You were betrothed to Martin when you were very young and Martin never touched you.'

She nodded. 'Yes, we made a vow.'

'A vow?' A dark eyebrow lifted. 'That is news to me.'

'We pledged to remain chaste until our marriage.'

Hugh held her gaze. 'I didn't know about the vow, but it doesn't surprise me. Martin never was a…woman's man.'

'What do you mean? Years ago, Edouard made a similar comment—I had no idea what he meant.'

Thus it was that Aude lay back on her pillows in the box-bed with Hugh in her arms, and listened with growing dismay and astonishment while Hugh gave a hushed explanation of what it meant when a man could not love women, but instead—

'Sir Jean!' Aude gasped as the realisation hit home. 'Martin loved Sir Jean!'

Sir Jean was a knight whose company Martin had seldom done without.

'During my time at Beaumont, Sir Jean and Martin were inseparable,' she said, thinking it through. 'I thought they were simply good comrades as you and Edouard are, but now…now I see it was quite different.'

'Quite different.' Giving a huge yawn, Hugh pillowed his head on her breast. 'Count Martin and Sir Jean were lovers.'

'And is it common, then, for one man to love another in that way?'

Hugh shrugged. 'Fairly common.'

'But it is obviously not talked about openly?'

'No, some consider it a sin.'

'Do you?'

He shook his head.

'What a fool I was not to realise.' Aude felt a frown form. 'Did everyone know that Count Martin could not love women?'

Lifting his head, he gave her a straight look, half-frowning himself. 'Some people undoubtedly did; as I said, it is not something that is much discussed.'

She gave him a little shove, and edged back. 'But you endorsed my betrothal to him!'

'Yes, I did.' A wary note entered his voice.

'You did this although you knew he would never really want me?'

With a grimace, Hugh propped his head on an elbow. 'Aude, Martin liked you. He was an honourable man who would have made a good husband.'

But Aude had not finished. It was as though this new understanding about the man she had been betrothed to for four years had broken a delicate spell, and the delicious melting feeling engendered by Hugh's kisses had entirely gone. Anger was taking its place. He had made a fool of her! 'You knew my marriage to Count Martin would have been a pretence? That Martin would never love me properly?'

'He would have done his duty, Aude, I am sure.'

'But what would he have felt? He would have hated it, he would have hated me!'

Hugh shook his head. 'Not so, there are many kinds of love. Martin was very fond of you. Aude, he came to love you, I am sure. He was always good to you.'

'Yes, but—' Aude fell silent while she struggled to digest what Hugh had told her. She had thought she loved Count Martin, but how could she have done? What she had felt for him had been a delusion. And that vow they had made—everything fell into place. 'I never knew him.'

Hugh sighed. 'Yes, you did. You knew you had a good man, one who cared for you while Edouard was fighting in England. And he did care for you.'

'Ye…es.'

'You loved him.'

'How could I have done, when I knew so little about him?' His hand came towards her, she batted it away. 'Everyone was laughing at me, I suppose.'

He shook his head. 'Not at all.'

'Hugh, tell me one thing—why did you endorse the betrothal, knowing as you did that any marriage between me and Count Martin would have been a sham?'

'You were a girl of thirteen when you went to Beaumont—how could you be told about such things? At any rate, after your father's death, Edouard and I were answering the Duke's call to arms. Time was short, the matter urgent. You asked for Martin. Aude, I thought you wanted him.' He hugged her to him.

'And that is why you endorsed the betrothal, because I asked for him?'

'I knew you would be safe with Martin while Edouard was in England. You could not be left at Crèvecoeur— the steward there was not to be trusted.'

Her anger receding, she tipped her head to one side. 'It was important to you that I should be safe?'

'Of course.' Hugh's voice was becoming slurred. 'Had to place you safely before we embarked for England.'

His hold on her was slackening, his body seemed heavier. Some hurt remained over this revelation concerning Count Martin and Sir Jean, but Hugh desperately needed rest. Aude couldn't bring herself to force more discussion on him.

She pressed a kiss on his forehead and inhaled his scent. Hugh. A male scent that for as long as she could remember had been entangled with various childish longings. With yearning for something she had never dared name, for the heir to the County of Freyncourt had been so far beyond Aude's reach that even the thought of an alliance between the two of them was forbidden. But the forbidden was not all that came to mind when she breathed in his scent. There were thoughts of friendship, of safety. Her heart swelled. It was good to know that four years ago in Dives, when he had been making battle-plans, he had wanted her safe.

And Hugh was in the right about one point: Martin *had* been good to her. She might not have known about Martin's love for Sir Jean, but she had been able to talk to Martin in a way that had been impossible with anyone else, except perhaps Hugh himself.

'Hugh?'

Silence. His head was a weight on her breast. His breathing was soft, his hold had loosened.

Asleep? Hugh could not sleep here, not in her bed!

'Hugh?'

No response.

Gently, she ruffled his hair. 'Hugh?'

Nothing. Not a movement, not a murmur. Just that large, beautifully muscled body lying relaxed and heavy beside her.

It was quiet in the main part of the hall, there were no murmuring voices on the other side of the bed hangings. Everyone save Cedric was likely to be asleep; no one would disturb her before morning. And Hugh was exhausted, it would be cruel to wake him when he was sleeping so soundly…

What harm could there be in allowing him to rest here for another minute or two? No one would know.

She opened the horn-lantern shutter and blew out the candle.

Yes, she would let him sleep for an hour before waking him. Then he must go back to the villa in Crabbe Wood, because when dawn came he simply could not be found in her bed.

Faint light was edging round the bed curtain and from the hall came the scrape and clatter of the boards being set for breakfast. Aude's mind was sluggish.

Someone laughed. A cockerel was crowing out in the yard and further off, she could hear the soft lowing of a cow. For the second morning running a heavy weight lay against her. A warm masculine scent teased her nostrils. Hugh.

Holy Mother, Hugh was still here!

The last traces of sleep fled. His face lay on the pillow but two inches from hers, his breath stirred her hair. His eyes were closed, those long lashes lying dark across his cheekbones. He was deep, deep asleep. One warrior's arm was wrapped round her waist and a long, well-muscled leg was hooked firmly over hers.

Heart pounding, Aude thought quickly. She had had little sleep on the previous night, which probably explained why she had nodded off rather than staying awake in order to see Hugh safely on his way. And as for Hugh, sleep had been scant for him in the last couple of months; exhaustion had him in its grip.

'*Hugh*!' She shook his shoulder.

His lashes lifted and those breathtaking eyes stared into hers. His lips curved into a smile, a smile that froze almost before it was formed.

'*Hell*!' He jerked upright, cracking his head on the planked ceiling. 'I should have been long gone.' Grimacing, he was ruefully rubbing the top of his skull when his eyes went wide and the colour drained from his cheeks. 'What's that? Do you hear it?'

The serving girls were chattering as they laid out the breakfast platters, but surely there was nothing that would make Hugh go pale like that unless…she caught her breath. 'Horses! Someone is riding into the village.'

There was more soft swearing from Hugh. He grabbed his sword and reached for the tapestry on the back wall.

Diving at him, Aude hooked her fingers round his belt. 'No! It is well past dawn, you are bound to be seen!'

'Brat, far better I am discovered outside, than in here, warming your bed.'

'Good day. Is this Alfold Hall?'

The faint chink of harness floated in; a saddle creaked as someone dismounted.

'Yes, sir.'

'And is Lady Aude at home?' The voice—surely it was familiar?—grew louder. The newcomer had entered the hall.

Clinging to Hugh's belt—Hugh's jaw was set as he worked at the planking—Aude braced herself for the reply.

'Lord Edouard, welcome!' Edwige said.

Lord Edouard! Her brother had arrived in Alfold!

'Good morning, Edwige. Where is my sister?'

The sound of Edouard's voice had Aude's blood running cold. She felt an insane urge to laugh. 'It is Edouard!' she hissed, conscious that she was teetering on the edge of hysteria. 'Hugh, Edouard is here!'

Hugh looked at her, a line between his brows. 'Of all the times…'

'What shall we do?'

Footsteps came briskly towards them and Aude wished herself, and Hugh, a thousand miles away. Her thoughts were racing.

The shame of being discovered together! Anyone would only have to take one glance at Hugh—looking so handsome and so disreputable, with the shadow of his growing beard—and they must peg him for a seducer. He had lulled her too well with his pretty words—'*I have longed to do this for an age.*' Lulled her, so that despite her shock at learning about Count Martin, she had relaxed enough to fall asleep herself.

Now she understood what people meant when they said they wanted the floor to open up and swallow them. If only the floor would open up, it could take her and the bed and Hugh, and...

Eyes wide, she gazed helplessly at Hugh.

'Let me see,' Edouard was saying. 'It is not like Aude to lie abed so late.'

The curtain swept open, light flooded in, and Aude found herself blinking into her brother's incredulous face.

We must look the picture of guilt.

Straightening her shoulders, hastily checking that the ties of her nightgown were in place, Aude twisted her hair over her shoulder and climbed out of bed.

Edouard was making a choking sound. Several gasps came from further down the hall.

'Good morning, Edouard.' Aude's voice was trembling, she hoped no one noticed. Everyone had frozen and the hall was held by an appalled, pin-drop quiet. She was vaguely conscious of Hugh emerging from the box-bed behind her, of him straightening his tunic, clearing his throat. She even caught the guarded look he flashed at Edouard.

Every eye moved from her to Hugh.

Edouard's mouth hung open. His chest heaved and a muscle jumped in his jaw.

'Welcome to Alfold, Edouard.' Aude forced lightness into her voice. 'It is good to see you.' Somehow, her feet carried her forwards to receive his kiss.

Edouard gave her the absent-minded kiss a brother usually bestowed on a sister, years of habit briefly overcoming his shock.

'Aude,' he began to sputter. 'You...you and...'

Reaching behind her, Aude fumbled for Hugh's hand. Firm fingers squeezed hers and then he was standing at her shoulder, eyes shielded.

'Good morning, Lord Edouard,' Hugh said, calmly.

'Hugh…' Edouard cleared his throat, his face very red. 'What the devil are you up to?'

'Did our letter reach you, Edouard?' Clutching at straws, Aude blurted the first thing that came into her head. Since coming to Wessex she had written to her brother, but that had been long before Hugh's arrival and she had made no mention of him. The letter she had sent had certainly not been a joint letter from her and Hugh, as she was implying.

Sir Ralph and Sir William were watching intently from their place by the hearth. Aude was uncertain of their loyalty. But worse that that was her brother's stunned expression. What might Edouard say? Caught off-guard like this, was he in danger of inadvertently revealing Hugh's true identity?

That must *not* happen!

'Your letter? Oh, yes, indeed I have your letter,' Edouard ground out, but his eyes said very clearly that he understood there had been no letter concerning Hugh.

Aude made herself smile. It was no easy thing trying to appear calm when everyone was fixed on your slightest move. She gripped Hugh's hand and hung her head. 'I know you forbade me to speak to Hugh of *Jumièges*,' she said, making a point of stressing Hugh's assumed name 'and that you consider an untitled man unsuitable, but I have to tell you—'

'A moment, Aude.' Edouard caught her chin and forced her eyes to meet his. 'Hugh of…Jumièges?' His lips twitched.

'I…yes.' Her chin inched up. 'I know you forbade me to associate with Hugh, Edouard. I am sorry I disobeyed you and I am sorry to make you angry—'

Hugh made a sharp movement. 'Aude, my dear…' His voice was soft, but it did not sound as intimate as it had done when they had been whispering in the illusory safety of the box-bed; it sounded dangerous. Insincere. He never called her *my dear*. 'I think it best that I do the talking.'

'No such thing.' Aude gritted her teeth, aware her cheeks must be crimson. Her thoughts were scurrying this way and that, searching for a way out. The panic almost engulfed her.

And then it hit her. Of course! The answer was obvious. If she dare.

She thought furiously. If only there was time to consider this fully, Hugh would be within his rights to be very angry…but there was no time, she must act and act swiftly.

She gave him what she hoped was a serene smile. 'Hugh, Edouard is my brother and I have disobeyed him. It is my responsibility to make him a full confession. We must tell him *everything*.'

Hugh's mouth was smiling, but his eyes were confused. He had no idea, Aude realised with a jolt, no idea what she was about to do.

I am trying to save your skin, and you may never forgive me. But I have to do this, Hugh, please understand. If you were indeed plain Hugh of Jumièges and you were caught in my bed, that would be bad enough, but should Edouard let slip that you are Count Hugh de Freyncourt…

She hauled in a breath and lifted her arm so no one

present could be in any doubt that she and Hugh were clasping hands. Her heart was pounding as though she had just run from Crabbe Wood.

'Edouard, I am glad you arrived this morning,' she said, in a clear voice that would reach the furthest corner of the hall. 'Because I have to tell you that last night Hugh of Jumièges and I accepted each other as man and wife.'

Hugh's breath caught.

Aude could not look at him, she dare not.

Edouard's eyes went wide. '*Married*? You and Hugh?'

'Yes, we are married.' Slowly, Aude lowered their clasped hands.

The stillness in the hall was uncanny; she had never heard such a stillness, the whole of Wessex must be in its grip.

What had she done?

'Lord!' Louise was the first to break the silence. She plumped down on a wall-bench.

Edwige's jaw dropped. A slow grin spread across Gil's face.

And Hugh? It was too soon to look at Hugh.

Outside, the cock crowed, but Aude scarcely heard it. Every muscle was tense lest Hugh should deny her.

'Aude, are you certain?' Hugh's harsh mutter twisted her heart. She was unable to lift her eyes to his face but she could tell his teeth were clenched. Out of the corner of her eye she saw him gesture curtly at their fascinated audience, voice pitched so that only she and Edouard would hear. 'You do realise—this amounts to a public declaration. I am hardly a prospect for any sensible woman at the moment, but if I agree there will be no going back—we will be married. This will have far-reaching consequences.'

There was a huge lump in Aude's throat. She had shocked him—no, it was worse than that, Hugh was beside himself with anger...the words 'sensible woman' had been uttered so scathingly. He had never used such a tone with her before—never.

What had she done? Unable to find her voice, she gave a jerky nod. She might not be a *sensible woman*, but she knew the traditions—a priest was not necessary for a marriage to be binding. Two things were necessary. First, that both parties consent and make a public declaration before witnesses and, second, consummation.

It was fast becoming commonplace to ask for a priest's blessing, but a blessing was by no means a necessity. Because their 'marriage' had not been consummated, it would be simple for Hugh to deny her. And if he did deny her? Well, events would then fall out as they must; she would suffer some disgrace, but that was a small thing. It was true that her declaration complicated matters, and yet...

Surely Hugh's position in England might be improved if he was Aude of Alfold's husband? For one thing, it would supply him with an excuse to remain in Wessex. And as long as she could persuade him to keep out of sight of the King, there was likely only a handful of others who had actually had met him in person and could denounce him as being the disgraced Count de Freyncourt.

Aude risked a glance. He was looking rumpled. That sun-streaked hair was tousled, it was obvious he had just woken up. There was a troubled expression in his eyes and his lips were tightly compressed. Her chest ached;

it was no good, she could not lie to herself. She was desperate that Hugh should not come to harm.

His sense of honour may make him refuse you.

It was true that if Hugh accepted her declaration, he would be putting her in some danger. It was no light matter to give aid to a lord who should not even be in England. Thinking to protect her, he could deny her.

Might he resent her for putting him in this position? Might he blame her for not sending him on his way last night?

Aude looked at her toes. If only she had thought before she opened her mouth. *Too late, it is too late to claw the words back.* She had spoken out because she loved him, she had done so ever since she was a child. He had been her hero and she had idolised him. But there was a world of difference between loving someone and falling in love with them, as she was fast learning.

The worst thing that could happen had happened. She had fallen in love with Hugh Duclair. And if he made a liar of her, her life would lie in ruins.

'Aude, you are certain?'

The hall seemed to rock as a wave of dizziness swept over her. Hugh did not want her. What had she done?

Chapter Twelve

Edouard was watching them, a tight smile on his lips. Aude loved her brother, but not in the same way that she loved Hugh Duclair, not at all in the same way. She folded her lips together, refusing to say anything of her feelings. Hugh was already under pressure here, she had no wish to make things even worse.

Her hand trembled. 'I am certain,' she murmured.

Hugh's lips formed a smile so cold it sent a shiver down her spine. His fingers bit into hers. 'Very well.' His gaze shifted to Edouard. 'Lord Edouard,' he spoke with distant formality, 'I have long wished to marry your sister and would have you know that we are fully contracted to each other. If it pleases you, all that remains is for you to witness our union as it is blessed by the Church.'

Hugh had long wished to marry her?

No, Hugh was playing to their audience, prettying up

*this mess by saying what he thought the others wanted
to hear. It meant nothing.*

Lines on his brow, Edouard was shaking his head in
a bemused way. 'Aude, you run away from marriage in
Jumièges—' his voice was low, confidential '—yet now
you have married Hugh?'

'Yes.'

Abruptly the lines vanished. 'I see it! You have been
nursing a secret *tendre* for Hugh for years…'

Aude lifted her chin. 'Nonsense!'

Both Edouard and Hugh were staring at her, everyone
was staring at her, but only Edouard and Hugh had heard
her lie.

Swallowing, she enlarged on it. 'I admit Hugh was
something of hero to me when I was younger, but as for
nursing a *tendre* for him—what nonsense!'

'Very well.' Edouard looked unconvinced, but he
drew himself up and glanced about the hall as though to
assure himself that he had everyone's attention. Loudly,
he cleared his throat. 'You, Aude de Crèvecoeur, have
taken Hugh of Jumièges in marriage?'

This then, was the declaration. There were certainly plenty of witnesses present—the entire hall—
Heavens.

'Yes.' It was terrifying how one lie led so swiftly to
another. Aude put steel in her voice. 'I do declare that
Hugh and I are married.'

'And I, Hugh…of Jumièges, do confirm it.'

Edouard was shaking his head again. Confused?
Angry? It was impossible to say. Aude hoped he was
not angry.

She was gripped by a sense of unreality. Part of her
was dreading the moment when Hugh would give her

his reaction, his *real* reaction. He would not do so here in public; here he was taking refuge in formality. But later, when they were on their own… God help her!

'Very well,' Edouard said. 'Let us pray that neither of you lives to regret it.'

'We won't.' Hugh sent Aude a smile of such cloying sweetness that she narrowed her eyes at him. Her brother might not be angry, but Hugh definitely was. Hugh's smile was telling her that she had overstepped herself when she had declared him to be her husband.

'A moment, Hugh, if you please.' Edouard gestured him to one side.

Hugh released her and the two men moved away, abandoning Aude by the box-bed. She was uncomfortably conscious that she was clad only in her nightgown, and that Edwige and Louise were staring at her as though they had never seen her before. On his pallet, Gil was leaning up on an elbow; he was focused on Edouard and Hugh, but there was a similar expression in his eyes. It made her realise the enormity of what she had done.

Hugh was her husband!

What were Hugh and Edouard saying to one another? Whatever it was, she wanted to hear it, but she could hardly chase after them in her nightclothes!

Hooking a blanket from the bed, she flung it round her shoulders and arched a brow at one of the round-eyed serving girls. 'The entertainment is over for the morning.'

'Yes, my lady.'

'Please continue preparing for breakfast. After that we will have to shift ourselves, there will be a wedding feast this evening.'

She remained the focus of all eyes. Louise was

grinning at her from across the hall. Gil raised his hand to her and Sir Ralph and Sir William inclined their heads in her direction. Sir Olivier she could not look at.

Guilt weighed on her with regard to Sir Olivier. She had made it clear to him in Jumièges that she would not marry him, but he was the most personable of her household knights and until a few moments ago she had thought it possible that she might change her mind. He had told her he would not give up hope; she owed him an explanation.

Later, though—Sir Olivier's explanation would have to wait. She must dress, and quickly! Hugh and Edouard were deep in conference, moving past the trestles towards the light spilling in through the door-way. Going out? Where? She gazed frowningly after them. Something was niggling at the back of her mind. It concerned Edouard's reaction when she and Hugh had emerged from the box-bed. That watchful way he had observed them, something about it had not rung true. Edouard had been shocked to see them together, but he had not seemed particularly surprised to see Hugh, which *was* odd. Her brother had then made some comment to Hugh, but try as she might, she couldn't recall it. And what were they were talking about now? Her very public declaration of marriage or something else?

Hugh scooped up a hunk of bread from a table as they passed it; he had missed the evening meal yesterday and must be ravenous. As he and Edouard went out, a muted babble arose.

'Such shameful behaviour, and she—a lady—she should know better!'

'Hastily patched together to conceal the most scandalous of affairs.'

'How long do you think that has been going on?'

'Her brother had no idea, did you see Lord Edouard's face?'

'Could such a marriage possibly last?'

'A shocking business, I always thought Normans were...'

Not wanting to hear any more, her mind in chaos, Aude hurled herself into the relative quiet of the box-bed. She yanked the curtain shut and snatched blindly at a gown hanging on the hook at the foot of the bed.

When she re-emerged, Gil was seated at one of the trestles talking to Edwige. 'You look much recovered, Gil,' Aude said.

Luckily her hand had fallen on the most demure of gowns, a simple green one in a lightweight summer weave. Her veil was white and it was pinned very firmly in place. After their rude awakening this morning, a demure gown was definitely called for.

Gil grinned. 'I feel much better, thank you.'

'Good, but please remember you should not be riding today.'

'I shall remember.'

Aude jerked her head at the hall entrance, where a splash of sunlight fell across the floor. 'Haven't they come back?'

'No, my lady.'

She stepped into the warmth outside. Edouard had brought a small retinue with him. Raoul and a couple of grooms were leading off the horses, and Aude's old travelling trunks—the ones she had left half-empty in the Abbey Lodge at Jumièges—were lined up, waiting to be carried in. Shame took her. She had deceived Edouard in

Jumièges, she had deceived him today. What a terrible sister she was.

'Good day, Raoul.'

'Good day, my lady.'

She ran Hugh and Edouard to earth in the village church. They were standing in front of the altar with Father Ambrose and a monk in a black habit who was a stranger to her. Edouard was gesticulating violently but the moment her shadow fell over them, he froze. It was obvious she had interrupted an argument.

Four faces turned towards her. Edouard was wearing his blackest expression; the priest and the monk looked politely concerned, but their reactions did not concern her. She looked at Hugh. Those dark brows were drawn together, his mouth was thin. Tension in every muscle, she approached them, skirts sweeping the beaten earth floor.

Hugh's hand reached out, drawing her to his side. 'Aude, permit me to introduce Brother Reinfrid.'

His hold was firm, but gentle. And it might be wishful thinking on Aude's part, but perhaps his expression did not seem as stern as it had done back in the hall. Some of her tension seeped away. 'Good day, Brother.'

The monk inclined his head. 'Lady Aude.'

'Did you accompany Lord Edouard from Normandy, Brother Reinfrid?'

Edouard made an impatient movement. 'He did, but what business it is of yours, Aude, I cannot see.'

Hugh gave him a straight look. 'Edouard, if Aude is truly to be my wife, this is very much her concern.'

Edouard grunted, 'You know my views. From the first I didn't want Aude sucked into your troubles, I am thinking of her safety.'

'Her safety is my concern too.'

'Damn it all, Hugh, if that is so, then why the devil did you come back to Alfold a second time?'

'You know the answer.' Hugh shot a sidelong glance at Aude. 'I have just explained how Gil was sorely wounded, he needed skills far beyond mine.'

Aude's sixth sense stirred, and again she found herself struggling to work out exactly what was bothering her about Edouard's reaction to finding them in bed together. There were dark undercurrents here. She had the distinct impression that there were two conversations going on, and the actual words being exchanged between her brother and Hugh were only half the story.

'*Mon Dieu*, Hugh, you didn't have to sleep with her!'

Hugh grimaced. 'That was an error, I admit I had no intention of doing so.'

'Then why the hell did you?'

Hugh lifted his shoulders. 'We were talking. I fell asleep.'

Brother Reinfrid was watching closely. 'Am I to understand that not only have you and Lady Aude made a public declaration, but you have also slept together?'

Hugh nodded. 'Yes, Brother.'

'Then all other considerations aside, I must point that you imperil her soul and yours, if your union is not blessed.'

'Brother, that cannot be right,' Aude said. The monk had placed a strange emphasis on the words *all other considerations aside*. This only served to strengthen Aude's conviction that she must discover what was being left unsaid. But before she discovered it, she simply could not stand by while Edouard and Hugh discussed her future in this way. She was no longer a child. 'A marriage is binding without the blessing, everyone knows that.'

Brother Reinfrid folded his arms, tucking his hands out of sight up the sleeves of his habit. 'Strictly speaking you are correct, my lady, but that is a state of affairs which the Church frowns upon and intends to change. Marriage is no light matter—why not accept the blessing of the Church to help you in your new life?'

Beside her, Hugh was muttering. Aude thought she caught something about the Church being 'hell-bent on extending its influence', but when she glanced enquiringly at him his face was a blank.

'What you are hinting at, Brother—' Hugh's voice was dry '—is that if I confirm this marriage, Lady Aude might find herself in harm's way simply by her association with me, but that if I do not confirm it, her immortal soul is at risk?'

Edouard laughed. 'Either way, Hugh, you are damned.'

'Yes, we have made, it would seem, a devil of a choice. On the one hand Aude's virtue is saved by our marriage, on the other, the marriage might put her in danger. There may come a time when she is accused of assisting a felon.'

A devil of a choice. Sweet Mother, would he ever forgive her?

Edouard looked earnestly at them. 'What do you want, both of you? I may not like the position in which you find yourselves, personally, I would far rather you had done things properly. However, I realise why that was impossible. I would have you understand that I will support you, whatever you decide.'

Edouard thinks Hugh loves me, Aude thought with a little *frisson* of astonishment. *Surely he must realise Hugh is trying to get me out of the pit I have dug for myself? Hugh does not love me, he is being noble…*

'Thank you. For myself,' Hugh said slowly, giving her one of those cold half-smiles, 'I would like this marriage. I am scarcely in a position to be marrying anyone, but since we find ourselves in this impossible position, I am content.'

This impossible position. Aude's stomach clenched. *I am content.* Was that the truth? Aude wished she could read him, but those eyes—grey at this moment—were on her, he was waiting for her reply. Grey eyes, Lord, that wasn't good.

Aude swallowed her doubts. 'And I,' she said.

Father Ambrose clasped his hands. 'Very well, we shall conduct the blessing at once.'

'Here?' Aude's eyes went wide. 'This instant?'

'Why not?' Edouard made an impatient sound. 'You may have put the cart before the horse in some areas, but that does not mean you should miss out on a Church blessing.' He gestured at the priest. 'Come on, Father, let's get it over with.'

Aude closed her eyes, praying with her whole being that Hugh meant it when he said that he would like their 'marriage' to stand.

'If you are content, Brat, then so am I.' Hugh ran his hand over his stubble-darkened chin with a grimace. 'Although I could have wished for a wash and shave… and a change of clothing first.'

Aude looked swiftly away, she would take Hugh in rags, *if he but knew it. If only he loved her, if only he could be restored to his proper status.* 'You shall have

both as soon as may be arranged,' she said. 'And food—
I'll warrant a proper meal wouldn't go amiss either.'

The blessing had been over before Aude had a chance
to blink.

The day passed in a haze of nervous anticipation as
the entire village, or so it seemed, threw itself into preparations for that evening's feast.

Her wedding feast. They would not allow her to
organise it.

'You are to sit there, my lady,' Edwige said, pointing firmly to a bench in the sun. 'You are not to lift a
finger.'

'But I *want* to help!' With a smile, Aude allowed
Edwige and Louise to push her onto the bench.

'Not allowed. We need space to work.'

Resigning herself to the inevitable, Aude gave in.
*Good, at least I will have time to think through the
consequences of this marriage.* In bright sunlight, her
bold declaration seemed recklessly impulsive.

*Had she done the right thing? Would Hugh come to
resent her for forcing him into marriage? Did he do so
already? Naturally, once the fuss had died down she
would offer him an annulment. An annulment might be
the last thing she would want, but if it stopped Hugh
coming to hate her, it would be worth it.*

*No, no, what was she thinking? An annulment?
Never! She loved him, she would fight to keep him. If
Hugh were to ask for an annulment, however, that would
be another matter.*

*In the meantime, it was perhaps no bad thing for
Hugh—temporarily at least—to be able to act as her
husband. It gave him a legitimate reason for being in*

Wessex and he could now assume another name, Hugh of Alfold. How English that sounded! Surely no one would suspect that Hugh of Alfold and Hugh Duclair, Count de Freyncourt, were one and the same person.

Yes, perhaps she had done the right thing after all. On the other hand, that cold look he had given her had chilled her to the marrow...

'My lady?'

A child with flaxen braids had come up and was offering her a posy of marigolds and lavender, picked no doubt from her family's field strip. Childish fingers had tied the flowers together with a few wisps of straw.

'For me?' Aude took the posy carefully, it was in imminent danger of disintegrating. 'Thank you. What is your name?'

'Fritha, my lady.'

The child wandered back to a woman who was hovering outside a nearby cottage. The mother was fair like her daughter and painfully thin, and as their eyes met, Aude recalled being told that she was a widow of what was referred to here as the Great Battle. Hastings. The woman gave Aude a brief smile and a nod that Aude realised was more shy than brusque and ducked inside the cottage.

Progress, Aude thought, her mood lifting. Two days earlier, Fritha's mother had ignored her when she had bid her good morning.

She ran her gaze over Alfold. The watch-point was manned. One or two of the villagers were back in their fields. Others must be in the barn, their presence there betrayed by the rhythmic beat of the flail and the dust sifting out into the sunlit road.

Edouard and Hugh came out of the hall.

Hugh caught her eye and waved. 'We're going to find the river,' he said, holding his tunic away from his chest with an expressive grimace. In his other hand he was holding something that looked very like her brother's best red tunic. 'A swim, followed by a bath.'

Aude nodded. As Hugh and her brother disappeared round the side of the hall, Oswy, his arm no longer in its sling, approached. He was holding a braided belt. 'Mother said to give you this.' He lowered his voice. 'She was afraid it might not be good enough, but it is her best one.'

The belt was pink and blue with cream threads running through it.

'Tell your mother it is beautiful, I like it very well.'

Oswy turned to go.

'Oswy, a moment, your shoulder…?'

Grinning, Oswy made a circle with his elbow. 'Better, my lady, it is better.'

'I am so glad. Oswy?'

'My lady?'

Aude gestured at the bustle inside the hall; at the people running in and out, at the cart setting off for last minute supplies from Winchester, at the cloud of smoke gusting through the vents in the cookhouse roof. 'There is to be a feast tonight.'

'Yes, my lady.'

'Please make sure your mother knows, we are hoping she will come. And would you please invite the other villagers too?'

'What, all of them?'

'Yes, indeed. I hope everyone will come.'

Oswy's eyes lit up. 'I'll tell them!'

As the shadows shortened, more people came up to

her bench. Some brought gifts, some their good wishes. By the time the sun was at its zenith, Aude felt like a queen. She had almost managed to relegate her misgivings to the back of her mind. She could not say what it was about her marriage to Hugh, but even villagers who had previously watched her with the most jaundiced of eyes came to introduce themselves.

Someone else coughed at her elbow. It was the miller, a tentative smile on his face.

'Good morning,' Aude said. Up until this moment the man had worn a permanent frown when in her company.

'Good morning, my lady, I hear you have wed that Hugh fellow, the one who helped Oswy and organised the watch-point.'

'Yes.' She held up a hand. 'But please could you speak more slowly, my understanding is better if you speak slowly.'

'Yes, my lady. I give you both my good wishes. I have been wanting to speak to you—the millstones need cutting. In the next few days, when you have a moment, please could you ask your husband to make arrangements for the stone-dresser to visit Alfold?'

'Certainly. And I hope we may see you at the feast,' Aude said.

'Thank you, my lady.'

The alewife approached with a wooden beaker brimming with ale. 'Here, my lady.'

Aude took a wary sip; she had tasted English ale before and generally it wasn't to her taste. But this ale... She smiled.

'You brew a fine ale,' she said, and meant it. 'It has a good flavour and it is most refreshing. Thank you.'

'You are welcome, my lady. It can't be nice being banished like this.'

'B...banished?'

The alewife sent her a strange look. 'From the hall, my lady. Goodness, whatever did you think I meant?'

Aude was saved from forming a reply as Hugh and Edouard reappeared at the far end of the lane, which led from the river. Their hair was dark with water and they were laughing together as they had done when they were boys.

Close by, the lane was smoky with the dust made by two girls winnowing corn outside one of the cottages. As Hugh and Edouard approached, it struck her that their manner with one another was almost too easy. Hadn't Edouard forbidden her to speak to Hugh back by the Seine in Jumièges? Aude puzzled over this as she sipped her ale. Had her brother ever really turned his back on Hugh? Given their long-standing friendship, it seemed unlikely. The rift between them must have been a blind...

As she watched, Edouard threw his head back, clapping Hugh on the back. At present, they were certainly behaving like men who had never exchanged a cross word in their lives.

What about that argument she had interrupted in the church, those undercurrents she had felt? A veil lifted. *Hugh had come to Alfold not to check on her well-being as she had assumed, but to make contact with her brother!*

Aude managed a casual nod when they looked her way, but she did not take her eyes from them as they turned towards the hut next to the cookhouse. Hugh had announced a wish to take a warm bath after his swim and this hut was the laundry. Water had been put on to heat, the great tubs were doubtless prepared. Aude had taken no part in any of this, and she certainly would not join them now to have it out with them, not when their every word might be overheard.

What else were they keeping from her?

Had her brother really come to Alfold to visit her? Had that been the real reason for his appearance? In the first shock of seeing him, that had been her assumption, but so much had happened since then…

She was married to Hugh—Heavens, what a tangle! She must tease it into order. Thankfully, sitting on this bench in enforced idleness, she had time aplenty.

It could well be that brotherly love was not the main reason that Edouard was visiting Alfold. Had Edouard arrived with another meeting in mind? Had he come knowing Hugh was nearby?

Yes, she would stake her life on it, Edouard had come here intending to rendezvous with Hugh. They must have arranged it back in Jumièges. And if Edouard had come to meet Hugh, then it followed that Hugh must have been intending to make contact with her brother not her, when he had arrived here a few days ago.

There was a chill in the air that put her in mind of autumn. Aude shivered.

How convenient for them that Richard of Beaumont had granted her this small piece of England. But where did that leave her? What must she now make of the kisses she had shared with Hugh? Of their time together? She had hoped Hugh was growing fond of her, but once again, it seemed she had misjudged a man.

Hugh was not fond of her, *he had used her.* His charm had made her forget how ruthless he could be. He had certainly not hesitated to steal her boat twice when he needed to. Stupid, stupid, when would she learn?

Men used women.

Edouard had used her to try to make a string of suitable marriage alliances. First with Count Martin who, while he had been kind, had used her betrothal with him to cloak the relationship he had had with Sir Jean. There had been Count Richard, who had set her aside in order to marry Emma of Fulford. There had been Sir Olivier, doubtless chosen because he was a landless knight and Edouard knew that Aude's life with their father would make her sympathetic towards him.

And finally there was Hugh. Hugh had come to meet Edouard, of that she was now convinced, but he had not thought twice about asking her to look after Louise; he had rushed straight to her when Gil had been hurt. In both instances, Aude had been glad to help, but there was a difference between helping a friend and in finding you had been used by a ruthless man whose one ambition was to recover his place in society...

'My lady?' The ale-wife was looking at her solicitously. 'Is something wrong?'

'No, everything is fine,' Aude said, pinning a cheerful expression on her face.

What were they talking about in the laundry house? And to think that she had been worrying about Edouard's reaction to her continuing friendship with Hugh—she had been worrying for nothing. Edouard's arrival in Alfold could only mean one thing...

Before Hugh had left Jumièges, he and Edouard had arranged to meet up in England. And despite Edouard ordering her, *ordering her,* not to speak to Hugh, the two men had remained friends, even allies, throughout.

There had been signs, Aude could dimly remember a subtle exchange of glances when she and Edouard had encountered Hugh at the Jumièges docks, but she had ignored them.

'They have made a fool of me,' she murmured.

'What's that, my lady?'

Aude shook her head. 'My apologies, I was but thinking aloud.'

Hugh and Edouard are working together!

I have been living in a dream to think that Hugh came to see me, that he trusted me. What man ever put his trust in a woman? Why, even the miller in Alfold must speak to a man when he wants his millstones dressing!

'Fine-looking man, your new husband,' the ale-wife said.

Aude shot her a look, but the woman's eyes were kind. 'Yes, he is,' she agreed, sadly, 'I have always thought so.'

'Known him long, have you?'

Aude had opened her mouth before she realised any reply might compromise Hugh's safety. 'Please,' she said instead, carefully moving Fritha's marigolds to one side and patting the bench, 'do join me.'

The woman brightened, sitting down with such alacrity that Aude realised she should have invited her sooner. 'Don't mind if I do.'

'The villagers seem content at my marriage,' Aude said. At least her English was standing the test of simple conversation.

'Oh, yes, my lady. Your Hugh of Jumièges seems a fine man, he was so quick with Oswy. It will be good to see Alfold in the hands of a practical man, a man of common sense. And his knowledge of military affairs—well, these days a village needs to be defended.'

Of course! To the Saxons here at Alfold, Hugh was an ordinary man, plain Hugh of Jumièges. They had no idea that by rights he was a powerful Norman count. As an ordinary man, he would fit in well with the English way of life. Ever since their Saxon thane had been killed and his land placed in the keeping of one of King William's most powerful men, the villagers must have been living in dread of the day he would come to claim Thane Frideric's land.

Everyone in Alfold was smiling because Hugh was *not* a great Norman lord. Aude had no knowledge of Thane Frideric's character, but this she did know— Thane Frideric had lived in the hall, among his people. He had not set himself apart in the way of a man intent on wringing every last penny from his estates.

Hugh's assumed ordinariness was working in his favour here. That, and his deftness and gentleness in the handling of small boys who fell off roofs.

His deftness and gentleness—pain sliced through her—Hugh was not all ruthlessness.

Aude handed the wooden beaker back to the ale-wife with a polite smile. Her stomach was starting to churn, but it had nothing to do with the ale.

Tonight, she and Hugh would be bedding down together as man and wife.

Had she done the right thing?

Tonight, when they retired, she would ask him whether he had come to Alfold to see her, or whether all along he had had it in mind to meet with her brother. She would make him tell her everything!

Tonight, when they retired…

Chapter Thirteen

With the babble from the wedding feast and the clang
of pots ringing in her ears, Aude touched Hugh's arm.
'Hugh, I will retire now.'

'And I shall join you.'

Ducking through the curtains into the box-bed, Aude
crawled on to the mattress. Hugh followed, drawing the
curtains behind him.

The small space was filled with light from two lanterns hanging from nails above the bed. The extra brightness did little to dispel a peculiar sense of intimacy that
Aude could only put down to the fact that this evening,
she and Hugh were married. They were both wearing
bright finery, she in a blue silk gown with a cream veil
and underskirts and he in Edouard's best red tunic. Aude
felt as shy as though they were neither of them wearing
a stitch.

'Wine, wife?' His voice was so harsh, she flinched.

Someone—Louise or Edwige—had put a flagon and

a couple of clay cups on the wall shelf. The bed linens were fresh and fragrant with lavender and little Fritha's marigold posy lay in the centre of the bed. Hugh shifted it to one side.

'No, thank you.'

During the celebration, nerves had got the better of her. Unable to make her peace with Hugh in public, Aude hadn't been able to eat much, and she had perhaps drunk a little more than she ought. There hadn't been a moment to question her brother either, but she was certain the two of them were in collusion. Most likely they had been working together long before Jumièges, when Edouard had forbidden her to speak to Hugh. Their lack of trust in her was galling, to say the least. She ought to have this out with him…

Hugh was reaching down a lantern and blowing it out. When he stretched, the mattress rustled. The borrowed red tunic was fractionally tight on him, which made it seem as though he was showing off his wide shoulders, though Aude knew he was not. Hugh was simply larger than her brother and most of his own clothes had been left behind in Château Freyncourt. Strong muscles flexed beneath the fine broadcloth.

Watching him through lowered lashes, Aude swallowed. She could well remember what his naked chest looked like—the image of him tossing her baggage off that river barge in Jumièges was vivid in her memory. She had married the most handsome of men, and tonight his body was devastatingly attractive. There had always been a dangerous edge to Hugh; oddly, knowing that he might resent their marriage did not put her off. The opposite, rather. A nervous excitement gripped her.

It was astonishing to think that tonight, he was hers.

Except—she must remember, Hugh was full of anger, and she was full of questions…

It was likely that the talking and laughing out in the hall would go on for some time. The boards were still up and Gil was the only one to have taken to his pallet. There was a dull thud as the main door slammed. The bed curtain shifted in the draught and someone let out a cheer.

'They must be bringing in more food,' Aude murmured.

'Or ale.'

Hugh stretched out his legs. Aude made herself focus on his cross-gartering, rather than those strong thighs. He had not removed his boots, but she was too shy to mention it. Another worry surfaced.

'Hugh, do you think it will amuse them to disturb us?'

'Not likely, the people don't know us well enough and…' his mouth twisted '…I had a word with Edouard. No one will bother us.'

Aude's cheeks scorched and she tore her gaze from his. She twined her hands together; this was probably as good a moment as any to discover what her brother and Hugh were up to. 'Hugh?'

'Mmm?' She almost jumped out of her skin when he covered her hands with one of his. It was something he had done many times before, but tonight, with the priest's blessing ringing in her ears and merriment from their wedding feast floating past the embroidered curtain, the gesture seemed laden with meaning. They were man and wife. Hugh had not even removed his boots, but there was a determined set to his jaw. Angry or not, she did not doubt that by tomorrow morning, she would no longer be a virgin.

His thumb moved slowly across the back of her knuckles. The starry tingles burst into being. Aude's questions froze on her tongue, Hugh's anger was forgotten. Indeed, at this moment he did not look the slightest bit angry. His eyes were dark in the light of the remaining lantern, his face was in shadow. Their silhouettes were splashed across the folds of the curtain at the foot of the bed, blurry and grey. Hugh's was the larger one, hers the smaller—they were very close together.

Soon to be closer, in mind as well as in body? Aude could not say, but perhaps she had grounds for hope. In her life she had faced many rejections—Martin had loved Sir Jean; Count Richard had chosen to marry Emma of Fulford; but Hugh…

She blinked at him.

'Aude, what is it?'

Hugh might not be thrilled by their marriage, but he had not rejected her. It was possible that hope was not entirely misplaced…

She swallowed. 'Hugh, you and Edouard—'

'Forget about Edouard.' Hugh released her hand—he was frowning at her belt, at her circlet and veil. 'Too many clothes,' he said.

Aude felt a distinct flutter in her belly. Slowly, as though he understood her nervousness and was determined not to startle her, Hugh lifted her circlet from her head and reached across her to put it on the ledge. His arm brushed her breast even as warm lips nudged the silk veil aside. He kissed her cheek.

Smiling, he slid the veil from her hair and it vanished

somewhere behind them. Long fingers lingered on her belt. 'This is pretty.'

'I…yes. It was a gift from one of my…our tenants.'

'You have won them over, they like you.'

'They like you too. There is bound to be some bad feeling against Normans but on the whole—' Aude bit off the words. She was babbling like a fool, not that Hugh seemed to mind.

He was leaning close, pressing more kisses on her cheek and all the while his fingers were busy in her hair, loosening it, spreading it out over her shoulders. 'I love the way it catches the light,' he murmured.

His expression was sharply focused, entirely on her, and something about it pushed the fears and worries to the back of her mind. So what if Edouard and Hugh had conspired together? So what if there were matters they were keeping from her? Hugh's resentment was a concern, to be sure, but he had backed her up when she had claimed him as her husband, he had not rejected her. This evening all that mattered was that he was gazing at her in that shockingly lustful way that never failed to melt her limbs. Heat centred in her belly. This was her wedding night and she was going to enjoy it! The questions, the recriminations—they could come later.

He breathed her name. 'Aude.'

Conscious of everyone on the other side of the curtain, Aude fought back a moan. She wasn't afraid, not of Hugh. It wasn't only lust she was reading in his expression. True, those stormy eyes had gone almost black, but there was softness there too, the familiar warmth.

And love? Was love to be found in Hugh's expression? An ache made itself felt in the centre of her chest—that was a question she could not answer. In any case, Hugh was leaning over her and one of those disorderly locks of sun-bleached hair had fallen out of place. Reaching up, she smoothed it back.

Afterwards, there would surely be time for talking.

Blue skirts whispered as he tugged them up. A hand found her thigh and began to caress her. So many starry tingles, low in her belly. Aude sank her fingers into his hair and brought their mouths together.

He nibbled at her lip, she played with his. His other hand stroked upwards and under her loosened gown, it closed over a breast.

Moaning, she tugged at his belt. 'You, too,' she said, arching into his caress. 'I want to touch you. I want to… admire you.'

'You want to admire me?' His colour deepened. How endearing to think that, with all his experience, she had the power to embarrass him.

He cleared his throat, hands going to his belt to unfasten it. He dropped the belt to one side and whipped off his tunic and undershirt. 'I don't think anyone has ever wanted to admire me before.'

Aude reached for his chest. It was beautifully sculpted, each muscle delineated by years of knightly training and exercise. Her fingers began to explore the fascinating mix of hard muscle and soft skin that was Hugh.

He bit his lip. His eyes had never been so dark. He was looking at her as though he would devour her. She loved it, she loved *him*.

The words were hovering on the tip of her tongue. Her heart squeezed. His hair was going its own wild way; his pupils were dark and that hint of colour on his cheekbones told of control, but barely held in check, of vulnerability. And she was the cause. She, Aude de

Crèvecoeur, rendered him vulnerable. *Not* saying the words *I love you* just then was one of the hardest things Aude had ever done.

A burst of laughter erupted from the benches. Biting her lip, Aude glanced at the bed curtain.

'It is alright, Brat, no one will disturb us.' His voice was husky.

'I hope you are right.'

Hugh was in a state of shock if Aude but knew it, but he would die before confessing it. Gently, he eased her gown up and over her head. A flimsy undergown followed. Aude made no resistance. In truth, she wriggled to help him. That done, she sat up again and in the most matter-of-fact way, seemingly oblivious of the effect her slender limbs were having on him, gestured at his boots.

Hugh's blood rushed to his groin and together they wrestled his boots off and unwound his cross-gartering. She did most of it—the sight of her slender white body had turned his fingers into thumbs.

Shock had held him the entire day, from the moment Aude had—in a piece of extreme folly, given the dangers—claimed him as her husband. Bad enough that she had run the risk of being caught with Count Hugh de Freyncourt within these walls...but to have declared that she had *married* him. Lord.

This marriage was damned inconvenient, but Hugh had accepted Aude at her word because he had always been fond of her. Her life had been far from easy, but at last she had Alfold. How could he have made a liar of her in front of her own people? There was no getting away from it—from the moment they had been found in bed together, their fate had been sealed. They must make the best of it.

Tonight, that did not seem a hardship. Aude's hair was a disordered cloud about her head, her limbs were creamy against the bedclothes. Naked, Aude was slender and delicate. Merely to look at her was to be tantalised by her. Hugh took her by the waist and gently brought her against him. Naked she appeared more fragile than her personality would allow.

Her arms wound round him, and her hands were sliding into his chausses, her fingers pressing into his buttock muscles, holding him to her. 'Nothing remotely fragile about that,' he muttered before he could stop himself. Her hair hung down her back like fire, tickling the back of his hands. He throbbed and ached where she pressed against him.

'Hmm?'

Hugh shoved down his chausses and braies, and fell onto the mattress with her. A couple of freckles on her breast caught his eye. 'I like your freckles,' he said, kissing them. The scent of musk and summer flowers filled his mind. He drew back and looked at her breasts. 'Beautiful,' he murmured.

Aude smiled and shifted against him and Hugh's sense of shock began to fade. This was Aude. His wife. Never mind that they should never have married, never mind that he ought not to touch her.

'Little Brat, who would have thought it?'

'Mmm?'

His fingers were wandering down her thigh. 'Irresistible,' he muttered, watching her face. Her eyes had closed. He watched as a look of pleasure stole over her face—it took the breath from his lungs. He throbbed for her, he burned.

'Aude, my love.' His unguarded use of an endearment he had never used with anyone checked him. *His love*? He was fond of her, certainly, but…*love*?

What he was feeling for her was desire, pure and simple. He had felt it before, it would soon pass.

She was moving sinuously against his hand. Her legs opened at his lightest touch. Gently, he eased a finger inside her. At the same moment a small hand wrapped round him. When she gave him an experimental squeeze, he jolted and bit back a groan. She was bringing him to her, positioning him…

'Wait, my love, wait,' he managed. 'You are a virgin, you are not ready, I can't just…just…'

His mind froze.

His body knew better. With one of Aude's hands pushing him to her, and the other tight about her neck— she was kissing his cheek, his nose, his mouth… Hugh let his body take over. He pushed.

She gasped as the warmth of her body tightened around him. Holding himself up on his elbows, he looked deep into amber eyes. She sighed and relaxed.

'Hugh.'

That was it, just his name. And then those sinuous movements started again and he must push, push, push into her and she was writhing under him and those imaginings he had had of Aude in his bed were as nothing. They had not conjured the heat of her, nor the heady scent of aroused woman, of Aude. His dreams had not told him how his guts would clench at the sight of a wild strand of copper hair trailing around his wrist. Nor had they conveyed exactly how the delicate perfection of her body would feel as she moved under him, as they found their rhythm together.

Aude was here in bed with him, this was their wedding night and the world, for once, was Heaven.

He eased back, smiling, wanting to convey something of what he felt. She clutched him to her and whimpered. On one elbow, he slid his hand between them. 'Have faith, my impatient love,' he said.

And then they were moving again, and he was playing with her in between pushes. Push, play, push, play.

He was watching her the moment the pleasure took her. Her breath stopped, her eyes closed, and under his fingers he felt the tremor of tiny pulses. One more push and the pleasure rushed at him, swallowing him so completely that there was no more Hugh and no more Aude, just one being, wrapped in bliss.

They had made love and it had been beautiful.

Hugh rolled on to his back and Aude snuggled into him with a sigh. Her eyes were half-closed and she was conscious of his gaze on her. She felt the moment he reached over to put out the remaining lantern.

Darkness fell over them like a soft cloak. There was just the faintest shimmer of light edging around the bed-curtain, the mutterings and mumbles from the hall seemed a million miles away.

Sleep was stealing over her when Aude remembered her questions.

'Hugh?'

'Mmm?' An eyelid opened, he caressed her cheek. Pushing a strand of hair out of her face, he twined it round his finger, released it, and watched it spring back into its natural curl.

'When you first came to Alfold you were hoping to find Edouard here, were you not?'

His face closed.

'Hugh, Edouard came here on your business, I am sure of it...'

'Aude, we can discuss this later.' He gave an exaggerated yawn. 'We should sleep.'

'I ask because I—' she choked back the words *I love you* just in time '—I want to help.'

'You have already done more than you should, with Gil and Louise.'

'It seems little enough. I want to help you as in the same way that I suspect Edouard has been helping you. I want to see you restored to your rightful place.' Frowning, she clenched her fist on his chest. 'I know you and Edouard are planning something. Why won't you tell me what it is—don't you trust me?'

'Trust is not the issue.'

'Isn't it?'

A large hand rested gently on the back of her head. His smile was sad. 'Aude, know that I care for you, know that I do not want you to be involved—'

'Not involved? We were married today!'

How was it, Aude thought with something approaching desperation, that a few moments ago they had been united in the most delightful, satisfying way that a man and a woman could be united, and *already* they were quarrelling?

She gripped his shoulder. 'Please, Hugh, I know you and Edouard are allies. Won't you tell me what's going on?'

His fingers slid round to her jaw, his breath stirred her hair.

'Since you insist, I will tell you this. Edouard and I are going to Winchester tomorrow.'

Goosebumps stole over her skin. 'You are going to see the Abbot of New Minster?'

He nodded.

'Isn't that dangerous?'

'We will be circumspect. I am not about to trumpet my identity until we know it is safe for me to do so. I shall be Hugh of Jumièges—' with a grin he hugged her to him '—or Hugh of Alfold until my innocence is proved.'

'But, Hugh…' Aude's voice was high, she moderated it '…last time you went to Winchester, men from the garrison set a pack of dogs on you! And Gil…' She chewed her lip. 'Lord, Hugh, how can you be sure that won't happen again?'

Pressing her closer, he kissed her forehead, and let his hand slide lower. His fingers curled possessively round her breast. 'We are going, Brat, so you can lose that scowl.'

His fingers moved suggestively over her skin, and immediately Aude's mind began to cloud and she became aware of that slow heat building at her core.

Hugh shifted, a strong leg hooked over hers, he leaned up on an elbow.

'Aude, kiss me.' His eyes were dark and compelling, his mouth tender.

'Didn't you say we should sleep?'

He grinned and bent to whisper in her ear. 'I think I have found my second wind.'

He was trying to distract her and he was succeeding; the goosebumps had gone. Aude felt herself blush. 'It is possible then, twice?' Her heart began to thud.

'Indeed it is, my innocent. And that question tells me that you are in need of a small demonstration...'

His teeth closed softly over her ear. He nuzzled her neck, head moving inexorably to her breast. His fingers were ahead of him, stroking her hips, setting off those starry tingles as he parted her thighs.

'Hugh...' her voice was little more than a breath '...oh, yes, Hugh.'

'My love.' His voice was full of satisfaction.

Grasping at the last shreds of reason, Aude buried both hands in his hair, tugging at it, forcing him to meet her eyes.

'If you and Edouard are going to Winchester in the morning, I am going with you.'

Hugh gave an inarticulate murmur and his lips returned to her breast. Desire coiled within her. Aude ached for him, she wanted nothing more than to surrender to the pleasure of his touch. It wasn't easy, but somehow she found words.

'Hugh?'

'Mmm?'

'In the morning, I am going with you.'

'Good morning, my lady.'

Slowly, Aude opened her eyes. Edwige was peering round the edge of the curtain.

'I have your water, my lady.'

Aude yawned. The mattress next to her was empty, a dent in the pillow being the only sign that Hugh had slept there. 'Thank you.'

Edwige stepped into the space at the foot of the bed and set a steaming jug on the shelf. A soft light filtered through from the hall, together with the clatter of knives and the mouth-watering smell of fresh bread.

Edwige selected a green gown from Aude's clothes hook, and put it over her arm. A coffer creaked as she opened it. 'Your dark veil today, my lady?'

Hugh must have been up early, his tunic—or rather her brother's tunic—was not to be seen. Aude's brows snapped together and she sat up with a jolt.

He wouldn't! Would he?

'Edwige, where is my husband—is he breaking his fast?'

'Indeed not. Lord H…your husband rode out at first light.'

'*What*?'

Edwige looked up, grey veil in hand. 'Didn't he tell you? Your husband and Lord Edouard have set out for Winchester.'

'*No*!' Aude leaped from the bed and snatched the gown and veil from Edwige. 'Did my brother's squire accompany them?'

'No, my lady.'

'Edouard's men-at-arms?'

'Why, no, my lady.'

Aude gritted her teeth. 'What about my knights—I don't suppose they went with them either?'

'No, my lady, they went alone.'

'God's Grace!' Aude bent hastily over the ewer and splashed her face. Her maid's mouth pursed; she disapproved of Aude's language. 'There's no need to look like that, Edwige, they should have taken someone with them.'

'Yes, my lady.'

Aude struggled into the green gown, heart banging like a battle drum. 'My lacings, and quickly.'

When it came to her veil, she batted Edwige's hand away. She didn't think there was time. 'I can manage the rest. Find Raoul. And Sir Olivier. Tell them.' She checked herself. 'No, *ask* them to saddle two horses at once.'

'You are going after them?'

'Yes. *Yes.* Hurry, *please*!'

With a swift nod, Edwige dived through the curtains.

'Sir Olivier, I am happy we are in accord,' Aude concluded, as the city walls of Winchester came into view. 'I would have been most upset if my marriage to Hugh had lost me a good knight.'

Sir Olivier gave her a straight look. 'I cannot say I was delighted, my lady, but from the start you explained that you would not marry me. I see now why that was. You have known your husband for many years, have you not?'

They were approaching the river, one of the city gates lay on the other side of the bridge. As they clattered over the bridge, Aude flushed and shot him a look. It didn't seem to matter what she said to the contrary—her feelings for Hugh seemed to be public knowledge.

She cleared her throat. 'Be that as it may, I would like you to stay on at Alfold, Sir Olivier. Whatever the outcome of my husband's affairs, I will still have need of a trustworthy knight to act as my steward.'

Sir Olivier's smile reached his eyes. 'Thank you, my lady, you honour me. I shall do my best not to disappoint you or your husband.'

Nodding, Aude looked blindly at the approaching gate. Sir Olivier had not taken offence at her marriage and it was a relief to have him accept the role of her steward. And it was certainly most heartening to have him act as though he never doubted that she and Hugh had a future together.

Dear God, please let that be true.

Chapter Fourteen

Hugh and Edouard had ridden unhindered into the heart of Winchester right up to New Minster itself. At the Abbey gatehouse, they had been asked to disarm and since to have refused would have roused suspicion, they had left their swords in the care of the porter while they searched out the scriptorium. Hugh could only hope swords would not be needed; the monks here were surely men of peace.

The doors of the scriptorium was latched open, and the desks arranged in semi-circles to make the most of the light. Several tonsured heads looked up as Hugh and Edward's shadows fell across their work.

Hugh caught a swift impression of rank on rank of desks, of black-robed monks bent diligently over creamy vellum. Of quiet concentration. The cathedral bells had been ringing, but as the chimes faded more subtle sounds could be heard—the diligent scratching of quills on parchment, the buzzing of a large blowfly lurching across the room.

The nearest monk was painstakingly outlining the blue robes of a golden-haloed angel who made up part of an illuminated letter. The blue was made, Hugh knew, from crushed lapis lazuli and was almost as costly as the gold. The manuscripts made in this scriptorium were the equal of any in Christendom, and this angel in his flowing robes was as likely to end up in the hands of Queen Mathilda as a prince of the church.

The monk's tongue peeped out as he worked on a fold of the angel's robe.

'Excuse me, brother,' Hugh said.

The quill went still and the monk looked up, squinting in a way that told of many years hunched over lettering. His eyes might be good for close work, but otherwise his sight would be poor.

'Which is Abbot Wulfric?' Hugh asked. He was praying Abbot Wulfric could tell him where Brother Baldwin was to be found.

'Abbot Wulfric? He's not here.'

Damn. Hugh exchanged glances with Edouard. 'We were told the Abbot was here.'

'You were misinformed, sir.'

Another monk rose from his desk and limped slowly towards them, the moth-eaten hem of his black habit dragging on the flagged floor. He had wrinkled red cheeks and a back that was bowed with time. 'I will deal with this, brother.'

The first monk returned to his angel, his quill dipped into his inkpot.

'Abbot Wulfric is at Nunnaminster this morning,'

the aged monk said. 'They are professing some of the novices and Abbot Wulfric is officiating.'

Out in the courtyard, a dog began to bark, and for no reason that Hugh could point to the hairs rose on the back of his neck.

Everything snapped into focus. Time seemed to stop. Light was still pouring in through the doorway, the sun was warm on his neck, yet ice slithered down his spine.

On the surface the atmosphere in the scriptorium remained the same, but was it his imagination or were that monk's ink-stained fingers clenched a little too tightly around his quill? Was the quiet here, rather than being one of calm diligence, one of expectation? Or dread?

But what the devil could a roomful of monks have to fear?

At his elbow, Edouard swore softly under his breath, apparently coming to the same conclusion.

'A blind alley,' Hugh muttered. 'We are in a blind alley.'

Simultaneously, he and Edouard reached for their non-existent swords.

The dog yelped and fell silent. Hugh heard the tramp of many boots and a soft chink which Edouard would recognise as easily as he.

'Armed soldiers,' Hugh murmured as he turned. A dozen mailed troopers faced them with the sunlight bouncing off their conical helmets. Men who would have no qualms about drawing their swords within the confines of a monastery.

Hugh's mind raced. Out in the courtyard they might have had a chance, but what sort of a fight could two unarmed men offer in an Abbey scriptorium? The place

was full of monks—resistance would only lead to innocent and holy men being hurt.

Behind him, a monk gasped. Stools scraped as they
were hastily shoved back. And then the soldiers were
on them.

'You there!' One of the soldiers looked directly at
Hugh. Their commander, he supposed. 'Give me your
name.'

Hugh hesitated—he did not want to give his true
name, but he disliked prevarication and his instincts
were telling him that this man already knew who he
was.

Edouard stepped forwards, an easy smile on his lips.
'This is Hugh of Alfold. And lest you are wondering, I
am the Count of Corbeil, Lord of Crèvecoeur. Hugh has
married my sister.' He lifted a brow. 'And who might
you be?'

'Captain Godfrey of Caen.' Behind his noseguard,
the man's eyes were sharp.

'You and your men are mercenaries?' Hugh asked.

If, as he suspected, this man did indeed know his
identity, it was possible his troopers were in the pay of
the Bishop of St Aubin. But whoever they answered to,
they were likely to be the men who had given chase on
his earlier visit to Winchester. These men had wounded
Gil. 'Who is your paymaster?'

The captain ignored Hugh's question, his smile
was cynical. 'Hugh of Alfold? I think not. I believe
I am addressing Hugh Duclair, the former Count de
Freyncourt. I cannot imagine what you are doing in
Wessex.'

How did the man know? Had someone from Alfold
informed on him? Sir Ralph? Sir William? No matter.

Hugh ran his eyes round the courtyard. The walls were too tall, even supposing he made it that far; those troopers were braced to fall on them the moment they so much as breathed. Incongruously, he noticed a rook, a black ragged shape flying across the clear blue vault of the sky.

'No, Captain Godfrey, you are mistaken,' Edouard was saying. 'This is Hugh of Alfold.'

Hugh swore under his breath. Edouard's unwavering loyalty had him hamstrung. Whatever he did, he would not drag his friend down with him. And that, Hugh thought, eyeing the troopers, was a definite possibility. For Edouard's sake, a dash for freedom was out of the question.

With a last regretful glance at the Captain's men pressing close behind him, at the high wall beyond, Hugh laid a hand on Edouard's arm. 'Enough, the time for denials is over.'

'Hugh, for God's sake—'

'*Enough*! Edouard, your friendship means much to me, but the rest of this road is mine to tread, mine alone.' He lowered his voice. 'Think of yourself, think of Aude.'

The Captain's lip curled and the point of his sword came to rest against Hugh's throat. 'Your life will be forfeit when the King discovers you have broken the terms of your banishment. You should not be here.'

The aged monk stretched out a pleading hand. 'No bloodshed, sir! I pray you, no bloodshed.'

The Captain let out a curt laugh. 'Never fear, Brother, this man's blood is not mine to spill. He goes to the King to explain his conduct; the King will decide his fate.'

In the doorway behind the Captain, the troopers stirred. Someone was forcing their way through.

'Let me pass! If you please, let me pass!'

Aude! Blast the woman, she should be safe at Alfold...

The point of the Captain's sword pricked coldly at Hugh's throat. Arms clattered and boots scraped on stone as the troopers parted to make a way for her.

Briefly, Hugh closed his eyes. *You fool, Aude, you have already dug yourself in too deep, I did not want you digging any deeper.*

Direct as ever, and with her head high, Aude went straight to the Captain. Sir Olivier was shadowing her. *Thank God she had the sense to bring an escort with her.*

Aude fixed the Captain with a look that Hugh had first seen her use in the midst of a childish quarrel with Edouard. 'If you please, sir, would you mind telling me why you have my husband at swordpoint?' To Hugh's astonishment, an imperious wave of her hand had Captain Godfrey grounding his sword. Nonetheless, the man's grip on his hilt remained firm.

The Captain drew in a breath. 'And you must be...?'

'Lady Aude of Alfold. Who are you?'

'Godfrey of Caen, Captain.'

Aude glanced swiftly round the scriptorium, taking in the monks huddled by the walls and those with their quills suspended over their desks. She nodded briefly at Edouard and himself. 'What is going on, Captain?'

'Your husband is under arrest.'

She went pale, her cheeks milk-white against the grey of her veil and the green of her gown. Hugh would have gone to her, but the captain's sword glittered and a pricking at his throat held him in place.

'Why?' Her voice was little more than a whisper.

'The former Count de Freyncourt has been banished from all of King William's territories. I am under orders to see that he is taken to account for his unlawful presence here in England.'

'Edouard…' She clutched her brother's sleeve. 'There must be *something* we can do!'

Edouard shook his head. 'Aude, we are powerless to prevent this. We are three men with—' Sir Olivier received a wry glance '—but one sword between us. What may we do against an entire troop?'

'Edouard's talking sense,' Hugh spoke through gritted teeth. 'But you should not have come, you must have realised I did not want you here.'

She drew her head sharply back, hurt large in her eyes. 'Where should I be but at your side?'

'I did not want you here.' Hugh was praying that Aude would keep her head. It was a struggle to remain calm because sight of her had his stomach in knots. If she were hurt… 'You may lower your sword, Captain. I will come quietly, I want no trouble for my wife and friends, you understand?'

The sword wavered and retreated an inch. 'You swear?'

'On my father's grave.'

The sword wavered and fell. 'If it comes to the King's ears that your friends have been supporting you, they may find themselves brought to judgement in any case.'

'If I make no trouble—' Hugh made his voice hard

'—I see no reason why their names should be dragged into this.'

Aude opened her mouth, but before she could speak Edouard took her hand and placed it on his arm. 'Come, Aude—' he turned for the door '—there is nothing we can do here.'

Hell, she was digging in her heels.

'*No*! Edouard, you cannot simply accept this!'

She wrenched free, the grey veil swirled, and she planted herself back in front of the captain. 'You are the King's man?'

'Yes.'

'You have his ear?'

'My commander does.'

'If the King knows Hugh Duclair as I do, he cannot believe there is a disloyal bone in his body.'

The sun flickered across his helmet as the Captain shook his head. 'My lady, the Bishop of St Aubin overheard him discussing sedition with one of the Flemish—'

'Bishop Osmund is a liar,' Hugh said, as calmly as he could.

The captain's mouth thinned, his knuckles whitened on his sword hilt—both signs of a temper held on a short leash. With half the brothers of New Minster as witnesses, Hugh doubted that the captain would strike Aude, but the sooner Captain Godfrey was away from her, the better. Cold sweat trickled down his back.

'The Bishop of St Aubin,' Hugh continued, pitching his voice so the monks at the far end of the scriptorium might hear, 'had my father's silver in mind when he made those accusations. He wanted to line his own coffers.'

'Silver? I've not heard of any silver.'

'Captain, you will know it is common practice to leave valuables in the care of the Church. Before my father died, he deposited several chests with Bishop Osmund for safe-keeping. My father, rest his soul, thought the Freyncourt silver would be safe. Sadly, that faith was misplaced. I am in England not to undermine the King's position, but to prove my innocence. How the devil can I do that if I am holed up in some God-forsaken spot in Apulia? It was necessary for me to come here in person.'

The eyes behind the noseguard were little more than slits. 'You're lying. This tale about Freyncourt silver is but a cover to explain your presence here while you work against the King.' He jerked his head at the soldier next to him. 'Sergeant?'

'Sir?'

'Take him away, we shall have the truth out of him before he is brought to court. The King is away in East Anglia at present, but when he returns...'

'*No!*' Aude flung herself at Hugh, fingers curling into his belt. 'You cannot take him!'

'My lady, stand aside.'

Hugh peeled Aude's fingers from his belt and pushed her towards Edouard. His arms were wrenched behind him.

'I have proof, Captain,' Hugh said. 'A document that has been signed and sealed. I had planned for witnesses to the signatures to back me up, but I would be grateful if you did take me to the King. Then I might present him with this proof in person.'

The captain sheathed his sword with a snap. 'You are a liar. The document you speak of is a forgery.'

'For pity's sake, listen!' Aude burst out. 'Hugh is no liar, if he says he has this document, then that's the truth!'

She believed in him. There was a slight catch in her voice, but conviction was shining out of her eyes. Hugh's chest ached—Aude believed in him. One good thing had emerged from this messy trail of lies and deceit and it was staring at him with large amber eyes. Honest eyes, eyes that he would hold in his mind till his dying day. He intercepted a calculating sneer from the captain—Lord, his dying day might not be so far off...

'This document, Hugh,' Aude was asking urgently. 'Where is it?'

'It is—'

The captain's fist shot out. Pain erupted in Hugh's jaw and everything went black.

Aude lurched forwards to break Hugh's fall, but Edouard got there first.

'You bastard!' Aude was shaking in every limb. 'There was no need for that!'

'There was every need. This man has been banished and his word is suspect. You and you—' the captain gestured '—remove him.' One trooper stepped forwards to take Hugh by the feet, another by the shoulders.

'*Stop*!' Aude could see she was wasting her breath, it was there in the set of the captain's jaw, in the emptiness of his eyes. Edouard's arm came around her.

The troops tramped out. Hugh's limp body was jerked unceremoniously over the threshold.

'Where are you taking him?' she demanded. A cold stone was sitting in her belly. Hugh had been furious with her, furious. He had not wanted her here. Even though they were married, even after last night, he was yet to trust her.

'The garrison lock-up. And my advice to you, my lady, is to apply for an annulment as quickly as you may. The penalties for those who harbour banished men are severe.' His smile chilled Aude to her core. 'So… go home, my lady. Pick up your embroidery. If you behave, I am sure your application for an annulment will be favourably received. No one will hold it against you that a felon forced you into marriage.'

Conscious that her brother's arm was holding her in check as much as it was supporting her, Aude made it as far as the doorway and stared after Hugh. With a cynical salute, the captain led his men out under the arch.

Flanked by Edouard and Sir Olivier, Aude stood frozen until the footsteps faded. Doves were cooing on the roof of the scriptorium, and for the space of a heart-beat the sound transported her back to Beaumont Castle on one of the days that Hugh had visited her there. Her eyes filled.

'Edouard, I mislike Captain Godfrey,' she said, blinking hard. 'I get the distinct impression that his methods of questioning may be…unscrupulous.'

Edouard hesitated. And that, Aude realised, was answer enough. 'You think as I do. You think he might torture Hugh!'

'Not necessarily.' A thoughtful crease formed between Edouard's eyebrows. 'He would have to answer to his commander.'

'The garrison commander, yes, of course! That is what we must do!'

Edouard eyed her warily. 'What?'

'We must go and pay our respects to Sir Guy!'

'Sir Guy?'

'Sir Guy de Mortain, he commands the Winchester garrison. Edouard, have you met him?'

'No, but—'

'We must to go to the castle, you ought to make yourself known.'

Edouard's expression lightened. 'Aude, that is a good thought.' He crooked his arm at her. 'Come along.'

A cross was carved into the stone archway that led out of the courtyard. As they passed under it, Sir Olivier at their heels, Aude found herself praying that Sir Guy would take their part. Otherwise she had grave doubts that Hugh would survive to meet with the King, never mind exchange the kiss of peace with him.

For Aude, the beginning of the ride from New Minster to Winchester Castle passed in a panicky blur. She was thankful for the company of Edouard and Sir Olivier.

Once Edouard had retrieved his sword—along with Hugh's—from the Abbey porter, they were soon trotting past the old Saxon Minster. Aude was so intent on finding Sir Guy that she almost mowed down a pilgrim who ran out under her horse's hoofs.

'Watch where you're going!' The man scowled at her from under his hood, his staff thumped the ground.

Swiftly, she reined in. 'My apologies, sir.'

The pilgrim gave her a brusque nod and joined the line of people snaking through the Minster door. They would be heading for St Swithun's shrine—Aude had been told it worked miracles.

'Perhaps we should visit the shrine,' she murmured, the encounter with the pilgrim temporarily breaking her focus.

Edouard looked blankly at her. 'What's that?'

'Miracles are to be had there and we certainly need one.'

'I would rather put my faith in Sir Guy.'

'And in Hugh's proof.'

'Yes.'

They left the Minster precincts and rode past the garrison hall. Sir Guy had quarters in the garrison, but Aude knew that his main residence was in the castle at the top of the hill.

Market Street sloped gently upwards. It was apparent that Alfold was not the only village to have brought in a fine harvest. Winchester at harvest time was, it seemed, busier than Rouen. Wheels rumbled on every side. The narrow street was lined with stalls, while the main thoroughfare was a-jostle with carts bulging with grain sacks, with donkeys labouring beneath over-laden panniers…

They reined in for a couple of boys sweating under the weight of sacks twice their size; they held their horses in check for several handcarts laden with fresh loaves and fragrant meat pies. At the market cross, a girl with hens in a wickerwork cage crossed their path.

Impatience was rising with every delay. After the famine of the previous year, Aude was glad that this year's harvest had been a success, but the image of Hugh being dragged over the scriptorium threshold dominated her thoughts. *What was happening to him? Where was the garrison lock-up? Was Hugh being hurt?*

If Hugh were reinstated, might he learn to love her? Foolish, foolish question. Love grew out of trust, and clearly Hugh did not trust her…

* * *

Their luck turned after they had been challenged by the guards at the castle gatehouse and had been given permission to enter. They clattered over the drawbridge into the bailey and no sooner had Aude dismounted than a *conroi* of horse soldiers rode in behind them.

Sir Guy!

With a sigh of relief, she handed her reins to Sir Olivier. 'Would you mind?'

'My pleasure.'

'Squire for me too, Olivier,' Edouard said.

After that it was the work of a few moments to arrange an interview with Sir Guy.

'Excuse my dishevelment, my lady,' Sir Guy said as the horses were led away and his squire had run up to take his helmet from him. He bowed over her hand. 'This is an unexpected pleasure, I had not looked for another visit so close to your last one.'

'Thank you. Sir Guy, I should like to introduce my brother, Edouard, Count of Corbeil. Edouard, this is Sir Guy de Mortain.'

Sir Guy inclined his head. 'My lord.' He waved at one of the doors leading off from the bailey. 'I am pressed for time today, but I have worked up the devil of a thirst. Would you join me for refreshments?'

'Thank you, but I should warn you, sir, there is a matter of some urgency we would like to bring to your attention.'

'This way, my lady.'

They were ushered into a lofty hall. The whitewashed walls were hung with rich tapestries, the floor was thickly strewn with freshly cut rushes. Plumes of smoke rose from the central hearth. Beyond the fire stood a couple of trestle tables, their polished surfaces gleaming in the light angling down from narrow windows.

A serving girl appeared with wine that smelt faintly of cinnamon, another offered a tray of blackberry and apple pastries that looked to be glazed with honey.

Aude took nothing, her stomach was churning too much to eat. 'No, I thank you, but, no.' She would eat again when Hugh was safe.

When the serving girls had moved away, Sir Guy leaned against the table and smiled at them over the rim of his cup. 'So, how may I help you?'

Briefly, with the words tumbling over themselves, Aude explained their dilemma.

Sir Guy's face lost its smile. 'A moment,' he said. 'I must tell you that the Bishop of St Aubin has already sent word about this man. I must also tell you that your version and the Bishop's do not fit well together. Let me see if I have your version aright. Count Hugh de Freyncourt was stripped of his title and banished on the strength of the testimony of this Bishop?'

'Yes, but the accusations against Hugh are false, he is innocent.'

Sir Guy held up his hand for silence. 'One point, however, does coincide. You admit that he broke the terms of his banishment?'

'Yes.'

'Lady Aude, did you bring Hugh Duclair with you to England?'

'No, I did not realise he was in England until he arrived at Alfold.'

Sir Guy frowned. 'And now you have married him?'

'Yes.'

The garrison commander shook his head. 'Don't you think that was rather…unwise, my lady?'

'Sir Guy, Hugh is innocent! His loyalty to the King is unshakeable, he would never involve himself in Flemish plots against the King. Why, Hugh and my brother accompanied the King to England at the time of the Great Battle, when King William was but Duke of Normandy.'

'Did he so?'

'Yes, and—'

The commander made an impatient gesture and Aude fell silent.

'And now you say Captain Godfrey has him in custody?'

'Yes,' Edouard said. 'Sir, we are concerned for Hugh's life. It is as my sister has said, Hugh Duclair is loyal to the King. Before he was arrested, he made mention of a document that has come to light. It proves the Bishop has reasons for seeking his banishment.'

'You have seen this document yourself, Lord Edouard?'

'No, but if Hugh has indeed got his hands on it—and knowing him as I do, I have every reason to believe him—then not only is Hugh's life at stake, but this also puts the loyalty of Bishop Osmund into question.'

'What does the Bishop hope to gain by lying?'

'Several chests of Freyncourt silver, as I understand it. The document is proof of the deposit Hugh's father made. A monk witnessed the Bishop signing it.'

Sir Guy's eyes widened. 'But with the Count of Freyncourt in disgrace and the documents missing, there is no proof the silver existed.'

'Exactly!' Aude gripped her hands together. 'Please

help us, Sir Guy. I cannot think the King may rely on the word of a bishop prepared to lie for gain.'

'No, indeed.' Sir Guy set his wine-cup down. 'We need sight of this proof.'

'If only Hugh had told us where he had put it,' Aude said. She was on the point of demanding that she be allowed to have speech with Hugh when a shiver rippled through her. 'Wait, I know where it might be!'

She grasped the commander's arm. This was the chance to prove herself to Hugh. If she found his document and brought it to Sir Guy, Hugh must learn to trust her, he must! 'Sir Guy, if we bring you Hugh's proof, will you ensure that no harm comes to him while he is in Captain Godfrey's custody?'

'Assuredly.'

Aude searched Sir Guy's face and knew him for an honourable man. If Sir Guy said he would ensure no harm came to Hugh, he meant it. 'Thank you.'

'My lady, before you leave, there is something you should know. And please note, both of you—' Sir Guy's expression was earnest '—what I am about to tell you is not common knowledge; word must not get abroad.'

'Sir Guy, you may rely on our discretion,' Edouard said.

Aude's pulse began to race. Sir Guy's face told her that what he was about to disclose did not bode well for Hugh. 'What is it, sir?'

'When you arrived at the castle just now I was returning from patrolling the city perimeters. It is not a task I myself would normally undertake, but I had good reason for doing it today. I have received word that the King will arrive here this evening.'

For a moment the floor seemed to shift under Aude's

feet. 'King William is coming to Winchester *this evening*?'

Edouard frowned. 'I thought he was on campaign in East Anglia.'

'And so he is,' Sir Guy said. 'But there are matters here, urgent matters concerning—well, that is of no matter. Be that as it may, the King will be here tonight and I will have no choice but to inform him that we have caught Hugh Duclair breaking the terms of his banishment.'

'Tonight?' Edouard muttered. 'Hell, that doesn't leave much time.'

'Exactly. Because of Hugh Duclair's former status, he must be brought before the King. It will be King William himself who will pronounce judgement on him.'

Aude clenched her jaw. 'The King will exonerate him when the truth is known. Hugh will accept the King's peace.'

'That is possible, my lady. But I am warning you that one way or another this matter is likely to be resolved tonight.' Sir Guy heaved a sigh. 'With the King's arrival imminent, I am sure you will understand that I have many matters pressing, but it strikes me that the best course might be for me to send someone to the lockup to observe Hugh Duclair's interview with Captain Godfrey.'

Aude bit her lip. Sir Guy was right, she wasn't thinking straight. Her head felt as though it was going to burst.

Tonight! The king would be here tonight!

She put her hand to her forehead. 'But Captain Godfrey knocked Hugh's senses from him.'

'He is unconscious?'

'Yes.'

'He will come round.'

Aude's sense of panic was rising. 'Yes, but when? There's no time! Besides, Hugh suspects Captain Godfrey to be in the pay of the Bishop—he will reveal nothing to him.'

'Then my advice to you, my lady, is to find that document with all speed.'

'Thank you, Sir Guy, we will.'

Aude gave the garrison commander a curtsy so brief it bordered on discourteous. Edouard grasped her hand and they started for the door.

'Lady Aude…' Sir Guy's voice followed them the length of the hall.

'Sir?'

'I hope you find your proof.'

Giving him a brisk nod of acknowledgement, Aude swept out into the bailey.

Chapter Fifteen

Hugh's sight was the first sense to return—he was in a place of shadows.

Prison cell.

Feeling flooded back—his jaw was throbbing mercilessly. He had been dumped on a mouldering pile of straw, thankfully, his arms were not bound.

An acrid stink informed him that the straw was more than simply damp. Shuddering, Hugh pushed himself to his feet and massaged his jaw. No teeth had been broken, thank God, but the throbbing continued. His mind felt muddy.

The cell was scarcely larger than a coffin. The walls gleamed with damp and the air was rank with the stink of mildew and fear. Clumps of grey straw lay haphazardly on the floor, and even as he looked, a clump shifted and something dark—a rat?—scuttled into a corner and vanished behind a bucket.

A narrow bench lay along one wall. Several slats were

missing and at one end there was a pile of rags that might once been a blanket. A mean sliver of light came from a window slit that was partially blocked by a luxuriant growth of moss.

And the door? Oak. Banded with iron. Hinged and doubtless bolted on the outside. There was a small window in the top of the door, barred with a crude iron grille. Hugh squinted through the grille.

He could not see much. The door of a cell opposite and, yes, it had thick iron bolts on the outside and rust-stained hinges. A shadow moved in the other cell, briefly Hugh caught sight of a shaved head. It looked remarkably like a tonsure. There was a monk imprisoned in here? Lord. Could this be the deposed English Archbishop Stigand? Stigand had been accused of pluralism, he had clashed with the King. The last Hugh had heard of Stigand he had been incarcerated at Winchester—this might well be he.

Hugh craned his neck, but saw little that might be of use to him. A gloomy corridor; wet stone with a damp sheen to it, so wet this place must be located close to the river. What was the name of the river? The Itchen. The course the Itchen ran outside of the city walls, Hugh had marked it on his previous visit. Was this prison outside Winchester?

Hugh was unable to recall a likely building near the river, though his memory was quick to give him images of the river flowing past the walls. He recalled a wooden mill by a bridge; a wash-house; a straggling line of peasant's cottages. He had seen nothing resembling a prison on either of his visits to the city.

He peered down the corridor in the other direction. There was a second cell opposite, a feeble light was coming through a grille in another door. And there, set into a flagstone in front of the cell, was a heavy iron ring.

Interesting.

Try as he might, Hugh could see nothing more. The occupant of the cell exactly opposite to his, Stigand or otherwise, had retreated. All was quiet. Indeed it was so quiet that for a moment he thought he could hear the rush of the river. His skin was shrinking with cold. A dark, earthy smell filled his nostrils. The damp in here was getting to him. Granted, water was practically running down the walls. He heard a distant clang, as of a gate shutting, and pulled back from the door.

Hell, he had to get out of here, he had to get that document. He rubbed his jaw, probing the bruise. The guards would probably feed him; he might not have long to wait. Crossing to the bench, he shoved the mouldering blanket aside and sat down.

Thank God, Louise and Gil were at Alfold, because if things turned out badly for him, Aude and Edouard would see they were cared for. He rubbed his forehead as a wisp of memory came slowly into focus. Just after Captain Godfrey had knocked his senses from him, he thought he had heard a mocking voice recommending that Aude should have their marriage annulled.

Truth? Wild imagining of his unconscious mind?

Hugh's mouth twisted and he closed his eyes, leaning back against the stone wall. He hadn't heard Aude's response, but perhaps she should heed that advice. There were a few things Hugh regretted in his life, but one of them must be that moment of weakness back in Alfold, when he had accepted her as his wife. He hadn't been able to resist her. What a blind, selfish fool. He had woken up in her arms, the air had been filled with that bewitching, womanly scent, and he had found himself wishing that every day could begin that way. For a moment he had believed that if you wished for something hard enough, it might be yours. He was a fool.

They didn't love each other. When they had been surprised out of bed at Alfold, Aude had admitted as much. Edouard had muttered something about her harbouring tender feelings for him and she had been very swift to deny it. She had been so blunt and so definite there was no doubting that her heart was untouched.

Well, no matter—Hugh damped down a confusing feeling of hurt—he didn't love her either.

What did he feel for Aude? Affection, certainly. Warmth and the hot ache of desire…but love?

Mon Dieu, what did this matter? He must get his proof to the King! Otherwise that moment of weakness on his part might leave poor Aude condemned to a lifetime of sharing his disgrace. King William had been betrayed many times in his life, it had left him full of suspicion; he was on occasion capricious. And without a witness to back up Hugh's story there was no way of knowing whether the king would exonerate him. Poor Aude. Bad enough that she had to grow up in the shadow of her grandfather's shame, she should not have to endure his too.

Captain Godfrey, damn his eyes, was right. Aude would surely be better off without him. She must apply for an annulment.

Another of those distant clangs brought his eyes to the cell door.

Footsteps, two set of footsteps, by the sound of it. Hugh waited.

The bolt scraped, the door creaked and a guard appeared in the doorway with a jug and the end of a loaf. It was one of the soldiers who had put him in an arm-lock in the scriptorium.

'Your rations,' the man said, lobbing the bread across. 'Captain Godfrey said to tell you he will be along later.'

Hugh stood to take the jug. 'I shall look forward to that.' The sour smell of spoiled ale wrinkled his nose. 'Guard?'

Insolent eyes met his.

'I would like to send a message to Lady Aude at Alfold. Would you see that it is delivered?'

The man's gaze found Hugh's purse. 'Maybe.'

Hugh opened the flap and sighed. Naturally, it had been emptied, save for one silver penny. He dug it out. 'I can only give you this.' He pressed it into the man's hand. 'But the lady will reward the messenger.'

The guard eyed the penny. 'And your message?'

'Please tell Lady Aude that her husband commands her to follow the advice Captain Godfrey gave her in New Minster.'

'Eh?'

It wasn't easy forcing the words out. 'I wish our marriage to be annulled. Your Captain suggested as much, if you recall.'

The soldier grunted.

Heart heavy in his breast, Hugh pressed on. God knew the last thing he wanted was that his marriage to Aude should be annulled, but with matters as they stood he had no future to offer her.

Aude deserved better.

'Tell Lady Aude she is to apply for an annulment. Her brother will assist her.'

'Yes, my lord.' With a curl of his lip and a ridiculous parody of a bow, the guard backed out.

The door groaned shut and Hugh returned to the bench.

With Aude's future a little more secure, he had some serious planning to do.

The sun was past its zenith by the time Aude and her escort arrived back at Alfold. The fields between the hall and Crabbe Wood were bathed in a golden haze that on any other day Aude might have called peaceful.

Hurry, hurry, we must hurry.

The last of the corn had been cut during the morning, it was spread out on sacking to dry out properly. A child was standing guard over it, flapping a rag in a desultory manner to keep the birds off the grain. The birds hadn't gone far, pigeons and hens were picking over the aftermath in the strips. A few of the villagers—the worst part of their work being done—were dozing in the shade of an apple tree. Swallows swooped over the quiet fields.

Hurry, hurry.

At the hall, the ladder was up. A man was astride the roof ridge, cutting away the old thatch. His knife flashed, his face dripped with sweat. Oswy was clinging to the top of the ladder, watching the man with a rapt expression on his face. Someone must have brought in a thatcher from a neighbouring village.

Hurry.

Carpenters were heaving the hall door back on to its hinges, pale new wood revealing the places where the rotten planking had been cut away and replaced. Up at the watch-point on top of the rise, a helmet gleamed.

Oswy glanced across and waved at the approaching horses. His face was bright with happiness as he jiggled about on the top rungs. 'Lady Aude! Lady Aude!'

'Mind you are careful, Oswy,' Aude said. Even though her mind was all over the place, it was a relief to see Oswy's mother sewing on the nearby bench.

'I will!'

Eadgytha bounced up from the bench, her face wreathed in smiles. 'I am watching him, my lady. And—oh, my lady—' Eadgytha gestured at the man tearing the grey thatch from the roof '—this is Chad. My husband is back!'

'Back?' Aude's saddle creaked as she blinked bemusedly at the man on the roof. She had understood that Chad was dead, killed when King William defeated the Saxons at Hastings.

Chad caught her eye and wiped his brow on his sleeve. 'My lady.'

Questions were forming on Aude's tongue. Where had Eadgytha's husband been? Why had he chosen this moment to return? But Aude had no time to find answers, not this afternoon.

Hugh! Until she found Hugh's proof and he was exonerated, she could think of little else. Later, she would have more time to learn about Chad.

She sent Alfold's thatcher a distracted smile. 'Welcome back, Chad, you have been sorely missed.'

'My lady, I came as soon as I could. It is good to find Alfold in capable hands. I want you to know that my loyalty—'

'My lady!' Cedric appeared in the doorway, towing a

young girl behind him. His usually dour face was transformed by a happy grin as he nudged the girl at Aude. 'This is my cousin, Goda.'

Goda? Wasn't this the girl who had disappeared with the thieves? Taken by force, or so Aude had been led to believe. More questions lined up in Aude's mind, but there was no time to learn more. Aude accepted Goda's curtsy with a smile that she hoped no one would see was forced.

Exchanging glances with Edouard, Aude set her jaw and turned her horse towards Crabbe Wood. She kicked him back into a walk. She was glad for Eadgytha and Cedric, but there would no peace for her until she had found Hugh's proof and had put it in the King's hands.

'Hang on, Aude.' Catching her reins, Edouard hauled her horse to a standstill.

On the ride back to Alfold, Aude had told her brother about the Roman villa that Hugh had been using as a camp. She had explained about the mosaic floor that sounded hollow when you walked on it, and had discussed the nature of hypocausts with him. Edouard had agreed that in theory it was possible that something might be concealed in the old workings.

'Aude, you don't know for certain that Hugh hid this document in the hypocaust.'

'Edouard, I am sure that he did. Hugh returned to that villa before he came back to Alfold that night that he…that I…'

'The night you were married.'

'Yes. There is a hypocaust under that floor, and that is where he will have put it.'

'I cannot allow you to ride off on your own. We need to plan—'

'Edouard, you heard Sir Guy, we have no time!' Aude lowered her voice so that only he would hear. 'The King arrives at Winchester today, we must find that proof at once.'

'And so we will. But when did you last eat?'

'Eat? *Eat*?'

'You won't be much use to anyone if you start fainting from hunger.' Ruthlessly, Edouard guided her horse to where Raoul awaited them in front of the hall. 'Besides, you can't simply ride off on your own.' She wrenched on the reins, but Edouard smiled and shook his head. 'Don't you think we should speak with Gil before we set out for the villa?'

It seemed like an age before they were riding into Crabbe Wood, but in reality the sun had hardly moved during the time they paused at Alfold. They delayed just long enough for Edouard to snatch a meal, and for him to force bread and smoked ham into Aude.

'Gil, are you fit enough to come with us?' Edouard asked, swallowing down a mouthful of ale.

'Try stopping me,' Gil said, turning his back on the mutters of protest from Louise and Edwige.

And so, not half an hour later, Aude, her brother and Gil had arrived at the sun-dappled crossroads in the woods. Aude led the way towards the creeper-clad ruins. Thrusting the ivy aside, they entered the room with the mosaic floor.

'Someone's been here, and I don't mean Hugh,' Gil said. 'The blankets have gone and another fire has been lit. And that smell—' He pulled a face. 'This place has been used as a privy.'

He was right, Aude realised, assailed herself by a distinctive reek that had not been there before. And a number of bones had been chucked into a corner.

'Several pigeons have been cooked and eaten here as well,' Aude murmured. 'Those bones, Gil, do you think Hugh…?'

Gil shook his head and Aude's stomach plummeted as she recalled Hugh telling her he had bought food from a farmer on the day he last came here. He had made no mention of pigeon…

'The hypocaust, Gil, do you know how to get in? Otherwise, we shall simply have to search through the undergrowth outside.'

'I am not certain, but I think it is this way, my lady.' Leading her back into the fresh air, Gil picked up a stick and began thrashing his way through a patch of nettles. 'Lord, *no!*'

'What?'

'This must be the spot, see how these weeds have been trampled.'

The nettles Gil was pointing at were bent every which way, their stems were broken and crushed. His shoulders sagged. 'Someone has beaten us to it.'

'Several people by the look of it,' Aude murmured.

'Yes, my lady.'

The rubble and earth behind the foliage had also been disturbed. Gil dropped to his knees. As he started heaving stones aside, Aude joined him. She was conscious of Edouard standing watchfully behind them, of the rustle of the wind in the leaves, but most of all she was conscious of her heart banging in her ears.

Someone had been here before them.

With a grimace—Gil's leg must have been paining

him—Gil succeeding in revealing a dark hole, no larger than the entrance to a badger's set. The chalky earth was criss-crossed with thin roots and peppered with chunks of clay and broken masonry.

When he made to reach inside, Aude gently pushed him aside. Her hand, she noticed, was trembling. 'Be careful, Gil, you mustn't damage that leg. Let me.'

Gil moved aside. Aude lay on the bumpy ground and reached in. 'Nothing,' she said. 'I can feel nothing but soil and pebbles and…wait!' Her fingers slid over something that felt smooth and flat, like leather. Grasping the edge, she withdrew it. *A saddlebag!* 'Hugh's?'

'Yes, that's Hugh's.'

Aude sat back on her haunches, undid the buckles and flung back the flap.

Nothing. She groaned.

'Empty?' Edouard asked.

Aude held the bag up for his inspection. 'Yes, quite empty. I'll look again.'

Throwing herself flat, she shoved her whole arm into the space, up to her shoulder. Earth, more stones, a thick root.

'Nothing?'

'No. Heaven help us. Edouard, you try, your arm is longer than mine.'

Edouard took her place on the flattened weeds. A shard of clay flew over his shoulder. Aude bit her lip. Another shard flew past. At length Edouard sat up. 'Nothing.' He shook his head. 'If Hugh did hide something in here, it is not there now.'

'Someone has stolen it.'

Brushing earth from his chausses, Edouard sighed. 'Could be. But you can't be certain he put it in here.'

'He did, I know he did! Where else might he have put it?'

Gil was leaning on the stick, easing his leg. 'I think Lady Aude is right. Hugh told me what he would do in the event of him finding his proof. This is where he would have put it.'

Aude stared at Gil, sick with dread. 'Hugh definitely said he had a document that would cast fresh light on the Bishop of St Aubin's testimony. If it is not here, where on earth can it be?'

There was no means of measuring the passing of time in the garrison lock-up, the light was unchanging and weak, which probably meant that Hugh's cell faced north. He was sitting on the bench running through various escape plans in his mind when his stomach growled. Would he be fed again? He was so hungry that even another lump of stale bread would be welcome.

It was ominously quiet. After what the guard had told him, Hugh had been braced for an unpleasant interview with Captain Godfrey, but since the guards had left the cells, he had heard nothing. Nothing, save the occasional moan from a prisoner further down the corridor, and the murmuring of prayer from the man in the cell opposite. Deposed Archbishop or not, that man was definitely in Holy Orders. And somewhere he would swear he heard running water. This place had to be close to the river or one of its tributaries.

Distant voices. A clang, and the distinctive sound of a large key grating in a lock. The guards were returning. *At last!*

Heartbeat quickening, Hugh stood. He stretched and flexed his fingers; his instincts were telling him that if he was going to make a bid for an escape, it was now or never.

Positioning himself by the door, he peered down the corridor. The light had strengthened, so the main door to the prison must be open. Hugh could not envision what lay beyond that door, when they had brought him through it, he had been senseless. From the muffled mutter of voices he would lay odds it was a guardhouse. It certainly made sense to position the cells close to the soldiers. And if that was so, any escape in that direction would be fraught with danger.

A guard—one only—came into view. He was wearing a short mail coat that reached his knees, but no helmet. The man must be relying on his companions in the guardhouse for back-up. Hugh's pulse speeded up.

He waited while the guard entered the cell next to his, rolling his shoulders.

He kept his breath steady while the guard locked that door and went to the opposite cell with food on a wooden platter. Hugh watched him drop the platter to the ground, unlock the door and boot it through.

Hugh flexed his hands while the guard secured the door. The whole business with the food had taken seconds. *One guard only. One. And while the man was being cautious, he was not being cautious enough.*

When the key scraped in his own door, Hugh stepped lightly back. The door swung open. As soon as the platter appeared, Hugh lunged.

His fingers closed round the guard's calf, he caught hold of the man's cross-gartering.

A memory shot through his mind—of Aude hooking on to his leg in much the same way when he had pulled her from the Seine. Had she received his message yet? How would she react?

Focus, Hugh, stay focused.

Hugh hauled. When the guard opened his mouth, Hugh dived. There was no room for finesse, Hugh simply flattened him. His elbow cracked against the stone doorway, he pressed his hand over the guard's mouth.

Grunting, he dragged the guard kicking and thrashing out of the corridor. After a desperate scrabble, Hugh was kneeling over him. He had him by the hair, wriggling and writhing like an eel in a trap. Chain mail ground into Hugh's thighs.

One carefully judged blow to the man's head and the thrashing stopped. Breathing hard, Hugh wrenched off the man's belt and took the keys. He wouldn't have long. A gag, he needed a gag. He ripped off a piece of blanket and stuffed it into the guard's mouth. The belt bound it in place.

A minute more and Hugh had taken the guard's place in the corridor. As he locked the door to his cell, the coat of chain mail weighed heavy on his shoulders. *Pity about the lack of helmet.* Glancing towards the guardhouse, he briefly weighed up his chances of shutting and locking the door before he was noticed. They weren't good.

He glanced the other way and found himself staring at a wall. This corridor ran nowhere.

Merde. It was the guardhouse, or nothing.

Unless…. Hugh frowned at the rusted iron ring set into the stone floor. Moving quietly towards it, he lifted the ring, braced himself and heaved.

The flagstone shifted, the sound of running water

intensified. One final heave and the stone grated aside.

It was black as pitch down there. Brushing bright rust from his hands, Hugh dropped to the floor. The dank earthy smell intensified. Water! Shiny black water was racing along a few feet below his nose.

An underground stream ran directly below the prison! The guards probably used it for sluicing out the cells.

Frowning, Hugh leaned further in. How deep was it?

More importantly, where did it come out? If it came out at all.

A roar of laughter rolled down the corridor. Hugh glanced at his cell door, it wouldn't be long before someone came to look for that guard…

He hung over the edge.

How deep? He had no way of telling.

What if there was no way out? It had been a dry summer in England as well as in Normandy, but Hugh had a clear recollection of rain pattering onto the thatch at Alfold. The water levels could rise as that rain filtered down from the outlying hills.

He leaned in as far as he could without overbalancing. Downstream, a faint glimmer caught his eye. Blink and he'd have missed it. But he'd seen enough. Any light down there could only mean one thing—a way out. And it was not far off either, just a little way—a very little way, he prayed—downstream.

Pity about the mail shirt, Hugh thought, grunting as he wrestled his way out of it. Unlocking the cell door— the guard remained unconscious—Hugh hurled the mail shirt on to the bench, closed the door and re-locked it.

At the trapdoor he didn't hesitate.

God help me. He lowered himself in, and let go.

Ice. The water was so cold it snatched his breath.

Mon Dieu!

He went down like a stone. His feet hit bottom, his skull cracked against something hard. A wall? A natural underground tunnel? It was impossible to see.

He came up spluttering, sucking in air. His shoulder scraped the side of the waterway, he cracked his skull a second time. The flow felt swifter than it had looked. Water was in his ears, it was in his nose. A jet-black darkness was closing in on him. Struggling to keep afloat, Hugh caught a last glimpse of the prison trapdoor, a shrinking oblong of light above him.

And then the light was gone.

The river carried him along. He fought to turn in the direction of the current, desperate to stay on the surface.

Light. A faint pinprick ahead. His heart was thumping; his ears ached with cold; his hands were going numb. Flailing out, he struck the side of the tunnel and barely felt it. A swirl of water took him briefly under. And then he was back on the surface, lungs aching, dragging in breath.

The light was a little stronger. He could see a glow, a striped glow.

Striped?

His foot scraped the bottom, he jarred his knee. A creature slid past him. Otter. Its dark head appeared in front of him and dipped out of sight.

Yes, there were black vertical stripes ahead, blocking out the light.

'Hell, *no!*'

Hugh was flung against metal. The river had washed him up against an iron grille.

'*Hell*!'

Pressed from behind by the water which flowed under and past him, Hugh found himself blinking out at the water meadows outside the city walls. The grille must block access to the prison via the underground river. He jerked at a bar. It shifted slightly. Hope filled him.

Ahead, the edges of the river were thickly edged with rushes. Small birds were flitting from reed to reed, warbling sweetly in the sunlit air. There were cress beds with yellow butterflies hovering over them. A swan. A brace of quacking ducks. And there, taunting him, the sleek head of the otter.

Chest heaving, Hugh leant his head against the bar while he got his breath back. A log had been washed up next to him. Like him it was pressed against the grille, like him it was too large to squeeze through the gaps between the bars. To judge by the rotten state of it, the log had been held back by the grille for some time.

Eyeing the idyllic afternoon on the other side of the bars, Hugh shifted his grip and prayed the water levels would not rise until after he had fought his way free. If the water rose first, Aude would not have to worry about seeking an annulment…

Chapter Sixteen

The evening light was streaming like a golden banner across the western sky by the time Aude and Edouard gained entry into Winchester Castle.

'It is a risky strategy,' Edouard said, shouldering his way into the crowd.

The Great Hall was crammed. Despite Sir Guy's attempt at discretion, word had spread about the King's arrival; people must have seen his entourage ride in.

'What else can we do? Hugh's proof is lost and if we don't plead for him, who will?' Aude drew her skirts aside to avoid them being caught on a knight's spurs.

Ahead of her, she could see nothing but heads and backs. Someone's elbow jabbed her in the ribs. 'Sweet Mother, is the entire district squashed in here? I have never seen so many soldiers.'

Edouard grunted. Reaching for her hand, he hauled her in the general direction of the central hearth, forcing his way past several troopers, a couple of archers,

a bishop in silken robes. Aude could see no one who
might be the King himself. Not that she had met him,
she had no idea what he looked like.

'Are you sure the King is in here?' She stumbled, and
at her feet a wolfhound snarled. She had trodden on its
tail.

Edouard fought forwards. 'The King is here.'

Another elbow caught her in the stomach.

'*Ow*! Is it always like this, getting to see him?' She
raised herself up on her toes. By the dais at the top end of
the hall, under a great banner, a row of silvered mailcoats
met her eyes. The King's personal guard? 'Edouard, I
think King William is behind those men and—'

'Lady Aude! Count Edouard!' Sir Guy was standing
before them, a harsh expression on his face. 'Did you
bring Hugh Duclair's document?'

'I…that is, no. We were unable to find it.'

Sir Guy let out an exasperated sound. 'Excuse me,
my lords, if you please.' He gestured and, as if he were a
sorcerer, a way was cleared for them. They found themselves at the side of the hall where it was less crowded.
'My lady, Duclair needs that proof desperately. Matters
have worsened since you were here this morning.'

Aude's throat tightened. 'Worsened?'

Sir Guy nodded. 'I sent word to the prison as I had
promised, but by the time I had done so Duclair was
gone. Indeed, at first we thought him drowned.'

Aude felt herself go very still. *Drowned? Not Hugh.*
'You *thought* him drowned?'

The garrison commander's expression softened.
'Never fear, my lady, he survived. He escaped via the
underground river—it comes out at Otterburn. The exit
is barred, but he broke through. As I understand it, he

came straight here.' He jerked his head towards the dais. 'He is there now, in conference with the King.'

Aude lurched forwards, one thought in her mind. 'I must go to him!'

Blunt fingers closed over her arm. 'It would have been better if you had found his proof.'

'Someone had been there before us. We have left his squire behind in Alfold making enquiries of the villagers, but...' she looked down at the hand on her arm, stomach twisting '...Sir Guy, I will speak for him, I *must*.'

Nodding, Sir Guy released her. 'He is fortunate to have such friends. But I warn you to be brief. The King came to resolve a dispute with the Church; he dislikes delay and he intends to leave again at first light.'

They stepped back into the crowd. With the garrison commander clearing their path, they reached the dais in moments. They were waved past another bishop, a couple of monks and a group of knights. They halted when they reached the wall of mailed soldiers that formed the King's bodyguard.

'Let them pass, Gérard.'

The captain of the guard saluted, and they stepped onto the dais and into the inner circle.

Aude's head was pounding, her hands were trembling, her knees felt as though they would not support her.

A stocky figure sat on a painted throne.

King William!

Aude received a fleeting impression of great energy, barely held in check, of bright, intelligent eyes. A firm chin. He was wearing a gold circlet, very plain, and a single finger ring. Nothing particularly ornate. Simple, practical clothing, save for the circlet.

Hugh!

He was kneeling in front of the King. The red tunic was ripped and filthy, his hair looked as though it hadn't been combed in a month. When he glanced her way, his eyes widened.

She dropped to her knees at Hugh's side and focused on the King's boots. This was William, King of England and Duke of Normandy. She must not let Hugh distract her.

'My liege…' Nerves getting the better of her, Aude stumbled into silence and bowed her head.

The King's fingers drummed on the carved arms of his throne.

'And you are?'

'Aude of Alfold, your Grace.'

Aude sensed, rather than saw, the King exchange looks with Sir Guy. 'I take it you have a petition for me?'

'Yes, your Grace.'

'Come on then, out with it!'

She lifted her gaze from his boots, thoughts racing. The King was not known for his softness—man or woman, he treated all alike. It was rumoured that he had lost his temper while courting Queen Mathilda. He was said to have dragged her about by the hair, to have beaten her…but whether this was truth or fabrication, Aude could not say.

Clearing her throat, she made her voice strong. 'My liege, I have come to attest to the good character of Hugh Duclair. I have come to tell you that I believe the Bishop of St Aubin was lying when he spoke of Hugh seeking to ally himself with disloyal Flemish noblemen. I have come to—'

Hugh grabbed her hand. 'Aude, don't!'

She could smell riverweed. And mud. She sneaked a sideways glance. Yes, she was right about the mud—it streaked his face, it dulled his hair. But he was still the most handsome man she had ever seen.

There was a movement behind them and the King made an impatient gesture. 'Count Edouard?' His voice had an edge to it. 'You have something to add?'

'Your Grace, I would endorse what my sister has said. Hugh Duclair does not have a disloyal bone in his body.'

The King lifted his hand. 'I well remember your support in 1066. I also recall that Hugh Duclair fought at your side.'

'Yes, my liege.'

The King sighed, his fingers tapped. 'Duclair has spoken at some length of money his father put into the hands of the church for safe-keeping. He has spoken of an ambitious churchman. I, too—' the King directed a black look at the bishop standing on the edge of the circle '—have difficulties in that regard, despite having taken pains to make my views well known. It is my opinion that a King is best placed to supervise the government of the Church within his dominions.'

'Yes, your Grace.'

'Some among us would do well to remember that Archbishop Stigand lost his liberty for taking more than was his due.' Another pointed glance went the bishop's way. The bishop flinched. With a small smile, the King's cool gaze returned to Hugh. 'But enough of that, I should like to have sight of this document.'

'Your Grace,' Aude said, 'the villagers at Alfold are searching for it.'

Hugh's fingers tightened on hers. 'Aude, I left it
in the—'

'Hypocaust. Hugh, we guessed as much and went to
fetch it. But it is not there.' She gazed up at the King.
'Your Grace—'

'*Hugh*!' Someone at the foot of the dais was waving
to attract attention. '*Lady Aude*!'

'Gil!'

The King sighed and cocked a weary eyebrow at
Hugh. 'Duclair, I suspect that this is yet another petition
on your behalf.'

Mind in turmoil, Aude could only watch as the King
waved the guards aside to admit Gil. He was holding
a parchment, and Brother Reinfrid—the monk who
had accompanied Edouard from Normandy—was with
him.

*Hugh's document? Dear God, let it be Hugh's
document*!

'Thank God,' Hugh muttered as Gil fell to his knees
and handed the parchment to the King.

Aude held her breath as the King unrolled it. She
clung to Hugh's hand.

'Gil, what happened?' Hugh hissed.

'It was the villagers,' Gil whispered back, the King
was engrossed in reading. 'Some of them had joined that
gang of thieves—'

'I thought as much.'

'They found our camp, and your document. They
kept it because they thought it might be worth something.' Gil sent Aude a smile. 'But after you and Lord
Edouard left for Winchester this afternoon, I…I hope
you do not mind, Hugh, but I explained everything to

them and once they realised how it would help you, they held a meeting. They gave it to me to bring here.'

'Gil, you have done well,' Aude said, smiling.

Gil nodded, but his expression was sober. 'I am only sorry I had to break your confidence, Hugh.'

The King rolled up the parchment. 'Yes, you did well, boy. But these thieves, do you have their names? One should not hesitate to punish thieves—' a rancorous look was directed at the nearby churchman '—whatever their rank or calling.'

Aude's eyes widened, as the penny dropped. Of course! The thatcher, Chad, must have been one of them! And Cedric's cousin, Goda? Perhaps. There were doubtless others, villagers who had joined the thieves when they had lost Thane Frideric. Perhaps they had not always been thieves, perhaps they had started out as rebels against the Normans. Villagers who had been fighting in hope of regaining their old way of life.

Firmly, she folded her lips together. She would say nothing. These villagers had come home, and in siding with Hugh, they had earned her silence.

'I am sorry, your Grace,' Hugh said. 'I did not see them.'

'Pity.'

Brother Reinfrid stepped forwards. 'My liege?'

The King looked down his nose at him. 'And you are?'

'Brother Reinfrid of Jumièges, formerly of St Aubin.'

The King's gaze sharpened. 'Formerly of St Aubin?'

'Yes, my liege.'

'Did you witness the signing of this document?'

'Not personally. But a fellow brother did witness it. I have found him.'

Aude's sharply indrawn breath was echoed by Hugh's.

The King looked searchingly over Brother Reinfrid's shoulder. 'Where is he? Why is he not here?'

'My liege, Brother Baldwin, he…he would not accompany me.'

'He refused to come?' The King's eyes were blank with disbelief. 'Did you stress the importance of his testimony?'

Brother Reinfrid bowed his head. 'Yes, my liege, indeed I did. But Brother Baldwin has become a solitary, he has withdrawn from the world.'

'Withdrawn from the world, eh? Where is he?'

'Establishing his hermitage near St Stephen's. He will testify to the truth, my liege, he did to me, but we will have to send to him. Is my word enough?'

Aude held her breath—Hugh's fate hung on a knife point. If Brother Baldwin's refusal to attend Winchester Castle angered the King, she suspected no amount of hearsay evidence would make him change his mind.

The King's gaze ran over the supplicants kneeling at his feet, Brother Reinfrid, Hugh, Edouard, Gil, herself…

He shrugged and getting to his feet, gestured them up.

'I find I believe you, Brother,' the King murmured. 'If only all churchmen were so dedicated to their faith as this Brother Baldwin. As I mentioned, I myself have found that far too many are overly interested in earthly matters. Sir Guy?'

'My liege?'

'Tomorrow, for form's sake, you are to visit St

Stephen's and verify Brother Baldwin's testimony.' He sighed. 'After which, you had best add the Bishop of St Aubin's name to the list of bishops in need of…firm guidance. We cannot have churchmen casting covetous eyes on my vassals' property; we cannot have them blackening the names of honourable men.'

Sir Guy bowed. 'My liege.'

'In the meantime, come, Count Hugh, let us do this properly.'

Count Hugh! The King had called him Count Hugh! Surely he would not do that unless the document and their testimony had convinced him of Hugh's loyalty?

The King held out his arms and Aude stood to the side, holding her breath while Hugh gave him the kiss of peace.

Thank God, Hugh thought. *Thank God.*

The King grimaced and stepped smartly back. 'I think a change of clothing is in order, my lord Count.'

'Yes, your Grace.' Hugh was grinning like a witless fool, he couldn't help it. This banishment had been hanging over him like a doom for too long. For so long, in fact, that he suspected it would take a while for the full ramifications to sink in. He was reinstated, but more importantly he had regained the favour of his King. Bowing, he retreated a pace. Freyncourt would be his once more! He smiled at Aude. She smiled back.

'One thing further, Lord Hugh…'

'My liege?'

'Your marriage. I should like to seal our new accord by granting you an heiress.'

Hugh's blood went cold. He hadn't thought it possible, but a doom worse than banishment was louring over him.

'An heiress?' *No*! In his mind's eye, Hugh watched in horror as a lock of copper hair unravelled from about his wrist.

'Indeed. I seem to recall that some years ago there was talk of you marrying one of my half-cousins—'

'*No*!'

The King drew his head back. 'I beg your pardon, Lord Hugh?'

'My liege, I have to inform you that I am already married.'

'Already? The marriage of one of my Counts is a political matter, I do not recall you asking my permission.'

'No, my liege, I am sorry. I can only say that I was not, at the time, one of your Counts.'

The King's eyes were like flint. 'You make light of this, Lord Hugh?'

'Never.' Hugh tasted bile. He looked at Aude and pain sliced through him. *Agony—to lose her—agony*!

Understanding crashed in on him.

For months, he had fought to regain the King's favour, thinking that was the sum of his desires. He had come to England with but one aim in mind.

But Aude...he could not lose Aude! Set against Aude, the favour of the King was but an abstraction. To lose Aude would be to lose half of himself. Aude was, quite simply, the most important element in his life.

How long had this been the case? Since they had bedded? No, Aude had been important to him before that.

Since their marriage? No, long before that. He loved her. He needed her. *Holy Virgin, he loved her*!

Since when? Jumièges? He had no idea. But he loved her.

'Whom have you married?' The King was waiting for his reply.

'The Lady Aude.' Hugh led her forwards.

King William looked thoughtfully at them. 'You are content, my lady?'

'Yes, your Grace.' Aude gave him a curtsy. 'But if…. if our marriage is not suitable, we can seek an annulment.'

Hugh went cold to his core. 'Aude?' *Hell, that damned message he had sent from the prison! She must be thinking of that message.* He gritted his teeth. 'I don't want an annulment.'

The King's lips twitched.

Well, I am glad someone is finding this amusing.

'Hugh…' large amber eyes searched his '…I do not want our marriage to…' there was a slight catch in her voice '…hold you back. I do not want you to come to regret it.'

He gripped her hand. His chest felt compressed, it ached with the thought of losing her. 'Aude, I will never regret our marriage.'

'Oh, very well.' The King sank back on to the throne. 'Have your marriage with my blessing. If you are half as content with your lady as I am with mine, you will be a happy man.'

'Thank you, your Grace.'

'Now go away, there are other matters that need my attention.'

Yes, your Grace.'

'And for pity's sake, take a bath, Count Hugh. You reek of river.'

* * *

Back at Alfold Hall, Aude gave the broad-shouldered form of her husband a sideways glance. He was sat next to her at the head of the table, raising a cup to Edouard at the end of what had turned out to be a meal of celebration.

In Winchester, Hugh had taken a bath as the King had ordered, and Aude had found a seamstress who had been able to provide her with clothing that fitted him. Tonight he was wearing a green silk tunic with a subtle pattern in the weave. The seamstress Aude had bought it from had insisted the fabric had been in a consignment shipped in from Constantinople. Aude had no way of knowing whether that was the truth, but Hugh certainly looked well in it.

Tonight he was every inch the lord. Hugh Duclair, Count de Freyncourt and Lord of Alfold. She felt slightly in awe of him. This was the old Hugh, the Hugh she had idolised long before her betrothal to Martin.

The torchlight flickered in the bronze hanging bowls above them; it glinted on the pommel of Hugh's dagger, on his belt buckle, his ring.

'My thanks, Edouard, for your support in Winchester,' he said.

Edouard raised his cup. 'You are most welcome.'

Aude gave a wry smile as the wine was drunk and more was poured. There had been much toasting. Hugh was restored to his rightful place in the world, and all was well. Count Hugh de Freyncourt. Her husband. Her smile faded.

In the Winchester Great Hall, Hugh had said that he did not want an annulment, but whatever way you looked at it, she was not a good match for him. Especially now that he was Count Hugh again.

Quite simply, she was not his equal. How could she be? Yes, her brother was a Count, but Crèvecoeur and Corbeil were insignificant compared to Hugh's vast acres. And as for Aude herself, all she had to bring him by way of dowry was a minor estate in Normandy, and Alfold. He deserved better.

'To Lord Hugh!' At the end of the board, Chad Thatcher reached for his cup. 'To a lord who knows how to protect his own! *Waes hael!* Good health!'

Dragging on a bright smile, Aude drank the toast. 'To Lord Hugh!' Hugh had not been here long, but the villagers had taken him to their hearts. They respected him for setting up the watch-point, for teaching them to stand up for themselves. They valued his military competence and his compassion for injured boys.

'And Lady Aude, to Lady Aude!'

'Lady Aude! *Waes hael!*'

Aude smiled and nodded as the cups were raised in her honour.

Eadgytha leaned forwards. 'My lady, we are so glad you came to Alfold. You and Lord Hugh between you will make it a proper hall again.'

'That is my wish,' Aude said.

'To Gil!' Dynne said, 'Good health!'

Cups were raised. Gil's health was drunk.

'To Chad, *waes hael!*'

'To Dynne!'

'To Brother Reinfrid!'

Aude pushed herself to her feet. Clearly, this was going to go on for some time. 'Hugh?' Blue-grey eyes smiled up at her. 'I am for bed.'

'And I shall join you.' Rising, Hugh took her hand.

Inside their curtained refuge, Hugh guided her to the bed.

'I thought you would want to stay for the toasting,' she said, as yet another ragged cheer floated in from the hall.

Deftly he unfastened her veil. He cupped her cheek with his palm and kissed her temple. 'What, when I have a beautiful wife to attend to? She might complain if I became insensible with drink…'

His lips found her neck and before she knew it she was lying on her back on the bed-covers, pinned there by a well-muscled thigh. Somehow her arms had wound round him and he was smiling down at her. He drew back.

'Aude, you have been very quiet tonight—is something wrong?'

She slid her fingers into his hair in the way that he loved. 'Hugh, I think I make a pretty poor wife, I am not fit to sit by your side at Château Freyncourt.'

He frowned. 'Nonsense!'

'No, listen, Hugh, please. Back at Dives, all those years ago, you actually thought I was unsuitable—'

'I thought no such thing! That was my father's view, not mine.'

'Your father was right.' She twined her fingers into his hair, playing with it, looking at it in the light. 'We should not have married. Hugh, I think you should reconsider an annulment.'

He eased back and her hand fell away. 'It's that message, isn't it? The one I sent you from the prison?'

'What message?'

He looked searchingly at her for a moment, and

grinned. 'You never got it? Thank God for that. I didn't mean it anyway. Sent it in a dark moment.'

'What message? Hugh?'

Shaking his head, he tugged her close, fingertips tracing a line down her cheek and around her ear. 'It was about an annulment, but I never meant it. I was afraid I was falling and didn't want you to fall with me.' A touch of uncertainty entered his voice. 'You do want me, don't you? I hoped…' He cleared his throat and fixed his gaze on her throat. 'I hoped you meant what you said to the King, that you were content with our marriage. I hoped you love me. Aude?'

She blinked at him through a blur of tears. 'Love you?' Her breath escaped in a rush of happiness. If he wanted her love, he *must* trust her! 'Of course I love you! I have loved you since…since…oh, always.'

Hugh's brow cleared. *'Always?'*

'I loved you long before I went away with Father. All my life.'

'You haven't known me all your life.'

She thumped his chest. 'Don't be difficult, you know what I mean. So…' She gave him a sharp look. 'We are not to talk of annulments.'

'No, indeed.'

He grinned and his hand came to cover her breast. Gently, she pushed it away.

Startled blue eyes met hers. Blue. Her heart swelled to see Hugh happy, but he had a confession to make and she would have it out of him.

Eyes narrowing, his hand crept back to her breast, shaping it through the fabric of her gown, sending starry tingles shooting to her toes.

Taking his wrist, Aude removed his hand a second time, this time placing it firmly on her waist.

'So, we will not speak of annulments?' she repeated.

He shoved his hand through his hair. 'No, I told you.' A large hand gripped hers. 'You are my lady. I need you.'

'And…?'

His eyes were serious, his fingers laced gently with hers. 'I wish for no other. I love you, Aude. My beautiful lady, my dear friend. My light in the darkness.' He caught hold of her chin. 'I love you and no other, Brat, is that what you want to hear?'

She nodded.

'Good, because it's the truth. I love you.' He sighed. 'Although I expect that since you have wrung that confession out of me you will insist I stop calling you "Brat".'

Slowly, smiling so much that her cheeks ached, Aude shook her head. 'No, it is most odd, but it is some while since I have minded you calling me "Brat". Something else was worrying me far more.'

'Oh?'

'I thought you did not trust me, but—'

'Don't trust you?' Hugh stared. 'I would trust you with my life!'

She ran a fingertip along the line of his jaw—he had shaved and it was smooth to the touch. 'I see that, now you have told me you love me. You would not love where you did not trust.'

Hugh's lips curved, he nuzzled her cheek. 'My Brat,' he murmured.

As their eyes met, Aude made a delightful discovery.

Her husband's touch was not the only thing that could set the starry tingles dancing in her belly. A loving look did too.

Sinking her hands into Hugh's hair, she guided his mouth to hers.

'I wonder,' she murmured against his mouth.

'Hmm?'

Aude was silent, she was too busy taking the taste of him on to her tongue, too busy wondering what other equally delightful discoveries the night—and their life together—might have in store.

* * * * *